I couldn't allow myself to *feel* this way, but no matter how hard I tried to convince myself not to, I *wanted* this feeling. Maybe there was something wrong with me. A part of my brain that couldn't be made to *understand* that I wasn't one of them. The thoughts that had hijacked my mind *belonged* to someone else, someone who would be allowed to eat dinner at the same table as a *boy*. Someone who could move slowly on a dance floor under sparkling lights *in his arms* in front of everyone. Someone who could let him kiss her and allow herself to *kiss* him back.

I wasn't that girl, but I *wanted* to be.

PERFECTED

PERFECTED

kate jarvik birch

Entangled Publishing, LLC
2614 South Timberline Road
Suite 109
Fort Collins, CO 80525

Visit our website at www.entangledpublishing.com.

Edited by Heather Howland and Sue Winegardner
Cover design by Kelley York
Interior design by Jeremy Howland

Hardcover ISBN 978-1-62266-268-5
Paperback ISBN 978-1-63375-304-4
Ebook ISBN 978-1-62266-269-2

Manufactured in the United States of America

First Hardcover Edition July 2014
First Paperback Edition November 2015

10 9 8 7 6 5 4 3 2

To my family.

One

"*R*emember. You'll never be one of them," Miss Gellner said, repositioning each of us on our divans in the sitting room so our gowns draped elegantly around our crossed ankles.

She stepped back and gazed at the group of us, her face pinched and stern like always, but I spotted a tiny glimmer of pride behind her rheumy eyes. Twenty girls, all lovely, demure, quiet. She was pleased with us, even if she wouldn't say it out loud.

Miss Gellner blinked, as if bringing herself back to the moment. "Things won't change once you leave here," she went on. "Simply because you'll be pampered and spoiled, your life's mission won't suddenly be any different. Remember that. Your *sole purpose* is to enrich the lives of your new owners."

As she said this, she lightly tapped her bamboo training stick against my back, not a hard whack the way she had done relentlessly when we first transferred from the Greenwich Kennels to the training center, where she and her staff could cultivate us into the sort of girls we were bred to be. This was just a warning tap, reminding me to sit so that my spine was a stem, and I was the flower resting atop it.

It was a pose we'd practiced daily for the past four years, during our Music and Etiquette and Dining lessons, even during our nightly baths. But the fluttering in my stomach distracted me, drawing me down into myself. My whole body felt fluttery—my hands, my feet, even my eyes. I worried that the moment the two grand doors leading to the reception room swung open, I might flap away; a feather caught in the wind.

Next to me, Seven bit nervously at her bottom lip. It was weird to think that by tonight she'd have a new name, a real one. The breeders at Greenwich assigned us numbers as names at conception: One through Twenty, since twenty was the maximum number of girls they were allowed to have each year. I was Eight, but not for much longer. By tonight, I could be anything.

Across the room, Miss Gellner took a few steps toward the grand wooden doors, resting her hand lightly on the knob before she turned to face us one last time.

"I want you to keep your composure when they come in. I've spent four years preparing you for this moment." She thumped her training stick on the ground for emphasis. "Four years. Don't waste them. Each move that you make, every turn of your head and pout of your lips, speaks to my effectiveness as a trainer, and I won't have that work tarnished. When I open these doors, I expect you to remember all the things I've taught you."

The stiff lining of my dress rubbed against my rib cage and I ached to shift to a more comfortable position, but I held still, staring straight ahead at Miss Gellner with a soft smile placed carefully on my lips.

"Be sure to hold your tongues," she continued. "*You* are not doing the selecting. Do not ask questions. Speak if spoken to, but keep your answers brief. We don't want to scare away a potential buyer with a girl who has too forward a notion of who's in charge."

Beside me, the other girls sat silently. We were perfectly trained, all of us. And lovely, too. In our new dresses, we looked like royalty. Miss Gellner had picked out a different shade of gown for each of us, our first piece of clothing that was distinctly ours. She'd deliberated long and hard on the color choices. She wanted us each to look different. It wouldn't do for the customers to think they were getting cloned girls even though there were plenty of differences between us to set us apart. Yes, we all had large eyes, spaced perfectly on our heart-shaped faces. We all had small noses, long, thin necks, and rose petal lips. But we each had distinct coloring. Seven's hair was nearly black. Sixteen's eyes were green, the color of fresh summer grass, and Twenty's skin was the same warm brown of the toasted bread that we were rewarded with on Sunday mornings. We were each unique. One of a kind.

I was happy with the dress Miss Gellner had chosen for me. It was the palest shade of blue, hardly a color at all. These dresses would be the only item that would accompany us to our new homes. Our new owners would provide everything else.

"We're lucky to have a number of congressmen and senators here today," Miss Gellner said. "Power, prestige,

wealth—you'll be surrounded by the best, which is why
it is important that you *be* the best." Miss Gellner sighed,
nodding her head once. "All right girls. It's time."

She turned and threw open the doors. "Ladies...
Gentlemen..." Her voice boomed as she glided into the
next room. "If you'll kindly follow me, I'll show you to the
sitting room. You'll have a chance to look over the girls
before you make your decision. As I told each of you over
the phone, the number on your tag will determine the order
of selection."

A moment later a stream of bodies and voices flowed
into the room. I drew a breath and held it, trying to compose
myself, but the fluttering inside me only grew worse. My
vision blurred as the men and women pressed closer, talking
loudly to one another.

"Oh my! They're so little," a woman cooed. "They look
like twelve-year-olds."

"I can assure you, they're sixteen," Miss Gellner said.
"They're fully grown; all measuring exactly five feet."

An older man grabbed a lock of my hair and rubbed it
between his fingers. "Like corn silk," he said to the woman
next to him. "Did you say you were hoping for a blonde or a
redhead? This one almost seems like a mix of the two."

"And it does have beautiful eyes. Look, they're practically
turquoise," she crooned. "But, I was hoping for a real redhead.
There's an auburn one over there we should look at."

I didn't dare turn my head to watch them walk across
the room to look at Ten.

A middle-aged couple finished looking at Seven and
circled around me. I blinked a few times, bringing my vision
back into focus as the man's dark eyes skated over me. He

was obviously quite a bit older than me, but his jaw was much stronger than the other men I'd seen so far, and his eyes were bright. A sprinkling of gray hairs dusted the dark hair at his temples. The woman beside him had probably been a beauty when she was younger, but now she was a different sort of beautiful—regal and refined. She was tall, even taller than Miss Gellner, with high cheekbones, a strong jaw, and long, arched brows perched overtop piercing blue eyes. Even though she had lines around her eyes and mouth, her hair was almost as dark as Seven's, without a hint of gray. Everything about her intimidated me.

"Now this has some promise," the man said. "Do you like this one?"

"Oh John, do we really need to do this?" The woman sighed, her gaze drifting around the room.

"Do what, darling?"

"You can cut it with the 'darling,' too. It's not like anyone's listening. They're busy choosing their own pets," she said, gesturing at the rest of the people in the room with an elegant sweep of her arm. "And you can stop pretending I have any say in your precious little project. You know I couldn't care less about getting her."

Her husband stepped forward, so close their bodies almost touched. "You know how it looks for us not to have one, don't you? After all the time I spent getting this bill to pass. People are saying things. You don't want them to think—"

"Whatever you say, *dear*." She took a step away from him, eyeing an old man who had turned his attention to their conversation. "I'm merely along for the ride."

"You can't argue that Ruby needs this," the man said.

"We agreed."

Her face softened. "I know."

He took a deep breath, and when he turned back to me, it was as if he'd flipped a switch, changing his face back to the same well-groomed look of prominence and stature I'd seen on it to begin with.

"Stand up and give us a little whirl, love," he said to me.

I hadn't anticipated the weakness in my legs, but I stood and turned slowly, the way I learned in my Poise lessons. I kept my chin up, neck elongated, my arms held out ever so slightly from my sides as if my hands were brushing the skirt of a tutu.

The man smiled once I faced him again. "And what are your talents? The kennel trainer said that you each specialize in two."

"My talents are piano, dance, and singing. Although my vocal range is not as diverse as some."

His forehead creased, his eyes narrowing, and my stomach flipped. If Miss Gellner had been standing next to me, she would have lashed me with her stick. We'd practiced our lines over and over and still I said it wrong. There hadn't been any need for me to point out my faults so blatantly. I should have only mentioned the piano and dance and not said anything about the singing. I was trying too hard to impress.

"Three talents?" he asked. "Marvelous. I suppose we'd be getting a little bit more bang for the buck if we go with you then, isn't that right?"

The man's phrasing confused me and I lowered my eyes to the ground and smiled softly the way we'd been taught to do if we ever didn't know how to answer a question.

"So which is your favorite?"

"Favorite?" I asked.

"Which one do you like the most?"

"I'm quite good at all three as long as the song I'm singing is written for a mezzo-soprano."

"But certainly you have a favorite?"

My mind raced, trying to think over all the scenarios we'd spoken about in our Conversation class, but I drew a blank. Those classes were meant to help us understand our new owner better, not to help *them* understand *us*. I couldn't come right out and tell him that I had a favorite. Miss Gellner would be outraged. Maybe I could try to change the subject? But then he might realize I was doing it to avoid his question, and he would know that I really *did* have a favorite.

It was too complicated an interaction.

The woman smiled slyly. "Maybe she doesn't understand your question, John. Sure, she's pretty, but they weren't bred for brains."

"I thought you said you wanted to stay out of this."

She raised her hands and took a step back without saying another word.

The man tried again. "What I mean to say is, which one of your talents do you prefer? Is there one that makes you particularly happy?"

I swallowed, hoping to push down the rock that had lodged itself in my throat. "Well sir, if there's one that *you* prefer, I'm sure I'd be delighted to perform for you."

The man sighed and shook his head. "Never mind. Why don't you sit back down?"

I smiled once more and sank back onto the divan, trying to hold my head high even though my eyes burned.

For the next hour, the groups of men and women circled around the room. They were all so much bigger than I'd imagined they'd be, not only in their physical stature, but their presence, as if the room couldn't contain them. They gobbled up the air.

Finally Miss Gellner moved us into the concert room. We'd each been assigned one talent to demonstrate to give the clients a better taste of what they'd be buying. Four and Five would each be performing an *adagio en pointe*, a few girls were playing the flute and the cello, but the majority of us would be playing the piano or singing.

Maybe it should have bothered me that I wouldn't stand out, but all I could think about as we sat down in the velvet seats arranged along the edges of the room was Debussy's "Arabesque No. 1" in E major, the song Miss Gellner had chosen for me to play. It wasn't an elaborate song. I could play solos that were so much more difficult like the piece by Prokofiev that I learned last year, but I was glad she hadn't chosen that one. Sure, I wouldn't be able to show off my finger work playing the "First Arabesque," but that didn't matter. I could already feel the notes of the song moving up through my fingers and arms, a soft vibration that settled somewhere at the base of my neck like the warm hand of a friend.

We moved in order: One, Two, Three, Four, on and on until finally it was my turn. As I climbed the stairs to the small stage at the front of the room and sat on the tufted cushion of the piano bench, it was as if a white curtain had been drawn down between the crowd and me. I took a deep breath, savoring the moment before I placed my hands on the keys and started to play.

My fingers floated over the ivories for only a short four minutes, but my heart and mind quieted. I didn't know if the other girls felt this way when they were playing, as if they were all alone and the rest of the world melted away, leaving the air awash in soft color. I'd always been too embarrassed to ask. What if it meant that I had something wrong with me?

Those four minutes didn't last long enough and before I knew it my fingers had stopped, hovering over the keys as the last notes died away. A polite spattering of applause brought me back to the room full of strangers. As I stood, I glanced out into the audience, allowing myself to imagine which of these people might be my future owner. Toward the back of the room I spotted the man with the salt-and-pepper hair and his wife. Neither of them was clapping, but for just a second he held my gaze and nodded ever so slightly.

That small gesture made my face burn with shame. He knew that I lied to him before when he'd asked me which one of my talents was my favorite. Of course it was piano, but I could never say it out loud. I was supposed to bring pleasure to my new masters, not to find pleasure for myself.

A cold sweat broke out across my back and I shivered, sitting back down on my chair to watch the remainder of the performances. If he could read me so easily, maybe everyone else could, too.

Two

*I*t didn't surprise me that Ten was the first of us to be sold. The old couple that had been looking for a redhead must have been pleased enough with Ten's deep auburn hair to choose her with the first tag of the day.

Ten rose and walked elegantly to stand beside her new masters, and Miss Gellner called the name of the next tag holder.

"Our second tag belongs to Senator Gibbs," she announced. "Senator, it's a pleasure to have you here today. Have you had a chance to make your selection?"

The elderly gentleman stood and smoothed his hand across the front of his suit. "Yes. They're all fine specimens." He smiled, nodding to the rest of the tag holders. "But I do believe I'll go with number Sixteen."

A few disappointed mumbles circulated through the crowd as Sixteen took her place beside her new owner. I couldn't take my eyes off of the senator as he stroked Sixteen's hair with his large hand, twining his fingers through the flaxen curls at the base of her neck.

Miss Gellner moved on to the next tag, and I tried to concentrate on the name she was announcing, but her words got lost in the low hum filling my head.

I wiped my clammy palms against the soft silk of my dress, trying to calm myself, but I couldn't look away. Miss Gellner had assured us that the tags weren't handed out to just anyone. All her clients were from the top one percent of society. She made sure of that. A customer had to put down twenty thousand dollars just to be entered in the lottery to get a tag. They had to charge such a high price to ensure we'd be owned by the best. People don't appreciate common things, Miss Gellner always said, so it was important that we never be common.

And even though she made it quite clear that it was beneath her to speak about money, Miss Gellner said it was also important that we know exactly how much our owners were willing to pay for us. Two hundred thousand dollars is as much as some people spend on their homes, Miss Gellner said when she told us how much it took to own a Greenwich girl. Not the homes our new owners would live in, of course—she was speaking about the general public—but it was a substantial amount of money regardless. We were to understand that our new owners would think of us as an investment, and we needed to spend our lives making sure their investment was worth it.

Still, the way the senator stroked Sixteen's hair didn't feel right.

"...choose number Eight," a voice said from the crowd, and I lifted my head at the sound of my name.

Miss Gellner smiled. "Thank you, Congressman," she said,

and I followed her gaze to the man who had just selected me with the third tag of the day.

The congressman smiled at me and nodded. It was the same small gesture he'd given me after my performance. But still it confused me. If he knew I'd lied to him about my preference for playing the piano, why would he use up a third-pick tag to choose me? I got shakily to my feet, trying to paste a demure smile over the look of stunned disbelief on my face before I wound my way through the crowd to stand next to him.

"Hello, love," he said, smiling. "It looks like three is our lucky number. Tag number three for the girl with three talents."

"Oh yes, what splendid luck," his wife said in a flat voice.

I knew she was being sarcastic. It was the sort of speech Miss Gellner commanded us never to use under any circumstance, but there had been a few times when I'd overheard some of the girls speak this way to one another when Miss Gellner wasn't listening.

"I have a headache," she said, turning to her husband. "I'll be waiting out in the lobby until this little pageant is over."

The congressman watched his wife disappear behind the two wide doors that led into the waiting room before he turned to me. "Don't let Elise scare you," he said. "She's been in a bad mood ever since she turned fifty."

I didn't know how to respond. In our Conversation classes, Miss Gellner said never to engage in a discussion about a woman's age or weight, but I was afraid to stand idly without responding.

"Yes, sir," I said quietly and raised my head to watch as Miss Gellner called the remaining tags.

Less than an hour later, each girl had been sold. Even the last clients, who had been left with Eleven, seemed quite pleased with their purchase. Miss Gellner thanked the crowd and led us out into the lobby.

"On behalf of Greenwich Kennels, I'd like to thank you once again for choosing us," Miss Gellner said. "Your paperwork should arrive within the next week. Please feel free to visit our website for care instructions, as well as read the brochures we've sent home with you. And please don't hesitate to call if there's anything we can do for you."

"Next thing you know, she's going to tell us to have her registered with the American Kennel Club," the congressman's wife said, standing up from the chair we'd found her in. "Can we please get out of here? I still need to get ready for Grace's reception, and at this rate, I'll be late again."

"Don't worry. I'll get you home with plenty of time to spare," the congressman said, touching her lightly on the wrist. It was the first sign of Tactile Affection that I'd seen between the two of them, and I turned away like I'd been taught in my Body Language class, not wanting to intrude.

Out front, the congressman handed a small pink ticket to one of the valets standing next to the wide, circular driveway.

The valet glanced down at the ticket and smiled. "Oh, the Austin-Healey. Is it a '63?"

"'65," the congressman said. "Back when they really knew how to make a car."

The valet nodded enthusiastically. "I hope you don't mind me saying so, but it's a beautiful car, sir."

"Of course I don't mind," the congressman said. "I've got a soft spot for beautiful things."

"You've got a soft spot for *impractical* things," his wife countered, watching the valet run off to fetch their car, but this time there wasn't any real malice in her voice.

The congressman glanced around the parking lot at the other clients leaving with their newly acquired girls. "You'd think for people with such good taste in pets, they'd have better taste in cars."

I followed his gaze. I didn't know anything about automobiles. It was true, most of the cars people were leaving in were large black ones that looked quite a bit like the cars the kennel used to transport us from Greenwich.

Then, rounding the corner came the valet in the congressman's car. It was not like any other car I'd ever seen before. In fact, it might have been the complete opposite of all those long, dark sedans with dark windows and jet-black interiors.

The car was small and rounded, painted in a soft shade of teal, a few shades darker than my dress, and the interior was cherry red leather that I could guess, even from seeing it from a distance, was as soft and supple as silk. The sight of this little car brought a smile to my lips. It might not have been as big and important as the other cars, but it was exciting in a way that theirs were not.

The valet pulled to a stop in front of us and climbed out, smiling, as he handed over the keys.

"Ladies," the congressman said, opening the passenger side door.

"You get in first," the congressman's wife said, gently pushing me toward the car. "I'm not spending a thirty-minute drive wedged in the middle."

I climbed in, and the congressman's wife followed. Inside,

I tried to make myself as small as possible, pressing my legs together and folding my arms across my lap, but it was impossible not to be pushed up next to either one of them after the doors slammed shut.

"So what do you think of my wheels?" the congressman asked, revving the engine before he sped out of the parking lot.

"The wheels?" I asked, suddenly worried that I hadn't paid enough attention to them. I'd been so distracted by the rest of the car that I hadn't noticed the wheels. "They're very...round."

The congressman threw his head back and laughed. "Yes. Yes, they are very round. But what do you think of the car?"

"I've never seen one like it," I said. "It makes me wonder why people drive those other cars when they can choose one like this."

"Damn right!" the congressman shouted into the wind that whipped through the open windows. "I know how to pick them, don't I, love?"

I wasn't sure if he was speaking to me or his wife, but when she didn't respond, I assumed he was, indeed, talking to me. Behind us, the training center receded in the distance.

"Yes, Master. You chose a lovely vehicle."

"Oh God," the congressman's wife moaned. "Please, don't tell me she's planning on calling you 'Master.' I don't know if I can stomach it."

The congressman chuckled. "You don't like it?"

"Seriously, John, it's completely backwards. Who in their right mind thought that would be a good idea?"

"I think it's kind of charming," he said.

"Charming?" she said, rolling down her window. "Maybe if you're trying to recreate the Old South."

"Don't be so melodramatic. Since when did you start comparing genetically engineered pets to slaves?"

Their conversation was starting to make me nervous, and I stared straight ahead at the other cars on the busy road, trying to figure out where all these people were going and why they were in such a hurry to get there.

"I don't. And I wouldn't be comparing her to a slave if she hadn't been the one to use the word 'Master.' Whether or not your constituents agree with buying these pets, I'm pretty sure you don't want them drawing any connections to slavery. Unless you don't want to run for reelection?"

"Oh please, I bet half the House and Senate own pets." He opened and closed his fingers around the steering wheel. "If you think it's such an atrocious word, we'll tell her not to use it anymore. Got that, love?" he said, giving me a little nudge in the side.

I swallowed, unsure how to address him, "Yes...sir."

He smiled and reached across me to squeeze his wife's knee.

Three

$\mathcal{T}$he drive to the my new house was much farther than the drive between Greenwich Kennels and Miss Gellner's training center, but I hardly noticed. I liked the way the congressman drove fast on the curving roads, zipping past tall trees and rolling hills spotted with large country houses.

I'd never seen countryside like this before. Both the kennel and the training center were near the city, so I'd only seen the rows of shops and a few tidy neighborhoods nestled in between. But out here, the houses weren't close together. They were spaced between large, green lawns with forests and valleys and dark, stone walls winding through the trees. I'd never seen such grand houses, never even imagined they existed, even though Miss Gellner always spoke of the luxury we'd be surrounded by once we went to live with our new owners.

"It's a shame you won't be home this evening," the congressman said to his wife. "Ruby will miss you. It's the third night this week."

"She'll be fine," she said, waving her hand dismissively. "Besides, she'll be completely distracted with the pet. Everyone will be. Nobody will even notice I'm gone."

"Ruby will notice," he said. "So will Penn, even if he won't admit it."

"I'm sorry, but I made a commitment months ago. Janet put me in charge of the silent auction. Besides, if I don't come out for this, why should I expect anyone to come out for the benefit next Saturday?"

The congressman shrugged.

For the first time since we'd been in the car, the congressman's wife turned to face me. "Our daughter, Ruby, will be excited to see you," she said with what sounded like real affection. She didn't look at me for long before she turned to gaze back out the window and her face returned to its pre-occupied and distant stare. "The room is all set up," she said, speaking to her husband now. "I sent someone out for a few last-minute items, so it's not like she'll need anything."

We drove in silence for a few more minutes until the congressman slowed the car, pulling into a wide driveway lined with high, trimmed hedges. I leaned forward in the seat, just as the tall, brick house came into view.

"And this," the congressman said, gesturing at the building, "is home."

He hadn't asked my opinion, but I couldn't stop myself from speaking. "It's the most beautiful place I've ever seen."

How could I have ever imagined during all those years living inside the small, austere rooms at the kennel that a building like this even existed? Even Miss Gellner's descriptions of castles couldn't compete with the beauty before me.

The path leading to the front door was lined with perfectly rounded hedges and a pair of small trees, bursting with small silver leaves, hung low over the brick walkway. Near the front steps, two large stone pots overflowed with greenery. Around the wide front door, the carved white molding drew my eye up, up, past the second story windows and bright green vines that climbed the whitewashed brick onto the roof toward the sky, which seemed as if it must have been ordered especially for them, because I'd never seen a blue so radiant.

The congressman stopped the car and turned to observe the look of awe on my face. "I think she approves."

"If only our friends were as easy to impress," his wife said.

Just then, the front door opened wide and a girl ran out, waving her arms at the car as if she were trying to flag us down, even though it was obvious we'd come to a stop. She was yelling something, speaking in such a rush of words that I couldn't understand a bit of what she was saying. Finally, as she drew closer to the car, her words became clearer.

"… for the past hour," she gasped, "and Penn was about to make me go wait upstairs and then you pulled up."

She stopped short at the side of the car, suddenly silent, and peered inside. Even though she was about my size, I guessed she must have been quite a few years younger than me. This had to be Ruby. She didn't look a thing like any of the girls from Greenwich. Her eyes were big and dark, like her dad's, and her skin was covered with a layer of soft brown freckles that looked as if they'd been smudged on. I wanted to reach out a hand and draw my fingers across the bridge of her nose to see if her skin felt as velvety as it looked. She had features that Miss Gellner would have called "unfortunate," but there was something charming about them, and even though each of her features was homely on their own, they turned into something sweet, and innocent, and undeniably loveable when they were placed together on that face.

Her mom stepped out of the car and Ruby moved closer, bending down to stare in at me through the open door.

"Is that her?" she asked.

"Of course that's her," the congressman's wife said. "Who else would it be? Now step back so she can get out. We don't want to leave her out here all day, do we?"

Ruby stepped back and stared, openmouthed, as I climbed from the car. My legs tingled from being cramped up for such a long ride, but a moment later the congressman was at my side, helping me to my feet.

"She's my size," Ruby said, stepping forward so we stood nose-to-nose. To be sure, she raised her hand up above our heads to measure.

Her mother sighed. "She's the same size as all the other ones. They're bred to be little, remember? Now don't crowd her. You're going to give her a bad impression of our family."

"Is this one my age?" Ruby asked.

The congressman gave his daughter a pat on the top of the head. "No, she's all grown. Now why don't we take her inside instead of standing out in the driveway like a bunch of transients."

"Do we really get to keep this one?" Ruby asked, but both her parents ignored her.

This one? "Is there another pet?"

"We don't have her anymore." Ruby frowned, paying no

attention to the fact that I'd spoken out of turn. "My mom says it's because—"

"Yes, we did have another pet," the congressman interrupted. "Sadly, she came down with something that we couldn't treat on our own. The kennel *insisted* that we return her so that they could give her the special care she needed. We were all sad to see her go. Especially Ruby." He ruffled her hair, turning toward the house.

I moved to follow him, but my legs went weak at the knees. Miss Gellner spent years threatening us with what would happen if our owners were dissatisfied with us. *Greenwich must eliminate imperfection*, she used to say, smacking her training stick against her palm, and my legs would start to shake, not because I was afraid of being hit, but because it made me feel like I was a little girl again, walking past the dark red door at the end of the kennel's long hallway.

Growing up, we'd feared that door more than anything; more than the dark, more than scary stories whispered at night. It remained locked, but somehow we all knew that it was the door that imperfect pets were sent through. And we all knew they never came back out.

When I finally turned to follow him, I noticed someone else standing in the doorway. I hadn't seen him before because I'd been so distracted by the congressman's story about the other pet, but there he was, leaning up against the doorframe with his arms crossed over his chest, his deep brown eyes staring right at me. I froze, and for a second the world went fuzzy around the edges. The only clear thing was this boy standing in front of me.

I knew immediately that he was the congressman's son.

They looked like different versions of the same person. Both had the same square jaws, shaded with just a hint of stubble, and the same dark hair, although his wasn't combed neatly like his father's. It was shaggy and a bit tousled.

I'd never seen a boy this age before. All the workers at the kennel were older men with thick waists and sagging chins. But the congressman's son couldn't have been much older than me.

I hadn't realized that I'd stopped short, staring at the boy, until Ruby spoke.

"Why is she just standing there?" she asked.

The congressman followed my gaze to where his son stood in the doorway, and when I turned back to him he was staring at his son, too. His eyes narrowed and his lips twitched, tightening. The look only lasted a moment before he put his wide hand on my lower back and gave me a little nudge. "Come on, love. Penn and Ruby will help show you around the house."

Penn sighed and uncrossed his arms. "I don't really have time to be a part of the welcoming committee," he said before he turned and disappeared back inside the house.

"Ignore my brother," Ruby said, taking my hand in hers. "He's just grumpy 'cause Dad made him transfer schools and now his life is ruined. He's only nice if you make him peanut butter cookies. I'll teach you how."

Her hand was shockingly warm and soft in mine and I held on a little tighter, letting her pull me into the house. Even the stately exterior couldn't have prepared me for the gleaming dark hardwood floors and the wide stairway that curved up to the second floor, where a giant crystal chandelier cast warm light over everything.

Miss Gellner had decorated a few rooms at the training center with rich carpets and fine upholstered furniture so they would be presentable for her clients, but they didn't compare to the inside of the congressman's house. I tried to compose myself, but it was hard not to stand slack-jawed with my head tilted back to take it all in.

The congressman's wife didn't bother to say good-bye. She swept past us and climbed the stairway to the second floor, her heals clicking on the wood floor as she disappeared down the hallway.

"Well, Ruby," the congressman said. "It looks like it's up to the two of us to show your little pet to her room."

Ruby didn't seem to mind. She dragged me forward through an arched hallway that led to a gleaming white kitchen.

"This is the kitchen, obviously," she said, waving her hand as if the kitchen was the most boring room in the house. "We'll take you to your room first, okay? Daddy had the workers build it last year. You're lucky because you can see the pool from your window and there's French doors that go out to the patio."

The congressman didn't interrupt his daughter and she continued chattering. She pulled me past a room with windows that ran along all the walls and up onto the ceiling. I stopped for a minute, rooted. I'd never seen a room with a roof made of glass. To imagine that you could lie down on the couch and stare up at the clouds, and the birds, and the green branches of the trees swaying in the breeze...it took my breath away.

"This is just the conservatory," Ruby said. "There isn't a TV in here, but it's a good room for reading."

She led me on, through the conservatory and down a wide hallway lined with potted ferns. On either side, tall windows looked out into the backyard over the clear, blue pool on one side and the wide expanse of green lawn on the other.

"Okay, here we are," Ruby said, stopping at a door at the end of the hall. "Close your eyes."

Before I could close them, the congressman stepped behind me, slipping his warm hand over my eyes. "Ready?" he asked, leading me forward. One step. Two steps.

"Open your eyes!" Ruby yelled, and the congressman drew his hand away.

I turned in a circle, blinking as I took in the bright room.

It was white, everywhere, clean and crisp and untouched: the bed, the dressers, the couch and ottoman, even the curtains that hung down to the floor on either side of the four-poster bed. Through the tall windows lining the walls, yellow sunlight streamed in, bouncing off of the pool outside and casting ribbons of light that rippled against the high ceiling.

Our rooms at the kennel and the training center didn't look anything like this. The only thing they had in common was the color. White. The walls in my little room at the kennel were plain and unadorned. The cover on my twin bed, which sat underneath a small rectangular window, had also been white, but it had never seemed like a color the way it did here. Instead, the white had always seemed as if it lacked something brighter, more distinctive.

There was a fireplace, a chandelier, a closet, and even though it was beautiful, it left me feeling small and out of place. I turned in a slow circle, trying not to let the discomfort show in my eyes as I took it all in.

"I think she likes it, Dad," Ruby said. She stroked my arm lightly.

The congressman swung open the door to the closet. "It looks like Elise set everything up," he said. He ran his hand across the row of gowns hanging along the wall. There were dozens of them, all soft shades of coral, and blush, and cream. "I have to run and make a few calls. Do you think you can manage to get her over to the dining room in time for dinner, Ruby?"

She nodded solemnly.

"Good." The congressman chuckled, smiling down at both of us. He stroked my hair. The touch was gentle. Not at all like how the senator had knotted his fingers in Sixteen's hair. "Make yourself comfortable." His hand lingered on my cheek.

I hoped the expression on his face said he was happy that he'd gotten me. Even though Miss Gellner had spent four years training us, I suddenly felt as if I didn't really have any idea how to live at this house with these people. How was I supposed to be good enough for them?

He turned to go. The door clicked shut behind him and in its place, the image of the kennel's dark red door flashed in front of my eyes. I blinked it away, but the unease lingered in my belly.

What if after a day or two they realized I wasn't special, that I was too common to be spoiled this way?

Four

"*W*hy can't she sit at the table with us?" Ruby asked for the fifth time since dinner began.

She was seated at the end of the long dining room table, picking at her food. The congressman had called it chicken piccata but the only thing I recognized were the bright green asparagus and red potatoes pushed to the edge of her plate. Every few seconds she would glance over to where I was sitting at the small, round table set up near the window and smile happily, waving her fingers at me.

Penn rubbed a hand over his face. "God, how many times are you going to ask? She's a pet. Get it?"

"But our other pet used to sit at the table."

"Honey, we're trying to create better boundaries this time," the congressman explained.

"I just don't think it's fair. Doesn't it seem like she'd rather sit here, by me?"

"The people we bought her from gave us special instructions on how to take care of her," he said. "Her food is special. It's different from our food. And they said it was best to make sure she had her own dining space. We don't want you slipping her something that will make her sick."

Penn rolled his eyes. "Yeah, we wouldn't want her to *come down* with something like the last one."

I took a small bite of my sweet potato, barley, and lentil stew. This was one of the staple meals from the kennel. It didn't taste bad, but the smell drifting over from the congressman's meal was making my mouth water in a way I'd never experienced before.

Miss Gellner said our meals were designed to give us the perfect balance of vitamins, protein, and carbohydrates. The kennel tested out dozens of food combinations on us while we were growing up, but they found that a rotation between five staple meal plans gave the best results. Our special diet was one of the reasons us girls from Greenwich were known for our shiny hair, soft skin, and delicate frames. The people from the kennel didn't want our new owners messing up that reputation by feeding us the wrong sort of food. And if sitting at a different table would keep me from getting sick like the last pet, I was happy to oblige.

"What if I promise not to feed her anything?" Ruby asked.

"How about this," her father said. "Instead of thinking about where we're all sitting, what if we come up with a name for her?"

Ruby dropped her fork and clapped her hands, but a second later her face dropped. "Is it okay if we do it when Mom's not here?"

"Yeah, something tells me Mom's not going to mind too much," Penn said, stabbing at a potato.

The congressman glared at him across the table but he didn't say anything.

"There's a girl in my class that got a pet and they named her Princess," Ruby said. "They got theirs from a kennel in Virginia because her dad knows the owner."

Penn put down his fork and folded his arms over his chest. "Princess? That's what they named her? People name their golden retrievers Princess."

"Well, I wasn't saying *we* should name her that," Ruby said.

I could tell her feelings had been hurt by the way her bottom lip jutted out as she glared at him, but I was glad Penn had said something. I didn't want to end up with one of those common names Miss Gellner said people were always giving their pets—names like Princess and Lady.

"What about Ravenna? It's prettier than Princess and it's a perfect pet name."

The congressman sputtered and coughed, shaking his head.

Penn kicked his sister under the table. "Don't be stupid! You can't name them all the same thing."

The congressman stopped coughing and brought his napkin up to his face, dabbing at his watering eyes. "What about Bette," he asked. "That's a pretty name. And there's no denying she has those big eyes like Bette Davis."

"That's an awful name," Penn said. "You might as well call her Mildred or Ethel. It's an old lady name."

"Fine," the congressman said. "Do you have any better ideas?"

Penn paused and turned to look at me for the first time since we sat down to eat. All at once my cheeks burned and

I cast my gaze down toward my plate, taking a delicate bite of my stew. I stared at my lap, chewing slowly, willing the heat in my face to fade. I could feel Penn's gaze on me, pensive, studying. Why did it feel as if he were touching me?

My body is a stem and I am the flower that sits atop it, I repeated in my mind. *I am a flower. I am a flower.* The words did little to distract me from the fluttering in my stomach. Finally I couldn't stand it any longer. I lifted my head, looking up to where he sat, still staring at me. Our eyes met.

"Well?" the congressman said, breaking the silence.

"Her hair's not really blond, is it?" Penn asked, not answering his father's question at all.

"I don't know what that has to do with naming her." The congressman's voice sounded gruff, aggravated. "I suppose people would call it strawberry blonde."

"Strawberry!" Ruby yelled. "That's a pretty name. Like Strawberry Shortcake."

"Well, I still think it's weird we have to name them at all," Penn said, laying his fork down on his plate with a bang.

The congressman pulled at his collar, loosening it. "If a person is going to spend a small fortune on a pet, the least they should be entitled to is choosing a name for it."

Penn didn't seem upset by the rise in his father's voice. "You're right, Father. It's the least you're entitled to."

"Don't give me lip about entitlement, young man. Not after what we've been through with your school."

Penn's jaw tightened. "I didn't ask you to move me."

"I know," Ruby said, clapping her hands. "We could name her after someone famous. I just read a book about Cleopatra. She was pretty cool. Did you know she died when an Egyptian cobra bit her?" She smiled, oblivious to the tension running between her brother and father.

Penn held his father's gaze for a few long beats until, finally, he turned away. "Cleopatra? Doesn't that seem a little pretentious?"

"We could call her Patty?" the congressman suggested.

Ruby scrunched up her nose. "Patty sounds like an old lady substitute teacher."

I swallowed, afraid my voice would fail me. I wanted to say something to bridge the gap between the congressman and his children. I hated to think of them fighting over a name that would belong to me for the rest of my life. I searched for the right words, words that would leave them all happy. What had Miss Gellner said was the real purpose of conversation? To leave your partner feeling as if the correct answer had been theirs all along? That was easy enough to accomplish when speaking to one person, but it certainly became more difficult when you added a teenage boy and a little girl to the mix.

"What about Ella?" Penn said after a moment.

Ruby nodded. "Ella's a pretty name."

"Ella," the congressman repeated. It seemed that almost instantly he'd forgotten the harsh words that had so recently passed between himself and his son. "Yes, I think that might be it. What do you think, love?" he asked, turning to face me. "Is Ella the one?"

"It's lovely," I said, relieved. "Thank you. I imagine most people would be thrilled with the chance to help choose their own name. Babies don't really have that option, do they?"

"No, they don't," the congressman said. The edges of his eyes wrinkled as he smiled.

"I definitely wouldn't have picked Penn. I don't know what you and Mom were thinking," Penn said, but he smiled at his dad anyway.

"I like my name," Ruby interjected.

"Well, I like *all* your names," the congressman said before he took a hearty bite of his meal.

*T*t was still light out after dinner. The warm western sun flowed in through the back of the house, turning the rooms to gold. It wouldn't have been difficult for me to believe that everything was gilded: the chairs, the walls, the thick molding that crowned the ceiling. It was as if on the strike of the hour they'd all been transformed.

We were sitting in the conservatory with the congressman. He sat in the corner in a large, wing backed chair reading the paper. Every few minutes he would pause and glance up at me before he went back to his article. Ruby sat on the floor in front of a large, square coffee table piecing together a puzzle of a field of wildflowers while I leaned back on the chaise lounge eyeing the baby grand piano that sat in the corner of the room. I hadn't noticed it when we'd walked through earlier, but now I couldn't take my eyes off of it.

The congressman hadn't asked me to play anything for him yet, and I knew it would be presumptuous of me to suggest it, even though my fingers longed to stroke the keys.

"Can I take Ella up to my room?" Ruby asked, shoving aside the puzzle piece she'd spent the last five minutes trying, unsuccessfully, to fit into a spot.

"You can stay up for an hour," he said "But that's it. One hour. You better be in bed by the time your mother gets home."

Ruby tugged my hand, pulling me through the door. I glanced back at the piano one more time, knowing I wouldn't have a chance to play it tonight.

Ruby's room was upstairs at the end of the hallway. She stopped outside her closed door and turned to face me.

"I don't usually have friends over," she said. "But you can come up here whenever you want. Our last pet hardly ever came up. She was always in my dad's office." She frowned. "But I heard my mom say that you weren't even allowed in there. So, you can visit me all the time. If I'm in here, just knock like this and I'll let you in, okay?" She tapped lightly three times, paused and then gave two harder knocks followed by one final tap, so soft that her fingers hardly brushed the door.

She stared at me, waiting. I wanted to ask her to tell me more about the other pet, but it looked like she was waiting for me to respond. I nodded to let her know I understood.

"No, you have to try it," she said. "So I know you can do it later, without me helping."

Tap, tap, tap, knock, knock, tap. I finished, waiting for her approval.

"Okay, it isn't perfect, but it'll do," she said, and opened the door.

It was no surprise that the inside of Ruby's room was as elegant as the rest of the house. On the far side stood a four-poster bed that looked quite a bit like the one in my room, aside from the soft pink bedding and rose-colored canopy that covered it. The bed wasn't the only pink thing in Ruby's room. Almost everything, from the wallpaper, to the curtains, to the loveseat and chair, were colored in some varied shade of pink. Coral, rose, fuchsia, magenta, I couldn't even name all the different shades.

"Is pink your favorite color?" I asked.

Ruby shrugged. "It's okay. My mom picks everything out."

She led me in, sitting me down on the tufted bench at the end of her bed before she plopped down on the floor and gazed up at me. Miss Gellner's instructions to always keep myself in a lower, subservient position to my master nagged at the back of my mind. I hoped I wouldn't get in trouble if the congressman walked in.

"So what do you want to do?" Ruby asked. "The old pet liked to color. She was really good at shading stuff in so it looked real. But sometimes she spent too much time on her pictures and it got kind of boring."

I folded my hands in my lap, trying not to fidget. I'd never been very good with the visual arts, but I didn't want to disappoint her. Ruby sprawled out on the floor, leaning back on her elbows with her legs splayed out in front of her. Miss Gellner would never have let us sit that way, but it looked so comfortable, so relaxed, that I wished I could lie down next to her on the soft carpet.

"I'm happy to do whatever you'd like, Mistress."

Ruby rolled over on her belly, laughing. It wasn't a very ladylike laugh, more like a high-pitched giggle interspersed with little snorts. Finally she calmed down enough to speak. "Why'd you call me that?" she asked.

"I'm sorry," I said, flustered. "Didn't the other pet call you Mistress?"

She shook her head.

I should have known better. If the congressman's wife had asked me not to use the term "Master," maybe I wasn't supposed to address any of my new owners with the titles Miss Gellner had taught us to use. Obviously the last pet had picked up on things more quickly.

"What would you prefer me to call you?"

She sat back up and crossed her legs in front of her, leaning her elbows on her knees. "Just Ruby. That's what everybody calls me."

I nodded and blinked back a few tears threatening to form at the corners of my eyes. It seemed as if everything I said was wrong and I didn't understand why Miss Gellner had told us to call our new owners by names they didn't like. If Master and Mistress were so wrong, shouldn't she have known better? What if everything she taught me was wrong? I couldn't afford to be anything but perfect.

Ruby cocked her head and her face became serious. "It's okay," she said, sitting up to pat me on the hand. "I wasn't making fun of you." And then, as if she was searching for some way to repair things, she said softly, "I think you're beautiful. You're even prettier than Ravenna."

"Thank you," I told her, trying to compose myself. I shouldn't care what the other pet looked like, but a part of me wanted to believe it was true. The thought was prideful and my stomach knotted with shame. "And I think your freckles are beautiful. I've never seen anyone with so many."

"No. They're not beautiful," she said, covering her face with her hands. "They're ugly. My mom bought some special cream that was supposed to make them go away, but they're still there."

I didn't know what to say. At a time like this, maybe it

was better to keep my mouth shut.

Ruby uncovered her face. "My mom doesn't think I'm pretty."

My voice faltered. "I doubt that."

She sighed deeply. "My big sister is pretty. She looks like my mom. They have the same eyes and the same shaped face, but I don't really know who I look like. Just myself, I guess."

"You have a big sister?" I asked.

"Yeah, Claire. She's in college so she doesn't live here anymore," Ruby said. "But sometimes when she comes to visit she does my hair."

I sat up a little straighter. "I can do your hair if you'd like."

She reached up to touch the wild mess of curls that stuck out from her head. They weren't like Twelve's curls, which fell in perfect ringlets over her shoulders. They were an odd combination of tight curls around the front of her face that tapered off into smaller waves and finally to a few patches of hair that were nearly straight on the ends.

While we were at the training center, we spent plenty of time learning how to groom our own hair and sometimes after our baths they let us practice on the other girls, too. I hadn't had a lot of practice with hair like Ruby's, but I'd taken a lot of care to learn to keep my own hair smooth and sleek. Most days I wore mine up in a thick braid that twisted around the crown of my head, but today Miss Gellner had insisted we all wear it down, so mine still hung down my back nearly to my waist, loose and untethered.

Ruby stood up to grab a brush from her dresser and then sat down in front of me. She scooted back so that she was lying across my legs with her head in my lap. "It might be kind of snarly," she said, handing the brush to me. "My mom doesn't really make me do it since it's summertime."

I ran the brush through the ends, working to free the tangles as I moved my way closer to her scalp, grateful to finally be doing something I was good at.

"And maybe I can do your hair, too," Ruby said softly. She sat, reconsidering that for a second. "Well, maybe I can just brush it, since I'm not very good at braids or ponytails. But you could teach me."

For years I'd been dreaming about what it would be like to move in with my new masters, but I'd never imagined someone like Ruby. All our Conversation classes centered around the adult dialogue that we were supposed to be able to follow and comment on. If the kennel had known that we were going to be around children, why hadn't they taught us how to speak to them, too? Maybe that's why the other pet had avoided playing with Ruby, not because she disliked her, or preferred spending time with the congressman. Maybe she was too afraid to make a mistake.

We sat in silence for a long time while I worked the knots out of Ruby's hair and began braiding it into two neat French braids to frame her face. After a while, her breath became slow and heavy. I was about to try to wake her when she spoke, moving her head slightly in the direction of the large bookshelf at the other end of the room. "Oh my gosh," she whispered, as if she was suddenly remembering something very important. "I forgot to ask you what your favorite book is."

Miss Gellner had made sure to introduce us to plenty of books at the training center. She read aloud to us while we practiced sitting still during Poise class. For hours at a time we listened to *The Vivian Masters Complete Book of Etiquette, Theory and Practice of Grace*, as well as *Rules of Manner and Conversation*, which she would quiz us on later to make sure we'd truly been paying attention. Pets were meant to be showpieces. To do so we needed to be able to quiet our bodies and learn to sit like statuary if we needed to.

Most of the books that Miss Gellner read to us were dry and boring, but every once in a while she would read us the biography of what she called "a great American." Those books were never boring. They were filled with stories of powerful men like the ones who would someday be our masters.

"Oh... I... I don't know," I finally said, my fingers stalling above her shoulders. "What's *your* favorite?"

Ruby snorted. "Well it changes every week, seeing as my favorite book is usually the last one I read. Like last month I was going through a classics phase, so all my favorites were obviously classics. But this month I'm kind of into fantasy. I just finished *A Wrinkle in Time* this morning, so right now that's on the top of my list, even though the author kept using the word "tangible," which kind of bugged me. But other than that, it's my new favorite book."

Miss Gellner had certainly never read us anything about time wrinkles.

Ruby's body had started moving while she talked and her voice was animated now, not sleepy at all.

"You can borrow my books any time you want," Ruby said.

My mind stuttered, trying to find the words to talk about something else. *If the conversation is drifting into areas you're uncomfortable with, simply change the subject*, I'd learned in countless classes, but my mind was blank.

"I...well...what time is it?" I finally said. "Your father said I was only to stay an hour."

Ruby groaned. "It's not even late yet. I don't want you to go." When I got to my feet she sighed with resignation. "Okay, but we'll do something really fun tomorrow, okay?"

I curtsied. "Good night, Mistress Ruby," I said, walking briskly out the door and shutting it behind me with a loud click.

Maybe it was easier to stick with the things I already knew.

Five

I lay on top of the covers of my new bed, staring up at the dark ceiling. A few hours earlier, I'd changed into my new nightgown, which oddly enough, was as fancy as the dress I'd changed out of. It was long and flowing, with billowy fabric that swung softly against my legs whenever I took a step. It looked new, but maybe it had been worn before. All the clothes in my closet might have belonged to the other pet. It should have been a comfort, to think that all of the things in my room had been shared with another pet, someone just like me, but the thought didn't console me. It only reminded me that she'd been sent back.

I fidgeted. The nightgown didn't feel anything like my normal cotton one and I was suddenly worried I'd be expected to sleep elegantly. I practiced lying the way Miss Gellner had taught us to recline on a divan or a chaise lounge during our Poise lessons: my feet crossed at the ankles and my arm draped delicately across my body. But I didn't think there was any way I could last the whole night in this position. I'd never given any thought to how I slept until this very minute, but now I was afraid to close my eyes, afraid that as soon as I slipped into sleep I would roll onto my stomach with my legs sprawled crudely across the bed.

It didn't help that the bed was luxurious, with mounds of pillows and a feathery comforter I sank into the moment I lay down. I fought to stay awake, but the bed was too soft. I rolled onto my side, wishing that I felt comfortable enough to close my eyes for just a few minutes.

The house had been quiet for hours, and even though I assumed everyone had long since fallen asleep, I kept glancing at the doorway, worried I would look up to see the congressman standing there, even though he hadn't even stepped foot in my bedroom since the afternoon. From outside I caught the unmistakable sound of laughter. It was a light, tinkling sound. I sat up in bed and peered through the window at the pool.

The underwater light turned the pool turquoise, a rectangle of clear blue against the dark night surrounding it. From where I sat, I could make out two people floating in the deep end. Under the water, their bodies looked small and undulating as they treaded water next to one another.

There was another small peal of laughter and a moment later they swam to the edge of the pool, pressing up against one another along the wall.

Curiosity drew me out of bed. I knelt in front of the window, moving as close to the glass as I could. There were no curtains for me to hide behind, and the tall bank of windows running from the floor to the ceiling left hardly any wall to conceal me. I just hoped the shadows would be enough.

The window was cold, but I leaned my forehead against
it anyway, peering out at the two people lit from below in
the crystal water. All I could see was the back of their heads,
but then they moved a quarter turn, and Penn's face came
into view. His lips moved, speaking to the girl, although I
couldn't hear their words from here inside. The girl laughed,
throwing her head back so the ends of her wet hair dipped
into the water. And then, before I could look away, he
leaned forward and pressed his lips against hers.

I scooted backward, pulling my knees up to my chest. I
didn't want to see anymore, but I couldn't take my eyes off
of them. His lips only brushed hers for a moment, but the
gesture made me catch my breath. I closed my eyes, trying
to push away the feeling that was moving up through the
middle of me like warm water rising through my limbs.

I didn't want to feel this way.

I climbed back into bed, a bed that the other pet
probably slept in, too. This time I crawled underneath the
covers and pulled them up around my head, burying myself
beneath the pillows, hoping I could hide inside them.

My hands shook and I tucked them against my stomach.
Why was my heart jumping this way? I willed myself to be
still. Images of Penn and that girl floated across my mind,
but I pushed them away, let them drift to some far corner
where I wouldn't have to watch them anymore. Slowly, I
sank down into the soft nest of blankets, into the cool, deep
place where even dreams couldn't find me, and before I
knew it, I was asleep.

*W*hen I woke, the sun lit my room with the blush of early morning. The house was quiet. Outside, the pool reflected the soft hue of the sky, as smooth and still as a mirror.

I rolled over from my stomach. Sometime during the night I'd stretched out so my arms and legs were flung wide across the queen-size bed, exactly as I feared I would. I glanced around, hoping no one had seen me in such a degrading position, but I was alone.

The view out my window was beautiful at this time of morning. I hadn't had a good chance to study the grounds the day before because I'd been so consumed by the house itself, but now I stood in front of the windows near the loveseat and stared out across the expanse of lawn that sloped down on the south side of the house. In the distance, the rows of manicured hedges and flowerbeds wove in and out of the grass, and beyond those, what appeared to be a small orchard of fruit trees. Out my other windows, beyond the pool and the patio, a white gazebo sat at the bottom of the hill.

If one of my talents had been painting, I would have picked up a brush that very second. It was intoxicating. Living at the kennel, and then at the training center, I hadn't had much of an opportunity to spend time outside. Now the grass and the flowers gently blowing in the breeze seemed to call me. I swung open the French doors leading out onto the patio behind my room and stepped out into the cool morning air.

The gauzy fabric of my nightgown wasn't quite enough

to keep me warm, but I didn't want to spend another minute inside looking for something else to wear. I wrapped my arms around my chest, aware that in the morning light the sheer white cloth was almost transparent. It wasn't appropriate to be parading around in my nightclothes, but the house was completely still. No one would see me.

The grass was wet against my toes as I made my way across the lawn. I didn't have any particular destination in sight. Instead, I wandered past the flowers, stopping every few feet to smell the blossoms or glance back at the sleeping house.

At the bottom of the hill I came to the gazebo. The tall topiaries that stood on the inside of each of the white pillars made it feel as if I'd walked underneath a floating roof. I sank down onto one of the soft lounge chairs in the center of the room and stared back up at the house. It didn't seem so intimidating from this far away. And for a moment, at least, it didn't seem so hard to believe I could live here now.

My gaze traveled across the windows along the back of the house. Ruby's room overlooked the front of the house, but one of those windows might belong to Penn. The thought of him made my face flush.

I shook my head, trying to clear it. My feet were cold from walking barefoot across the lawn, and I laid them in a patch of sun at the bottom of the cushions and closed my eyes, breathing in the sweet smell that drifted off the vines growing along the railings.

Instead of thinking about Penn, I imagined the wall of books in Ruby's room. I shouldn't have let it worry me the way I did. Not being able to read was nothing to be ashamed of. I wasn't brilliant, but I wasn't a dolt. Sure, Miss

Gellner hadn't read us any fanciful tales, but we'd listened to biographies on all the American presidents and last year we'd spent months learning about the Kings of England. If our masters had wanted pets that could read and write, Miss Gellner would have trained us to do so. Besides, I could read music. That was a kind of reading. The next time Ruby asked about books I would point that out to her, instead of running off the way I had the night before.

The sound of footsteps brought me out of my reverie, and I opened my eyes to see Penn standing on the other side of the gazebo holding a tattered notebook in his hand.

"Oh, sorry," he said when I turned to face him. "I didn't mean to wake you."

"No, pardon me," I said, tucking my legs up underneath me and folding my arms across my chest, trying to cover up my thin nightgown. "I didn't realize there was anyone out here."

"I was just going to work on some lyrics." He shrugged. "I can do it somewhere else."

"I... I'm sorry," I stuttered. "I didn't realize…"

"You don't have to apologize to me," he said. "You've got as much right to be here as I do. It's your house, too, right?"

His words appeared kind, but his tone of voice confused me. It was cold, detached. He pressed his notebook to his chest and turned to leave.

"Wait…you don't have to go."

Penn stood with his back to me. Finally, he turned back around and lowered himself onto the edge of one of the chairs.

His gaze traveled slowly over me, finally stopping at my

face, but still he didn't smile and I folded my arms a little tighter across my chest.

"It's very beautiful down here," I said. "I've never seen so many flowers."

"Yeah, my parents went a little overboard with the landscaping," Penn said. "They'd like you to think it looks like this naturally, but believe me, it takes a half-dozen gardeners to keep it this way. I guess it's pretty, but I like things a little wilder."

"I think it's lovely," I said. "It's so much better than being inside."

Penn cocked his head and narrowed his eyes. The expression on his face made me think I'd said something wrong.

"They didn't let you go outside?"

"Oh no. I…they let us…I mean…we went outside. Every day," I stammered. I shouldn't have said anything about my life before. This wasn't what I meant. I only wanted to compliment the flowers. "I just meant that it wasn't like this. It feels like I'm inside a painting."

"Yeah." Penn nodded and slumped back in the chair, staring out at the flowers. His eyes were distant.

I plucked nervously at the hem of my nightgown. The silence was heavy, but I didn't dare speak again. Everything I said seemed to be wrong.

Finally, Penn spoke. "I didn't think my dad was actually going to go through with it again. Not after…" His voice trailed off and he shook his head. "You'd think he'd at least wait a little while. Out of respect, or whatever. But instead he just plows ahead and pretends like nothing even happened. He's so obsessed with what it would look like if we don't have one after all the time he spent getting the legislation passed and everything."

I wanted to ask him to go on, but the scowl that pulled at his mouth told me it wasn't a subject he was too happy with.

Penn stared down at the notebook in his lap, silently playing with the worn cover. After a few minutes he shook his head. "I think I'll go back inside."

As he stood to go, he leaned down to pluck a pink flower out of one of the large pots next to my chair. "Sometimes I think my dad likes beautiful things a little *too* much," he said, spinning the blossom between his fingers.

He leaned down and placed the flower behind my ear. When he pulled his hand away, his fingers brushed the side of my cheek.

"See ya around, Ella."

As he walked back up the path toward the house, I reached up and touched the velvety petals of the flower he'd placed in my hair. I could still feel the warm touch of his fingers against my cheek, and his words felt like they'd left their own heat behind in my mind.

I took a deep breath and closed my eyes, trying to quiet my breathing. I didn't dare head back to the house so obviously agitated. By the time I finally stood, the pounding in my heart had subsided. It was completely light out now, and I wanted to get back to my room before the others woke up. I didn't know yet what the congressman expected of me. Maybe he would be the kind of owner that simply wanted me to sit quietly on the furniture, smiling prettily.

Something told me life here wouldn't be that dull. I'd probably be spending a lot of time with Ruby. Even though

I hadn't been trained to play with children, I didn't mind the idea of spending time with her. She was lively and friendly, far more interesting than spending hours sitting perched on a couch.

But as much as I enjoyed Ruby, I was really hoping the congressman would ask me to play the piano for him today. I usually spent at least a few hours playing each day, but the past week had been crazy with the preparations for meeting our new owners. The short concert we'd performed at the training center was the only time I'd had a chance to play all week, and I was aching to sit down at the keys.

At the top of the hill, I stopped, the wind whipping lightly at my nightgown while I stared back at the gazebo one last time.

"There you are."

I jumped at the sound of the congressman's voice and spun around to see him stepping out of the French doors that led to my room.

"You had me nervous for a second there," he said, walking to stand next to me. "I came in to tell you that our housekeeper, Rosa, will be serving your breakfast on the patio near the pool. When you weren't here I worried that you'd run away during the night." He laughed, but his eyes weren't smiling.

My voice caught in my throat. "I was just looking at your beautiful gardens."

The congressman took a step onto the little patio behind my room and sat down on one of the small wrought iron chairs. He glanced at the yard as if he was considering its beauty. "Yes, this is the loveliest time of year. It seems like everything blooms at once."

His gaze skimmed my nightgown and then quickly went back up to my face. The blush that crept up my neck and onto my cheeks made me feel more exposed than the sheer fabric, but I didn't make a move to cover myself for fear I'd offend him.

Finally he spoke. "Once when I was little, we had a beagle that ran away from home. I hung signs all over the neighborhood, offered a huge reward, but we never got her back." He frowned as he wrapped a strand of my hair around his finger. "You wouldn't ever run away, would you, love?"

I paused, trying to find my voice. I didn't like being compared to a dog. Maybe I was misinterpreting his story. Maybe he'd simply been trying to tell me about a time when he lost something important to him...something he loved. I swallowed. "Of course not," I finally said. "Why would I ever leave a place as beautiful as this?"

Six

*E*ven though the morning started out crisp, by the afternoon the day had turned muggy and humid. Ruby and I sat in the conservatory working on her puzzle while the fans buzzed above our heads. She sighed and flicked another abandoned piece into the lid.

"This is too hard," she whined. "Let's go swimming. There are plenty of games we can play with two people. We can dive for rocks or do Marco Polo. I'll let you be Polo if you want. Maybe we can even talk Penn into playing and then we'll have three."

I didn't know what it meant to "be Polo," but the idea of going in the pool made me clammy with fear. I didn't want to tell Ruby that I didn't know how to swim. In the bathtubs at the training center, the most I could do was hold my breath underwater, but that was only for play, and the tubs weren't anywhere near as deep as the congressman's swimming pool.

"*Pleeeease*," Ruby whined again.

"I don't think that I have any swimwear," I said, hoping to deter her. "Maybe we could go up to your room instead. I could do your hair again."

She shook her head. "I'm sure my mom bought a swimsuit" She grabbed my hand and leapt to her feet, pulling me in the direction of my room.

It only took her a minute digging through the drawers to find the swimsuits. She pulled out two and held them up.

"Black or white, you choose," she said.

I'd never worn a swimsuit before, but both of the ones Ruby held up didn't look like they were made of much more fabric than my underwear. I couldn't imagine they would cover enough of me.

"Won't it show too much skin?" I asked, reaching for the black one. It was small and sheer, like my nightgown, and it seemed like there would hardly be enough fabric to cover one foot, let alone my whole body, but Ruby only laughed, shoving me toward the changing screen in the corner.

"Just put it on already. Meet me out by the pool when you're done."

I slipped out of my dress and wiggled into the suit, clasping the strap behind my neck. In the mirror, a spindly girl stared back at me. She was nothing but long legs and soft white skin. But luckily the suit covered me in the most important places. When I smoothed the fabric out, I was relieved to see that the fabric was only see-through along the waist. I wrapped myself in a towel and tiptoed out onto the patio where the congressman's wife sat underneath the covered patio, drinking something out of a sweating glass.

"You're going swimming?" she asked.

I clenched the towel a little tighter across my chest. "Ruby said she would like to swim and asked if I'd accompany her," I told her.

"Let's see how the suit looks," she said, motioning for me to lower the towel. "I had a stylist in New York who specializes in clothing for pets order all the clothes, but I never had a chance to see the suits."

I lowered the towel onto a lounge chair and did a full turn the way Miss Gellner had taught us to do whenever we were asked to show off our clothes, but my stiff arms stayed close to my body.

"You look just like Grace Kelly," the congressman's wife crooned. "That suit is beautiful."

I glanced down at the suit, trying to see what she was seeing, but I didn't really know what it was supposed to look like.

"The ruching is exquisite," she went on. "It makes your waist look miniscule, which I suppose it is."

"She thought it would show too much of her skin," Ruby said, walking up behind me. "She almost wouldn't come outside, and it's not like it's even a two piece." She laughed. "It's practically an old lady suit."

"It is plenty modest," the congressman's wife said, standing to walk around me. She pulled and rearranged bits of fabric so the tiny folds lay smooth against my skin. "Don't forget to put plenty of sunscreen on her, Ruby," she said, turning to face her daughter. "The last thing we need is for the pet to end up with a bunch of freckles like you."

The comment didn't seem to faze Ruby. She rolled her eyes. "I know."

"I'm not kidding," the congressman's wife said. "She's a

pet—it's not like we can expect her to do anything herself. It's your responsibility. Got it? We all need to take better care of her than the last one. And I can assure you, your father will not be pleased if he comes home and finds out that she's all red. He's already worried enough about having to be gone all day."

"I've got it, Mom," Ruby said, rolling her eyes again. "Stop nagging me."

The congressman's wife narrowed her eyes and looked at her daughter as if she wanted to say more, but then she reconsidered and strode back to the patio table, grabbing her drink before she went back inside through the kitchen door.

Ruby grabbed my arm. "Come on," she said, dragging me into the shallow end of the pool. She pulled on some goggles and then dove in with a gigantic splash.

I stood on the first wide step, shivering, not from cold, but from the thought of stepping down into an entire pool full of water. Surprisingly, the water was so warm it practically disappeared on my skin, as if it was the hot summer air that was swirling around me instead of thousands of gallons of water, but the sensation did little to calm me.

"Come *on!*" Ruby yelled again when she popped up. Rivulets of water ran down over her goggles and across her cheeks. She dove back under and wriggled along the bottom of the pool until she finally came splashing up near my legs. "Why are you just standing there?"

She propped her elbows on the cement and leaned back, sitting on the step at my feet, staring up at me. Her hair was still pulled back in the two French braids I'd put in the night before, and the goggles she wore pushed down on her ears, making them poke out comically from the side of her head. The goggles were funny. They made me think of the bulgy eyes of the flies that got inside the kennel during the summertime, but I was too nervous to laugh.

"Aren't you supposed to play with me?" Ruby asked when I didn't move any deeper into the water.

I bent down and splashed a bit of water in her direction.

She crossed her arms and glared at me. "That's not playing. You have to get wet."

I opened my mouth to tell her I wasn't really that sort of pet—I'd been trained to sit at the periphery of things looking pretty—when all of a sudden she lunged for me, wrapping her wet little body around my legs. I toppled into the pool and the water swallowed me. I sputtered and gasped, flailing to find my footing. My nose and throat filled with water and I blinked, but I couldn't see.

I came up, choking and sputtering and took a quick gulp of air before Ruby jumped on top of me again. Laughing, she pulled me under.

The water burned in the back of my throat and I fought to get another gasp of air. Underwater, Ruby's giggles sounded muffled and far away. I came up and gasped again, but my mouth filled with more water.

I fought to take another breath just as two large hands grabbed me around the waist, pulling me up out of the water.

"What are you trying to do, kill her? Can't you tell she can't swim?"

Penn dragged me out and laid me on the side of the pool, brushing back the slick of hair that covered my face. I pressed my cheek into the warm concrete and coughed up large gulps of water.

"Are you okay?" Penn asked, leaning over me. His shirt and shorts were sopping wet, but he didn't make an effort to mop up the water puddling around him.

I nodded slowly, trying not to look into his eyes. I drew in a few deep breaths. "I'm all right," I choked out.

In front of me, Ruby poked her head out of the water and grabbed onto the edge of the pool. "I'm sorry, Ella," she said. "Why didn't you tell me you didn't know how to swim?"

"Just leave her alone," Penn said, swatting his little sister away. "She's not a toy."

He grabbed my towel from off of the chair and dabbed the water from my face. "Do you want to try sitting up?"

I nodded and pushed myself up, dangling my feet over the edge into the water.

"Thank you," I whispered, trying to smooth out the mass of wet hair dripping down my back. "I think I'm all right now."

He hovered next to me a moment longer before he turned to go. "I'm going back inside," he called to Ruby, who was bobbing in the deep end. "Take better care of her or Dad's going to kill you."

"You don't have to be rude about it," Ruby called after him.

A breeze swept past me, bringing goose bumps to my skin as I stared at the broad back of Penn's shoulders as he stepped into the kitchen, trailing water behind him. Even now, with my throat and eyes stinging from the water, I could still picture the look of his bare skin floating in the pool the night before.

Ruby swam past me, zipping by my feet like a fish and

I closed my eyes, letting the sun warm my skin. Now that I was sitting on dry land, I was feeling a little bit better. Ruby wasn't thrilled that I was sitting poolside instead of in the water with her, but after a bit she seemed to forget that things would be more fun if I knew how to swim and made the best of what she had, which, at least, was someone willing to throw rings in the water for her to dive for.

"Throw it really deep this time!" Ruby yelled, treading water at the very end of the pool next to the diving board. "See if you can get it to go on the drain."

I reached for one of the rings she'd brought to me and tossed it into the water. It slowly sank to the pool floor, not quite landing on the drain. She took a deep gasp of air and dove down. For a second her bottom bobbed up above the water and then she was swimming down, down, down.

She didn't realize how lucky she was to be able to swim, or read for that matter. She was only ten and already she could do more things than I could do. Maybe I'd have to get her to teach me how to swim. It didn't have to be *soon*, I thought, with the sting of the water still sharp in my nose and my throat, but sometime.

She popped out of the water and swung the bright blue ring above her head. "I got it on the first try," she gasped.

The kitchen door swung open and Rosa, the Kimball's housekeeper, stepped outside carrying the telephone.

"Miss, the telephone's for you," she called, waiting patiently while Ruby swam to the edge of the pool and climbed out, reaching for the phone.

"Use the towel first," Rosa reprimanded. She held the phone out of reach while Ruby hurried to dry off as quickly as possible.

"Who is it?"

Rosa shrugged and handed the phone over.

"Hello," she chirped into the phone, obviously excited to be getting a phone call.

She sat down on a lounge chair, still dripping even though she held a towel between her knees. Rosa tapped her foot and crossed her arms across her chest impatiently. I wanted to ask Rosa if this was something special, or if she got calls all the time, but Rosa didn't seem like the type of person I could ask questions of.

She served me all my meals, and earlier in the day she'd come to collect my laundry, but she hadn't spoken to me besides giving me a brief nod when the congressman introduced us. And even though I couldn't quite figure out what I could have done to make her dislike me, I got the distinct feeling that she wasn't happy to have me here. A few times I had caught her staring at me, but as soon as I tried to meet her eyes she would shake her head and frown ever so slightly before she glanced away.

"Oh no." Ruby paused, frowning, "I don't think I got invited." She rubbed at her wet arms. "Yeah, have a good time. I hope you find a ride." Her voice cracked slightly at the end, but she kept her tears in until she hung up the phone and handed it to Rosa.

"Who was it?" Rosa asked.

She didn't answer. She shook her head, her face crumpling before she turned and ran into the house.

"Is she all right?" I asked. "Shall I go after her?"

Rosa turned to look at me full in the face for the first time since I'd arrived. Her eyes narrowed. "I don't know what you could do," she said. "The girl doesn't have friends. I don't think a *pet* can help with that." She spat the word "pet" as though it was something dirty.

I stopped moving my legs through the warm water and sat still, unsure how to respond. I ached to run after Ruby, but I sat unmoving, staring down into the clear water until Rosa turned around and walked inside.

I couldn't stop thinking about the way Rosa had said the word "pet," as if I was something sour, something repellent. It reminded me of the look on Penn's face when he talked about getting me. He hadn't thought his father would get *another one*, that's what he'd said, and the words looked like they left a bad taste in his mouth. At both the kennel and the training center, the word "pet" had always been used with pride. We were special, important, prized—at least that's what they'd always told us—so why did it seem different here?

Or maybe the thing that upset Rosa and Penn had nothing to do with me.

Seven

*W*hen Rosa returned to the house, I sneaked back into my room and got dressed. From there I crept through the conservatory, the congressman's book-lined study, the empty living room, and finally up the stairs to Ruby's room.

The door was shut, so I tapped lightly and moved my ear against it, listening for an invitation to come in, but the only sound I could make out was a few muffled sniffs from the other side.

I was about to leave when I remembered the secret knock. I put my ear to the door once more and repeated the series of knocks and taps. Holding my breath, I listened for her to call to me, telling me it was all right to come in, but there was only silence.

Just as I turned to go, the door cracked open.

"It's good you remembered the knock," Ruby said. "At first I thought maybe you were Rosa."

"May I come in?" I asked.

She left the door open without inviting me in and climbed back onto her rumpled bed, where I imagined she must have been lying before she answered the door. She buried her head in her pillow and I stood outside a moment longer, wondering if her open door was an offer to come in. When she didn't speak, I finally decided to enter.

I pulled the door shut quietly behind me and sat beside her on the bed. Her swimsuit was still wet from the pool and I rested my hand on her cold back, trying to rub a little warmth back into her. When she didn't speak, I lay down next to her and rested my head beside hers on the pillow.

After a few minutes of the two of us sitting in silence, she finally raised her face from the pillow and turned to face me. Even though her eyes were puffy from crying, they still held a faint mark from her goggles.

"That was Sarah. She needed a ride to Jayne Miller's party." She sniffed. "I guess she didn't know I wasn't invited."

"Did you want to go?" I asked.

She shrugged. "I guess. I never really get invited to anything."

I didn't know what to say to her. I didn't know anything about little girl's parties, so I couldn't even imagine what she would be missing out on. Maybe Rosa was right. What could a pet do to help?

Ruby wiped her eyes and fingered the end of my hair, which was almost dry from the pool. "I'm sorry I pushed you in the water."

"I should have told you that I couldn't swim," I said.

She sat up. "Yeah, you should have. I thought everybody knew how to swim."

"Did your last pet swim?" I asked.

She shrugged. "I don't know. We got her after the pool guys put the cover on and we had to give her back before they opened it back up."

She reached over to a frosted glass jar on her bedside table and pulled out a little gold wrapper. "You want one?" she asked, handing it to me.

I held out my hand and she placed the gold wrapper in my palm.

"What is it?"

"A butterscotch," she said. "My grandma sends them from Boston. There's a big candy store there that she takes me to when I visit."

She tugged on the ends of the wrapper and pulled out a small honey-colored butterscotch which she popped into her mouth, smiling. When I didn't do the same, her smile faded. "Don't you like them?"

I stared down at the shiny wrapper in my palm. "It's not one of the foods in my diet."

Ruby laughed. "Candy isn't a food in anyone's diet. That's why it's so good."

I pulled on the ends of the wrapper the way I'd seen her do it and picked up the hard candy.

"Go on," Ruby said. "Put it in your mouth."

I placed the butterscotch on my tongue and closed my mouth around it. The candy was tiny, but the flavor was immense inside my mouth, the sweetness filling up my whole head.

She giggled. "It's good, huh? But you probably shouldn't tell anyone that I gave it to you. My mom's always going off about cavities and getting fat and stuff."

I rubbed the candy gently against the top of my mouth,

careful not to suck it too quickly. This was a taste I wanted to keep in my mouth forever, something I wanted to savor and remember while I fell asleep at night.

As my candy slowly melted down to nothing, I eyed the wall of books on the other side of the room, and when the last bit crumbled away, leaving only the memory of sweetness in my mouth, I took a deep breath.

"I can't read," I said softly.

"What?" she gasped, pounding the bed with both fists. "You can't swim or read and you've never had candy? How are you supposed to survive? Those are like the most important things." She hopped off her bed, face flushed, eyes shining. "This is unacceptable!"

The excitement on her face made the tightness in my stomach disappear. She ran to the bookshelf and reached up on her tiptoes, stretching to grab a big red book on the top shelf.

"We'll start with this," she said, cradling the book in her arms before she plopped back down on the bed beside me. "This was my favorite book when I was little. It's got all the Grimm Fairy Tales. But don't worry—they're not like little kid fairy tales because they're full of scary stuff. My mom always used to say that they were too gruesome for girls, but I don't care."

She flipped the book open and ran her fingers over the page as if they were something soft.

"I've never taught anyone to read before," she said. "Maybe to start, I could just read out loud to you. That's what my mom and dad did when I was little. Then we'll start teaching you your letters."

I nodded and smiled, too afraid that if I spoke she'd

change her mind, or realize that pets weren't supposed to know how to read.

Ruby flipped through the pages, stopping to show me the ornate drawings every few pages. "Here, we'll start with this," she said, smoothing out a page in front of her. "*The Pink*, it's one of my favorite stories. You'll love it."

She leaned up against me, her little body warming my side and I smiled, letting myself relax for the first time all day.

As she started to read, I stared down at the delicate picture of a woman whose fair hair was crowned with jewels and flowers. The woman was beautiful, sound asleep on the banks of a river. She looked so perfect sleeping there, except for the three spots of blood that splattered her gown and the dark figure that crept away into the woods. None of the books that Miss Gellner had read to us had pictures like this.

Ruby ended up reading four stories to me and completely forgot about not being invited to Jayne's party. When I left her room, images of fire-breathing dogs and talking ravens were still clouding my vision. I'd never heard stories like those before, and even though I knew they were make believe, I could already feel the way they would haunt me, as if they'd found a soft spot to make a new home inside me.

I hurried in the direction of the stairs, hoping I could get back to my room before lunch was served. After what Rosa had said to me earlier, I didn't want her to find out I'd been upstairs. I didn't need to give her a real reason to dislike me.

Across the hall, the door to Penn's room was shut tight, but soft music wafted out from underneath it, drawing me toward the sound. It wasn't like the music we listened to at the training center. It wasn't Bach or Mozart, or even one of the lovely operas we used to sing during our Voice lessons.

The voice coming from behind the door was gruff and slightly shaky, and filled my heart with an ache I'd never felt before. The pain in my chest was sudden and completely unexpected, and I leaned up against the doorframe and closed my eyes tight, trying to hold on to the sound even though it hurt me. I couldn't tell whether it was sadness or joy pushing against the insides of my ribs, threatening to break me open.

I didn't even realize I was crying until the rattle of the doorknob made me open my eyes. The wetness on my cheeks startled me and I quickly wiped at it, stepping backward, but it was too late. He'd already seen me.

"What are you doing?" he asked.

"I... I..." I tried to catch my breath, but the music still played in the background. It wasn't muffled by the door now and I was so distracted by the pulse of the beat, and the sorrow in the man's voice, that I could hardly think. "I'm sorry," I said. "I heard your music."

Penn looked over his shoulder, as if the music was something he could see. "Yeah?"

"I didn't mean to bother you," I said, backing away. "I just haven't ever heard anything like it."

"You've never heard Ray LaMontagne?"

"No, I..." My voice trailed off.

He was staring at me with the same confusing expression I'd seen on his face every time he looked at me. It left me feeling like some strange, repulsive creature. I didn't know what reason he had to dislike me, but it was clear that he did.

"What, they didn't have music at the puppy mill?"

I didn't know what he was talking about, but the tone of his voice was hateful.

"We had music, but it was all classical. Nothing like this. This is so…" I fought for the right word, but I couldn't decide what to call it. "…so beautiful," I finally said.

His face softened slightly. "The song's called 'Trouble.' It's the title track to his first album. If you want to you can—"

Just then, the sound of raised voices drifted up the stairwell, distracting him, and he stepped past me, moving to the landing at the top of the stairs where he could get a better view of the commotion.

Timidly, I stepped up behind him and peered down to the foyer where the congressman's wife stood next to the open door with her arms folded across her chest. Standing half-in, half-out of the doorway was an older-looking woman with a pinched face and untamed gray hair that stood up on top of her head. Even though their clothes were almost identical, they didn't seem to belong in the same world.

"I really don't see how it's any of your business," the congressman's wife was saying.

This was obviously the wrong thing to say because the woman stepped farther into the foyer, pointing a long, skinny finger at her.

"Of course it's my business. It's a complete injustice. I thought you'd come to your senses, but apparently I was wrong. To think that you and your husband are bringing this sort of barbarity into our neighborhood a *second time*. It's unbelievable!"

"Barbarity?" The congressman's wife kept her voice calm, unlike the near shrieking tones the other woman's voice was climbing to.

"I'd say barbarity!" the woman yelled. "You're keeping another human being prisoner. You think you're so high and mighty that you can *own* another life. Well, I won't stand for it and I'd bet most of the voters in our district won't stand for it, either."

"I'm sorry you feel that way," she said. "What does Patsy have to say about it?"

The woman's face grew red. "Patsy is a schnauzer. You can't compare a person to a *dog*. It's a completely different situation. She's completely dependent on me. Besides, I treat her like one of the family."

"I don't want to argue with you, Rhonda," she said. "But I think it's exactly the same situation. We are the owners of a pet that the United States of America has deemed entirely legal in all fifty states. Whether or not you agree with it is beside the point."

"That's because people like your corrupt husband have passed legislation to make this sort of sick thing legal."

"If you're going to start calling my husband names, I'm going to have to ask you to leave."

The woman raised her arm, looking as if she might strike, and I instinctively took a step out from behind Penn, closing my hands around the railing to steady myself. Maybe the movement from upstairs distracted the woman, or maybe she realized how inappropriate it would be to actually hit the congressman's wife, because she lowered her arm.

Our eyes met.

"Is that her?" the woman asked, her voice suddenly becoming quiet, almost kind.

Penn, who had been standing utterly still during the entire scene, stepped forward, pushing me back from the railing so that his body was between the woman and me.

"I think it's time for you to be going now," the congressman's wife said, guiding her lightly by the elbow to the door.

"No, I only want to see her. You don't have to hide her from me," the woman said. She grabbed onto the doorframe and her voice rose again. "You! Girl!" she yelled at me. "Don't let them trap you here." Her voice was frantic. "Let go of me, Elise!" she bellowed. "You can't keep that girl locked up here. She's just a child. Look at her. I can help her!"

And with that, the congressman's wife shoved the woman back through the front entrance, slamming the wide wooden door with enough vigor that the picture frames shook against the wall.

Eight

I sat in my room on the couch near the window, staring out at the last bit of gold staining the sky. I couldn't place the feeling growing inside me. It was as if the flavor of Ruby's butterscotch and Penn's music still lingered on my tongue, a taste that was both bittersweet and totally divine.

This place was more beautiful than I ever could have imagined, but it was more confusing, too. It felt as if a conversation was going on around me, but I could only hear bits and pieces of it, and now I was trying desperately to string those bits together to make a sentence that I could actually understand.

The room was growing dark, but I didn't feel like turning on the bright light of the chandelier that hung at the end of my bed. In the shadows, I almost became a part of the room.

Miss Gellner had always admonished us to go to bed by nine o'clock each night. "Sleep feeds beauty," she always used to say. But I wasn't at all tired.

Just as I was about to get up from the couch to crawl into bed, there was a small *tap* at the door. Before I had a chance to respond, the door cracked open, letting the yellow light from the hallway spill into the room. The congressman's large body stood silhouetted in the doorframe.

"Ella?" he called, poking his head into the room.

I sat up straighter on the couch and arranged a content expression on my face.

"Please, come in," I said, pressing down the tremble in my voice.

The congressman strode into the room and sat beside me on the couch. The light was nearly gone from the sky and the only bit of illumination in the room was the yellow rectangle of light in the doorway. Sitting in the dark next to him felt too intimate, and I wished I had at least turned on a lamp.

"How was your first full day in your new house?"

"It was lovely." My face flushed at the lie, thinking of all the things that had happened during the day that I knew I shouldn't mention. Had he heard about that woman, Rhonda, and her crazy rant? Or about my swim in the pool? Or the forbidden piece of candy Ruby had given to me? I feared all of my secrets were written on my face as clearly as the words in Ruby's book of fairy tales, but the easy look on his face suggested he couldn't see them.

"I brought you a little something," the congressman said.

I hadn't noticed the small box he held until he placed it in my hands. The box was flat and rectangular, covered in soft, white satin.

"Go on, open it," he said.

I cracked the lid and stared down at the gold chain that

glittered ever so softly in the dim light. On the end of it was a round pendant. I lifted it up and held it to the light so I could see that the gold pendant was encircled with a ring of shining diamonds. Inside something was engraved in loopy script.

"It's your name," he said, reaching out to run his finger over the lettering. "And on the other side it has our address and phone number." He cupped the side of my face in his hand. "Let me put it on you."

My hands shook and I turned away from him, lifting the hair from off my back. The scooped back of my nightgown left me feeling bare, and without my hair to cover me a chill brought goose bumps to my skin.

The congressman reached his large arms around my body so the cold metal of the pendant rested across my collarbone.

"Now you'll never forget where you belong," he whispered next to my ear.

I reached down and touched the front of the pendant. "It's beautiful," I said. "Thank you for thinking of me."

"You're easy to think about, Ella."

My name sounded peculiar on his lips.

His hand still rested against the bare skin of my shoulder, but he didn't attempt to move it. Leaning forward, he brushed his lips lightly against my cheek.

When I raised my gaze, the congressman's wife was standing in the doorway. In one fluid motion the congressman removed his hand from my shoulder and scooted away from me.

"Elise, what wonderful timing," he said, standing. "I just gave Ella her new tag."

He stood and flipped on the light to the chandelier, casting the room with such bright, yellow light that I had to shield my eyes. Even so, I didn't miss the strange look that passed across his wife's face.

"Wonderful," she said, walking across the room to where I sat. "Let's have a look."

She only gave the pendant a passing glance before turning to her husband.

"It's late. Don't you think we should let Ella get to sleep?"

The congressman nodded, smiling at his wife. "Good night, love," he called behind him. A moment later the two of them closed the door, leaving me alone under the bright lights of the chandelier.

I don't know how long I sat on the edge of my bed, running my finger along the gold necklace, but eventually I switched off the light and lay down in the dark, waiting for the other lights in the house to blink out one by one. Finally, after what seemed like hours, I climbed out of bed and crept out onto the patio.

The house was dark and the light to the pool was off, but bits of moonlight glistened on the smooth surface. I sat down on the edge, dipping my feet into the water. They looked like two white fish moving back and forth beneath me, and for a minute I envied Ruby's ability to swim. If only I knew how, I could peel off this nightgown and lower my whole body down into the black water. What would it feel like, floating there in the dark staring up at the blue-black sky?

My fingers flittered up to the pendant at my throat. I couldn't stop touching it. Even after the metal warmed to my skin, I could still feel the cold place it had made on my chest. And even though it was a beautiful piece of jewelry, the first I'd ever worn, I longed to unclasp it and lay it back inside the pristine white box it had come in.

On the other side of the pool, the door to the kitchen clicked shut and I glanced up to see Penn walking toward me. It was too late to slink back into my room, so I sat still, hoping he wouldn't notice me.

"You look like a ghost in that nightgown," he said.

It was impossible not to think back to the moment I'd witnessed between him and that girl the night before. Would she be arriving soon? My cheeks flamed and I leaned away from him to run my hand through the water. "I hope I'm not interrupting you."

"No," he said, sitting down not too far from me and dipping his feet in beside mine. "I wasn't tired. Sometimes I come out here when I can't sleep."

"I can leave," I said, moving to get to my feet. "If you're expecting someone else."

He put out his hand to stop me, and for a long moment he stared at me, unblinking. Finally a smile cracked his lips. "You didn't happen to look out your window last night around midnight, did you?"

I opened my mouth to answer, but I was struck dumb, mortified, that he knew I'd been spying on him.

"I keep forgetting someone's in that room again," he said. "Don't worry about it. I'm not mad or anything. It was stupid of me. Really. My parents' room is right there." He pointed to the wing of the house that jutted out symmetrically to my room. I hadn't realized the congressman's room was so close to mine and suddenly I worried that he was watching us through the window.

Penn followed my gaze. "Don't worry, he usually goes to sleep pretty early. All that pandering to the public can really wear a guy out."

Beneath me, the water was as still as glass. It seemed like ages ago that he had pulled me out, and even longer ago that I'd seen him swimming with that girl. How could time change so suddenly? Years could go by in the blink of an eye and then you meet somebody and one day feels like an eternity.

"Is she your…friend?" I asked. "The girl you went swimming with last night?"

"Lexie?" Penn asked. "Yeah, I guess you could call her my friend." He reached down and splashed a handful of water across the surface of the pool. "Lexie and I used to go to school together, before my dad decided it was too scandalous to have a son in a performing arts school. Next year I'll be going to Briggons Academy because he thinks it's more important for a congressman's son to learn about economics than music." He shrugged. "Lexie and I were both just a little bored last night. It's not really anything."

I didn't know what being bored had to do with what I'd seen the night before.

"Is that why you touched her that way?" I asked. "Because you were bored?"

It was a bold question. I don't know what had made me ask it.

"Touched her?"

I shook my head. "I'm sorry. It was an inappropriate question. I've just never seen anyone do that..."

"Oh God," he groaned. "Listen, it wasn't like that. Really. We were just goofing around. It wasn't anything serious."

"Goofing around? Is that what it's called?"

"Yeah...oh...well...no," he stammered. "Come on, seriously? They didn't teach you any of this? Like in a video or anything?"

I shook my head. "I've heard that men touch their lips to a woman's hand, as a greeting, but I didn't know..." I swallowed. My throat felt so dry that I was finding it hard to talk. "I didn't know that they sometimes touched lips to lips."

Penn laughed, but only for a second before he cocked his head and stared at me, eyes squinted ever so softly. "You're serious, aren't you?" he asked. "They really didn't teach you about kissing?"

I touched my cheek, remembering the way the congressman had brushed his lips against my skin. But before I could untangle the knot of questions jumbled up inside me, Penn leaned forward quickly and brushed his lips against mine. They only rested against mine for a moment, but the touch sent a spark buzzing to the very center of my body. I pulled back, gasping for air as if I'd been dumped in the pool again.

"There," Penn smiled. "Now you know what it feels like."

"I don't—" I began, but then we were interrupted by voices coming from his parent's room.

"Don't act like it's not a big deal, John."

The voice that drifted out the window sounded as if it was right beside us.

"You need to let it go," the congressman said. "It was only a little kiss on the cheek, that's all. Keep your emotions in check."

My stomach twisted. Had the congressman felt the same spark when he'd kissed my cheek as I'd felt when Penn kissed my lips? Penn glanced uncomfortably in my direction. Did he know they were arguing about me? I started to stand up, but he grabbed my arm.

"Don't worry," he said. "As long as we're sitting down they can't see us. The potted palms cover the view from their windows."

"It's *your emotions* I'm worried about, not mine." The congressman's wife's voice didn't soften. If anything, it got louder. "You've already proven you can't control yourself with one of them around, and now you expect me to turn right back around and do this all over again. I don't want to have to relive your same stupid mistakes over and over again."

Penn ran a hand over his face and shook his head. It was obvious he didn't want to hear his parents fight.

"It wasn't *my* mistake."

There was a long pause.

"Fine, you don't believe me," the congressman said. "But don't take it out on her. How many times do I have to say I'm sorry?"

"I don't want you to keep saying you're sorry. I want reassurance."

"That was a completely different scenario," the congressman said. "You know that isn't why I got her."

"Isn't it? You were sure quick to replace the last one."

"How do you think it looked?" he snapped. "If I'd

waited, people would start talking. They'd think I didn't support my own bill, but worse than that, they'd start digging. That kind of speculation would ruin us. Besides," he said, his voice softening. "This will be good for Ruby."

"You can stop pandering to me," she said. "You already know that she's the *only* reason I agreed to this again. And it better be different this time. This time the pet is for Ruby, not you. It's not healthy for a ten-year-old to spend all her time alone in her room reading. So yes, maybe I'm hoping it will get her out more. Maybe I'm hoping she'll lose a little weight and start caring about how she looks. Is it so wrong for a mother to want that for her little girl?"

The congressman was quiet and I held my breath, waiting for someone to speak.

"I care about Ruby, too," he finally said. "Can you please just try to be happy about this?"

"I'm trying to keep an open mind. You're the one who's refusing to listen. If you would just consider having her—"

"I'm *not* getting her spayed." His voice was sharp. "It's a ten thousand dollar procedure that we don't need to have done. It'll take her weeks to recuperate. Why do that to the poor thing?"

There was no answer. After a moment of silence, I heard a door shut. Beside me, Penn clenched his hands, looking at me out of the corner of his eye.

"What does that mean, spayed?" I asked.

"Ella…I…God, she can't be serious," he said. "This whole thing is totally screwed up."

"Please, tell me what it means," I said. My body was already shaking, imagining being taken back to the kennel. I knew they did things with needles. I'd seen them on a table behind the red door. Sometimes we saw the workers emerge from behind it and we'd hide in our rooms, but their voices would drift through the vents, carrying words like "pentobarbital" and "euthanize" and even though I didn't recognize those words they terrified me. Just like the word "spayed."

Penn studied my face, but he didn't move. The night seemed eerily quiet. Even the crickets had let their music die away.

Finally he spoke. "It means you won't be able to have babies. They'll make it so you can't."

"I could have babies?" I asked, unable to hide the shock in my voice. All this fuss was about babies?

"Yeah," he said quietly. "You could."

"Penn?" I paused. Maybe it wasn't the right time to ask, but I had to know. "Why did you give the other pet back to the kennel?"

"Didn't my dad read you the press release?" Penn asked, his voice suddenly harsh.

"He said she got sick," I said.

"Yeah...sick." He shook his head. "Sadly, she came down with something that we couldn't treat on our own. The kennel *insisted* that we return her so that they could give her the special care she needed."

His words sounded familiar.

"But—"

"There's stuff you don't know, Ella. Stuff you probably shouldn't hear from me." He climbed to his feet. "I'm sorry. I've gotta get out of here."

He paused and looked at me one last time before he turned and strode out into the night, down the paths toward the gazebo. I didn't want him to leave. The night seemed colder and darker without him there. I wrapped my arms around my chest and pulled my wet and wrinkled feet from the water before I headed back to my room.

The cool air blowing from the vents made me shiver and I climbed under the covers, pulling them tight around my chin. Lightly, I traced my fingers over my lips, remembering what it had felt like to have Penn's mouth on top of my own, even if it had only been for a second. Just thinking about it made my body tingle, but I wanted to feel it there again. I wanted to feel that spark, even though I knew it was wrong. I wasn't supposed to feel this way. What would the congressman do if he found out about the thoughts that were running through my mind? If they'd given one pet back to the kennel, maybe I'd get sent back, too. I'd assumed when they bought me that I'd live here forever.

It hadn't occurred to me that my stay might be temporary.

I pressed the heels of my palms against my eyes, trying to block out the memory of the kennel's red door, but it was useless. The image had already stained my thoughts, a shock of red as bright as blood against the dark.

Nine

$\mathcal{I}$ rose early and picked one of the gowns Ruby preferred when she last stopped by my room. It was the softest shade of blush, the same creamy pink of my cheeks. The closet was full of dresses that were almost this exact shade, each one as lovely as the gown Miss Gellner had spent so much time picking out for me. I'd already been at the house a week and I hadn't worn a third of the dresses in the closet.

This dress was elegant. The bodice was covered in fine lace with a thin satin bow accentuating my waist. Below that, yards and yards of soft chiffon billowed out like the upside-down petals of one of the beautiful flowers I'd seen in the garden. I knew, even without looking in the mirror, that it was stunning. It gave off the exact impression a pet was supposed to convey: beauty, prosperity, purity. But even so, I longed for something simple, like the plain cotton dresses we'd worn as girls in the kennel.

The other people in the congressman's family didn't

dress in fancy clothes every day. Ruby wore shorts and a
short-sleeved shirt if she wasn't running around in her bathing suit, and Penn's wardrobe didn't seem much different.
Even the congressman's wife, although always tailored and
put together, mostly wore clean, pressed slacks with silken
blouses. They were the sort of clothes someone could be at
home in.

But my dresses made me feel as if I was constantly on
display. Miss Gellner would have given me a sharp whack
with her stick and told me that's exactly what their purpose
was, and for me to get used to it. People didn't buy a pet
so that it could blend into the background. They bought a
showpiece, a thing of beauty. And after the conversation I'd
overheard between the congressman and his wife, I didn't
want to be anything but perfect. On the outside I needed to
look exactly like the pet I'd been raised to be. Maybe then,
my inside would begin to match. Maybe I'd stop wanting
things I couldn't have.

Outside, the day was cool. The grass was wet with dew
and even though my bare feet were becoming accustomed
to the feel of it, the luxury of being outside at dawn still
hit me anew each day. Today, I ambled down the broad hill
and veered left in front of the orchard, following the small,
stone path through a patch of bushes overflowing with
round white blossoms to the shade of a row of tall trees that
grew along the fence. Following the trail, I tilted my face
skyward and listened to the lonesome call of a single bird.
The early morning sun slanted through the trees, turning the
leaves golden. Up ahead, it reflected off of the windows of a
carriage house on the other side of the fence.

As I drew closer, I noticed there was someone outside.

Her back was turned to me and she stood hunched over a garbage can, scraping some dirt out of a bucket. Under my foot, a branch cracked and she spun around, putting her hand up to shield her eyes from the light.

"Who's there?" she called, her voice quivering slightly.

My voice caught in my throat. "I'm so sorry. I didn't mean to startle you. I was just out for a walk."

"Out for a walk at this hour?" she barked. "I thought I was the only one foolish enough to be up this early."

She lowered her hand from her eyes and her face came into view. I recognized her immediately—the pinched face, the wild gray hair. It was Rhonda, the lady who had stormed into the congressman's foyer the other day, screaming about how awful pets were.

My legs shook and I stepped farther back into the shadow of the trees. I didn't want her to see me. I only wanted to get back up to the house where everybody else was.

"I'm sorry I bothered you," I choked out, turning to go.

"No, wait. Please," the woman said. She stepped forward, taking off her gloves and tossing them down on a wooden table that ran along the back of the garage.

I stood frozen, wishing I could run, yet pulled by her command to stay.

"Don't go," she said again, closer now. "I'm Ms. Harper. I live here." She gestured behind her. Through the trees I could make out the pale yellow paint of her house.

"You're the girl from the Kimballs'," she said, nodding. I expected her to start yelling at me the way she had with the congressman's wife, but her face stayed calm. "It's nice to meet you up close."

She reached out her hand for me to shake, but I wasn't sure. What if the congressman's wife found out? Would it be a betrayal to shake hands with this woman?

"It's a pleasure," I finally said, curtsying slightly.

She withdrew her hand. "I guess I should apologize for the way I acted the other day," she said. "I can get a little overheated when it comes to politics. It burns me to the core to think slavery is alive and well in America."

I nodded as if I understood. "Please, excuse me. I need to be getting back."

"Wait!" Ms. Harper grabbed onto the edge of the fence. "Please, let me say one thing before you go."

My heart pounded in my chest, but I stood still.

"I can take you away from here," she said, looking straight into my eyes. "It's wrong what they're doing to you. People should *never* be kept as possessions." Her voice was desperate, pleading. "I can take you to a better place, give you your own life. I *know* people."

She reached out and grabbed at my arm, her cold fingers digging into my skin with a grip that made the hairs on the back of my neck stand on end. I pulled my arm away.

My legs shook, but I tried to keep my voice calm. "That's so kind of you, Ms. Harper, but please believe I'm fine where I am."

"They just have you brainwashed into believing that."

"I can assure you. I'm very happy," I told her. "Now if you'll excuse me, I really should be getting back. The Kimballs are expecting me."

"If you ever change your mind, my offer stands," Ms. Harper called after me. "I can help you. I can set you free."

$\mathcal{B}$y midafternoon the house was completely silent. The congressman had left right after breakfast for a meeting, and his wife was taking Ruby into New York for the day to go shopping for a new dress to wear to their big fundraising party. Penn had driven away earlier in the morning in his dad's convertible, but he hadn't returned yet. Even Rosa was gone. She'd been complaining about all the extra shopping she had to do that day.

Maybe I was the only one who had nothing important to do.

I stood at the window in the living room as the congressman's wife pulled out of the driveway. Ruby glumly waved good bye. She wasn't excited to be shopping with her mother. According to her, they'd already been on three unsuccessful shopping trips and had come away empty-handed. They were running out of time to find something suitable for her important party.

I waved after Ruby and stood for a minute longer, making certain they were truly gone.

The seconds ticked slowly and my hands began to itch. I'd been hoping for this moment since I arrived, the moment I could finally sit down at the grand piano in the conservatory and play. For the past week all of the songs I'd been thinking about felt as if they were piling up inside me. If I didn't get them out soon I'd explode.

As badly as I wanted to hike up my skirts and sprint straight to those perfect black and white keys, I forced myself to walk. There were some rules I just couldn't break. And even though I was certain Miss Gellner wouldn't be happy with the idea of me playing the piano without first being invited to do so, I decided that was one rule I would choose to disobey.

In the conservatory the piano sat in a bath of sunlight in the corner. The black top was polished to such sheen that the white puff of clouds floating above the skylights were mirrored in its reflection.

I circled the perimeter of the piano, running my hand gently over the keys, so softly that they didn't even make a sound. For some reason it didn't feel right to simply sit down to play. I needed to introduce myself, to let this beautiful instrument know who I was before I used it.

Finally I pulled out the cushioned bench and scooted up to the keys. Gently I pressed the middle C, listening to the sweet, soft tone that rang through the room, one single, perfect note. My eyes clouded with tears, grateful for the chance to play.

I took a deep breath, spreading my fingers across the keyboard, and closed my eyes. The notes moved up through my spine until I could actually feel them leaving my body. Until each one of those notes that had been held captive inside of me broke free.

Miss Gellner wouldn't have been pleased with the way I moved, letting the music take control of me this way. "Save your movement for ballet," she would have said, but I couldn't keep my body stiff and straight when there was this sort of sound surrounding me.

I moved through all my favorite songs. Vivaldi I played so softly that the song was merely a suggestion, the thought of sound. Later I pounded out Mozart with such force that it seemed as if bringing these songs to life was something violent, a raw and savage act.

Dewy sweat formed along my brow, and my breath came in quick bursts, like I'd been running, fast and hard to keep up with the music. I struck the last few chords and sat slouched and panting at the keys.

"Wow."

I turned around to see Penn sitting in his father's chair. He leaned forward. "Seriously," he said. "That was amazing. I don't even know what to say."

I sat up straight and smoothed out my skirt. "How long have you been sitting there?"

"I came in during the Chopin piece, at least I think that's what it was." He shrugged. "I'm not usually a big classical music fan."

"Yes, it was Chopin." I nodded, brushing the back of my shaking hand across my forehead. I hoped he couldn't see the sweat that beaded my brow. It was bad enough that he'd seen the way I'd lost myself in the music.

Penn fidgeted in the chair. "I'm sorry I didn't say something sooner, but it just felt wrong to interrupt you. You looked so..." He paused, as if trying to find the right word. "Consumed."

"I've been hoping your father would ask me to play, but he hasn't yet. I probably should have waited, but I figured that since everybody was out of the house for the afternoon, I wouldn't be bothering anyone."

"Not to disappoint you or anything, but your music won't be important to my dad unless there's someone to impress."

He must have caught the bitterness in his voice because he stopped himself. "I'm sorry," he said. "I just wanted to tell you how amazing your playing was. I didn't realize they taught you to play like that at the..."

He stopped talking and closed his eyes, shaking his head before he stood to go. I turned back to the piano, sorry to say good bye to it so soon.

"Ella?" Penn asked.

I turned around. He stood in the doorway, looking back at me. "Yes?"

"If you ever want to listen to more of the music I was playing the other day, you can always come up to my room. I've got a ton of stuff I could play for you."

"Oh," I said, surprised by the invitation. "I'd like that."

I couldn't hide the smile that broke across my face. My gaze fell to his lips and immediately my skin flushed. Could he tell that I was thinking about the way they felt?

He smiled back. "You can come up now, if you want."

*T*he inside of Penn's room didn't look a thing like the rest of the house. Maybe at one point his mother had had a hand in decorating it, but it was hard to tell because of the lengths he must have gone to cover it up. The bones of the room were strong and masculine: solid, wooden furniture stained a dark, deep cherry. But besides the furniture, the rest of the room appeared to be one giant battle against any influence of his mother.

The walls, which had once been painted a soft shade of green, were plastered over with posters of people and old, rusty road signs. The far wall above his bed was almost entirely covered with instruments. I didn't recognize most of them, but there were a few of them that I could name: a couple of guitars, a mandolin.

"Do you play those?" I asked, pointing to the wall.

"Yeah, most of them…at least a little," Penn said, glancing up from his speakers. "But I'm only really good at a few. Mostly I play the guitar."

I looked around for a place to sit, but most of the surfaces were covered in discarded clothes and towels. Apparently Rosa didn't pick up the laundry in his room the way she did for everyone else.

I stood awkwardly amidst the mess, glancing at the photographs that covered the mirror above the gigantic set of dresser drawers. There were pictures of Penn at the beach, and of him playing the guitar in front of a roaring bonfire. There were pictures of him clustered amidst groups of his friends. I searched their faces, trying to recognize the girl from the swimming pool, but none of them seemed familiar.

"Okay," he finally said. "I'm starting you out with Amos Lee since you liked Ray LaMontagne so much."

He hit a button and music started playing, sounding as if it was coming from all four corners of his room.

I closed my eyes to the soft sound of the piano, both familiar yet totally new. It was always enchanting to hear a new composition after hearing the same ones year after year, and this one was no exception. The notes were lonely, full of melancholy that reminded me a bit of one of Beethoven's sonatas. But I wasn't prepared for the ache I would feel once the singing started. I took a shuddering breath.

"Are you okay?"

I nodded, afraid that if I opened my mouth I wouldn't be able to speak. I closed my eyes again and let myself drift into the music. It wasn't until the song faded out and

I opened my eyes again that I realized Penn was sitting next to me. He was staring at me again, that same puzzled expression on his face.

"That was beautiful," I choked out, before he could ask me again if I was all right.

"Yeah." He smiled. "It's one of my favorites. Who would have guessed I'd have the same taste in music as a pet from Greenwich Kennels?" It was the first time he'd mentioned my past without sounding angry.

"You can play me something else if you want."

Penn put on another song and flopped down on the bed next to me, pushing a notebook and a pair of pants onto the floor.

"Sorry about the mess," he said. "Here, you can scoot over if you want."

I scooted closer to him, settling into the music. Both of us sat perfectly still and listened to the strum of the guitar and the beat of the drums that played underneath like a heartbeat. Next to me, I could feel the heat of Penn's leg seeping through the fabric of my dress, making my thigh burn.

He leaned in. This close I could see the bursts of gold inside his eyes, but all I could think about was that kiss, the way his lips had felt against mine. So soft. So warm. I wanted to feel that again.

There was a knock at the door and Penn scooted away from me, but not fast enough. His father threw the door open.

"Thank God," he said, striding over to us. "I looked all over the house for you, Ella. Didn't you hear me calling?"

"With the music playing, I must not have heard you," I

said. "I'm terribly sorry, Master."

Out of the corner of my eye I saw Penn cringe. I should have remembered that I wasn't to use that word, but I was so nervous, and the congressman's face was flushed and red, distracting me. I couldn't think straight.

The congressman turned on Penn. "What were you thinking, taking her up here?"

"I was just playing her some music. It's not like I—"

"Your music is the last thing I want you to introduce her to. If I remember correctly, you need to be focusing on catching up on your school work, not wasting time listening to songs."

"Dad, I—" Penn started to say, but the congressman didn't seem at all interested.

"Not now. I've got two campaign donors waiting in the conservatory to meet Ella. I've wasted ten minutes looking for her, so I really don't have time for your excuses right now."

As the congressman took me by the elbow and led me from the room, I chanced one last glance back at Penn.

He had already turned away.

Ten

*D*ownstairs in the conservatory, the congressman's colleagues sat waiting with their arms crossed over their chests and their legs folded at the knee. There were two of them, big men who seemed as proud and intimidating as my own master.

"Sorry to keep you waiting," the congressman said, leading me gently into the room. "It seems my son was trying to commandeer her."

"Well I can't blame him," one of the men said. He must have been a little older than the congressman, because his hair was almost completely white.

The congressman sat down in his usual chair and motioned for me to sit on the ottoman at his knee.

"So...I wasn't joking, was I?" he said. "This is the reason everyone was so excited about Bill 467." He gestured to me and smiled broadly, leaning back in his chair. "If it wasn't politically unethical I'd be buying stock in Greenwich Kennels

myself. As it is, I'm just happy to be able to recommend
them to people like you. Actually, I thought that you two
might be interested in applying for the lottery. The owners at
Greenwich are still grateful for my work on passing the legislation; one of the perks being that I have a little sway with
getting names moved up on the waiting list."

The congressman's colleagues both nodded, smiling
as their gazes moved back over me. I could see them each
imagining how it would be to own someone like me.

"And you're sure they're less care than your typical
pet?" the other man asked.

"No comparison," the congressman said.

"How about a teenage girl? I've already had two
teenage daughters and believe me, that's not something I
want to live through again. Although, I must say, this little
beauty brings me close to seriously reconsidering." He
leaned forward and picked up my hand, turning my palm up
so that he could stroke the soft skin along the inside of my
wrist.

The muscles in my arm twitched, but I didn't dare pull
away. Why hadn't Miss Gellner warned us that we'd be
touched this way? It didn't seem to bother the congressman,
but my skin crawled.

The congressman grinned, oblivious to my discomfort.
"I can assure you, Tom, they've been trained to be practically self-sufficient. Sure, you'll need to spend some money
on them. This little gal is a luxury; of course you're going to
want to outfit her with the best. But the payoff...well, who
wouldn't want to see this face over breakfast every morning?"

I should have been used to hearing people boast about

how great we Greenwich girls were. Miss Gellner had certainly done it enough. But hearing it come out of the congressman's mouth made me feel oddly small and inconsequential. Not important at all.

"I have to be honest, John," one of them said. "I heard that you'd had some sort of trouble with your first one. Did you have to take it back?"

The congressman waved his question away. "Oh, I wouldn't call it trouble," he said. "We did have another pet before we got Ella here, but she came down with something that we couldn't treat on our own. The kennel said it was a fluke and they *insisted* that we return her so that they could give her the special care she needed. But they were wonderful about putting our names at the top of the list for the next lottery and, of course, they waved all the fees."

The men nodded, seemingly unbothered that the other pet had been replaced so easily. Nobody cared. Maybe we were really that disposable. The other pet's sickness might have made her defective, but what about the improper thoughts that kept running through my head? Did those make me defective, too?

"Well, I really can't get over it," one of them said. "Who would have imagined when we were first starting out that they would come up with something like this?"

The congressman nodded. "It's going to completely redefine what it means to be one of the elite. Nowadays it seems like everyone has a yacht and a villa someplace. But these pets...they're a completely new indicator of class."

For a minute the three of them sat back in their chairs, chewing on their ideas as if they were feeding some barely disguised hunger inside them. I did as Miss Gellner had instructed and looked eagerly between their faces. It wouldn't do for them to think I found their conversation boring. Even if they assumed I didn't completely understand their conversation, I was still to appear engaged.

"She really is charming, John," the silver-haired man said. "What did you say I'd have to do to get my name on that list?"

"I'll go over all the details with you in just a moment," the congressman said. "But first let's have Ella play us a little something. Did I tell you they're classically trained in an instrument? Our Ella plays the piano."

He gave me a nod and I rose from the ottoman and made my way over to the piano, carefully arranging myself on the bench so my gown billowed out beside me on either side. I knew the picture I made sitting before them was as important as the music I produced.

I folded my hands in my lap and turned slightly so they could see my profile as I spoke. "Is there a song that you would prefer to hear?"

"Oh no," the congressman waved his hand. "You go ahead and play us anything, love."

I nodded. "Very well."

I turned around to face the piano, my fingers shaking. It seemed so strange to think that less than an hour ago I'd ached to play this instrument. But it felt tainted now. In my mind I kept replaying Penn's words.

Your music won't be important to my dad unless there's someone to impress.

I didn't want to play the piano out of obligation. I wanted to play it out of joy. Even if that joy was only bringing a bit of pleasure to my owner. But what pleasure was he getting from this? I was only a replacement.

As I played, I kept my eyes wide open, staring out at the trees that grew outside the window. It would have to be enough to bring the music into the room, without becoming a part of it. I wouldn't close my eyes. I wouldn't let my body dance.

When the song was over I folded my hands back in my lap and turned around to face the men again.

They clapped loudly, congratulating the congressman on his wonderful taste and I let my eyes glaze over a little bit. Maybe Miss Gellner was wrong. Maybe they didn't care if I was engaged in their conversation. They certainly didn't seem to care if the music came from my heart. It was enough just to have my fingers move. I could be a mechanical girl as easily as I could be a living one. All that mattered was how things looked on the outside.

Eleven

$\mathcal{A}$s the summer days grew longer and hotter, the novelty of my arrival wore off. A few weeks and my presence no longer shocked them. When they entered a room I happened to be in, they stopped looking surprised, as if they'd stumbled upon some unusual creature, a bird that had flapped through an open window and nested on their couch.

By the time the congressman's annual fundraising party rolled around, I'd figured out how to make the best of the time I was alone in the house, finding a few minutes of stolen time here and there to pound out enough songs to keep my soul fed.

On Saturday morning I sat on the patio, the way I'd made a habit of doing each morning since I'd arrived, but it was obvious that this morning was different. It was only six thirty, but already there were people buzzing around the backyard, getting a start on the millions of small tasks that needed to be completed before the party in the evening.

On the patio next to the pool house, a group of young men were setting up long tables for the hors d'oeuvres and the drinks. It was hard to imagine they would need so many tables just for food and drinks. Past the long tables, more men were setting up a large white tent out on the lawn.

Men and women in white buttoned shirts had already started unloading boxes out of large trucks they'd parked in front of the carriage house, and as much as I wanted to walk over and peer inside the boxes to see what sort of things they'd needed for one party that would take up so much space, I kept still, posing with a weak smile while I sipped a cup of warm green tea.

"Good morning."

I turned to see Penn walking across the patio. He was dressed in shorts and a T-shirt, but his hair was still damp from the shower.

"I was hoping you'd be out here," he said, stopping to stand at the foot of my chair. From behind his back he pulled a bouquet of flowers. "I got you something." He handed over the thick bunch, so full and heavy that they bowed their heavy heads in my lap, dropping fuchsia petals onto my skirt.

"Thank you," I said, looking up at him. "You picked these?"

"No." He laughed. "But the florist didn't look like they'd miss them. Besides, they're prettier in your hands than in one of those vase things."

He shuffled back and forth on his feet. "Do you mind if I sit?"

I nodded and scooted my legs to the side to make room for him on the cushion by my feet.

He glanced at me. The sun wasn't high in the sky, but even this early in the morning the light caught his eyes as he talked, turning them the loveliest shade of warm amber.

Across the yard, the door to the kitchen opened and his father stepped out. He was already dressed in khakis and a pressed shirt instead of his normal blue robe. In one hand he held a steaming mug and in the other a stack of papers. He glanced up and his mouth tightened into a thin line when he saw us. He set the cup and papers down on the patio table, then joined us.

Penn got to his feet.

The congressman glanced between the two of us and then down to the flowers in my lap. "Good morning, Penn. Good morning, Ella."

He took another step closer to me and Penn scooted back onto the grass. "Out helping with the floral arrangements, are we?" the congressman asked, putting a hand on my shoulder.

Penn didn't answer his father. Instead, he turned to me. "I gotta go. See you, Ella." He turned toward the house, shoving his hands in his pockets as he began to walk away.

"I hope you've been working on that essay for the internship instead of wasting your time with flowers," his father called after him and gave my arm another squeeze. "I'm just dying to show you off tonight, love," he said. "You'll be the belle of the ball." He stroked the hair back from my forehead.

"It looks like the party will be exquisite," I said.

"Yes." He nodded, glancing around the yard with a satisfied smile. "Make sure you get a nap in this afternoon. I don't want you getting distracted with all this party planning nonsense."

He took the flowers that were already beginning to droop in my lap. "I need you to be rested and perfect for this evening," he said, then walked away.

The congressman's wife, who had been flitting throughout the yard making sure everything was ending up in the correct place, watched her husband gather up his papers and walk back inside the house.

She broke free from the group of men she was speaking to and came over. Over the past few weeks she hadn't gone out of her way to speak to me, although on the occasions we were together she was always polite, even if she was brief.

"Good morning, Ella. Quite a show they're putting on, isn't it?" She didn't wait for a response from me before she went on. "If you think this is something, wait until tonight. Things are really going to look spectacular with the band and the lights. It will be truly magical."

She stopped talking and stared at me for a long moment, making sure I was paying attention.

"This is a very important event," she said. "I've been planning it for months and if I'm lucky we'll raise enough money for the Ghana Orphan's Fund to build the community center we've been saving up for. And, of course, we have the added bonus of getting plenty of John's constituents out at the same time. It's never too early to start campaigning for a reelection."

"That sounds wonderful," I told her, trying to keep my response as brief as possible. I doubted she cared what I thought about her event.

She pulled a chair over and sat next to me. "A lot of John's colleagues already know we got a pet from Greenwich, and although I'm sure he's planning on showing you off tonight, there are a number of women from the charity who aren't crazy about the whole…arrangement."

She brushed at the front of her blouse even though there wasn't a crease on it. "What I'm trying to say is, I'd rather not draw attention to you if I can help it. Not that I want to hide you during the party or anything, but I just thought if we can maybe have you keep to the perimeters of it, tone down your gown, so you don't draw quite so much attention…you know."

Her forehead crinkled and I realized just how uncomfortable it made her to not be completely in control.

"Of course," I told her. "I'm happy to do whatever pleases you."

"Oh wonderful." She sighed, obviously relieved. I wasn't sure how she was imagining our conversation could have gone any differently. "Actually, I already picked you out a dress. It's a black, tea-length Valentino. Really beautiful. You'll look gorgeous in it, believe me, but it is a bit more subdued than your normal attire."

She motioned to the gown I was wearing now, a floor-length, rose-colored dress made out of crushed silk and organza, embellished with so many tiny crystals over the bodice that it shone in the sunlight. Certainly not the subdued look she was going for.

"I'll have Rosa bring it to your room before the party," she said. "And if you could do me just one more little favor and not tell John about our arrangement, I'd really appreciate it."

I sighed with relief, knowing that I'd have an excuse to not be in the spotlight at the party. I gave her a nod and a conspiratorial smile.

The congressman's wife was correct. I did look stunning in my gown. Standing in front of the full-length mirror mounted beside my closet, I admired the way it changed my appearance. Even though the other gowns I wore were beautiful, they made me feel like the pet I'd been raised to be. I was fair and innocent, one of the beautiful princesses in Ruby's fairy tales.

But the black Valentino dress made me look different. I turned in a slow circle, trying to figure out why I felt so strange.

The dress was short, cut right below the knee where the silk chiffon fanned out ever so delicately. Around the waist, a broad black bow accentuated my figure. But my favorite part was the top. The silk was patterned in a soft, sweetheart neckline, and above that was a sheer voile top with long sleeves and a delicate collar that circled my collarbone, giving the dress a sophisticated air unlike anything I'd worn before. I stopped turning and let my hands fall to my sides. In this dress I hardly looked like a pet at all.

The party had already begun by the time I slipped out my double doors and onto the patio. Rosa had brought my dinner to my room instead of feeding me in the dining room because the congressman's wife had been worried it would seem peculiar to the guests if I were seen eating one of my meals. But even though I'd just eaten, the smells that drifted over from the long tables by the pool house made my mouth water. What would I give to be able to try just a nibble of all those fancy foods? I'd seen them all pass through the house on their way to the tables: dishes of dainty finger foods arranged like tiny pieces of art on the overflowing trays.

The patio was sparkling with the white lights strung from the pool house and along the top of the new tent. In the pool, glowing orbs floated on top of the water. The night was warm, but not hot, and the music drifting out of the tent at the bottom of the hill floated over to me on a light breeze. I stopped to soak it all in. It was hard to imagine there had ever been a more beautiful evening in the history of the world, and here I was, able to enjoy it all.

Across the patio I took in the groups of people buzzing around the tables and talking in clumps by the edge of the pool. They all seemed so grand, so important, smiling to one another over fluted glasses full of sparkling drinks.

The congressman and his wife stood amidst the clump of guests. They looked striking. His wife was remarkable in her everyday wear, but tonight she seemed like an entirely different person. The soft light illuminated her honey-colored gown, reflecting in the tiny gold beads scattered across the bodice, which slowly disappeared as they neared the ground. It was sleek and elegant, accentuating her broad shoulders and long, slender body. Next to her, the congressman stood with his hand around her waist, staring at her unwaveringly while she spoke. It was so different from the way he looked at me.

I hovered at the edge of the party near the pool house and watched as the guests orbited one another.

"They really went all out, didn't they?" Penn walked up next to me wearing a crisp black tuxedo.

I stared. He looked handsome in this change of clothes, polished and refined. His father would be happy to see his son blending in so well with his colleagues. But this new version of him made me nervous. It wasn't until I looked up at his tousled hair and warm eyes that I relaxed, grateful that his new clothes couldn't hide the real him.

In each of his hands he carried a long fluted glass. "I guess they don't really get the concept of excess," he said, handing one of the glasses to me.

I cradled the glass in my hand and took a tiny sip. The drink was utterly foreign. A million bubbles fizzed in my mouth. "It's magical," I said, looking out at the sparkling lights.

Penn smiled and stared at me before he turned to look out at the crowds of elegant people. Finally he looked back down into his own drink, where the bubbles climbed up the side of the glass like tiny strands of lights. "Sorry for being so cynical. Sometimes my parents bring out the worst in me."

We stood silent for a minute, listening to the sounds of the other guests. Their voices were a soft hum, punctuated every now and again by the sound of laughter and clinking glasses.

After a minute Penn turned back to me. "You look different tonight. I'm sorry I didn't tell you at first...when I came over. You're really...beautiful. I guess I'm so used to seeing your hair down, but it's really nice up like that."

"Thank you," I said, reaching up to touch the thick braid that wrapped around the top of my head. It was the same way I'd worn my hair for years in the training center, but it did feel different tonight.

"Do you want to go see the dance floor?"

"I promised your mother that I would stay toward the edge of things. She asked me not to draw too much attention to myself."

Penn shook his head, as if he should have expected this

from his mother. "It's impossible for you not to draw attention."

He grabbed my hand and pulled me onto the grass. In front of us, the tent was alive with light and noise. A wide wooden dance floor had been laid over the grass at the other end of the tent, and past it, the band stood on top of a small stage pouring music out into the night.

"I really wanted to dance with you," Penn said, frowning as he looked out over the crowded floor where his father stood talking with a large group of men.

The ceiling inside was covered with large lanterns, which reflected off of the glossy wood, and as much as I wanted to stand beneath them, I didn't want to disobey the congressman's wife.

I shook my head. "I'm sorry, Penn. I can't."

Watching the sweet way his face fell in disappointment made me laugh.

"Oh, you think hurting my feelings is funny?" he asked.

"No." I smiled, covering my face with my hands.

Penn turned his head away from me, but his smile was impossible to disguise. "Good thing I don't give up easily," he said. He pulled me around the corner of the tent and down the dark hill into the shadows. "We'll just have to dance out here."

With a quick flick of the wrist, he grabbed me again by the hand and drew me into his chest. My breath caught in my throat. After all the Dance lessons we'd been given at the training center, this was my first time dancing with a man.

A wild tingling spread through my chest, as if all those tiny bubbles in my drink had begun exploding inside me the moment he began to move me across the grass in a slow waltz. He wasn't a great dancer, but his arms were firm, his hand warm and strong against my back. I leaned my head on his chest, letting myself breathe in the clean smell of his starched shirt and the lingering fragrance of the bubbly drink on his breath.

"Ella?"

"Yes?"

"I...I'm sorry if I've been an ass. It's just... I can't figure out what to think of you. I didn't want to like you," he said, pulling me ever so slightly closer to him. "When my dad said he was getting another pet from Greenwich... God, I was so pissed. Not just because of what happened before, but because I don't want us to be one of those showpiece families my dad wants us to be. And I guess I thought you'd be another plastic girl, one more plaything for my midlife-crisis dad, or something, and it made me sick. But then I met you..." He paused, looking down at me. "You aren't anything like that other one. I mean, when I heard you playing the piano the other day... You can't teach a pet to play that way, you know? With so much heart. I don't know if I've ever seen a person play like that."

I wasn't sure if the heat in my face was the exhilaration of dancing, or modesty from hearing someone compliment my piano playing. But was it really a compliment to tell me that I didn't play the piano like a pet from Greenwich? Because that's what I was. And even if he hadn't liked the other girl, I couldn't imagine how we could be that different.

"Thank you," I said, trying to keep some decorum in my voice the way Miss Gellner had taught us to do when someone gave us a compliment, even though I still wasn't sure if it was a compliment, an apology, or a confession.

The only thing I did know was how good it felt to be held by his strong arms as we moved in small circles across the grass.

"It's a perfect night," I finally said.

"Yeah." He grinned. "What did I tell you? My parents don't really hold anything back."

"I didn't mean the party," I said, only realizing the words were too bold once they'd already left my mouth. But it was too late to take them back.

I looked back up at the gleaming tent. The congressman and two other men emerged, each holding a drink in their hands. He squinted up toward the house and then out across the lawn, obviously scanning the party for someone. My stomach flipped, knowing that someone was me.

Penn followed my gaze and the smile on his face disappeared. He grabbed me by the waist and pulled me farther down the hill where a stand of lilac bushes bordered the grass. My heels sank into the dirt, and branches smacked my arms as he dragged me in behind him. Cool green leaves enveloped us.

"Shh," Penn whispered, pulling me closer to his side.

I held completely still. My heart hammered in my throat, drowning out the sound of the music drifting down to us.

"He didn't see us, did he?" I whispered after a minute had passed.

Penn pushed aside a few branches and glanced back up to the tent. "I don't think so," he said. He stood up and smiled.

"What?"

He shook his head, laughing. "It's just funny," he said. "Hiding like this from my dad. I feel like I'm a little kid or something."

His laughter was contagious, and I covered my face with my hands.

Penn cocked his head and studied me. "You know, if you're really trying to escape the party tonight, I have a much better place for us to hide." He reached his hand out for mine. "If you haven't seen a secret garden at night, you've never truly lived."

I took a deep breath and grabbed his hand, stepping out of our hiding place.

"If you'll kindly follow me, madam," he said, plucking a stray twig from my hair before I wrapped my hand around his arm.

We wound our way along the back of the yard until we came to a small gravel path that wove its way through the orchard. Overhead, the moon shone on the pale stones making the path seem lit, even in the darkness.

We walked in silence for a minute, heading into the fruit grove. I'd never been there, even during the day, but in the moonlight, the garden looked completely foreign, all the colors compacted and condensed into cool silvers and blues.

Up the hill, the party was still in full swing. My feet crunched softly on the empty path and I took a deep breath, grateful to be away from it all.

"It's right past the orchard," Penn said as we traced our way between the trunks of gnarled old trees. They reached out to us with branches like withered, old arms, reminding me of the witches from Ruby's stories, and I held a little tighter to his arm.

Finally we came to a tall hedge running along the back of the orchard. An archway was cut into the center of it with a rusted wrought iron door that stood slightly ajar.

"I used to come here all the time when I was a little kid," Penn said, gently swinging the door inward. "Nobody else comes here because it's so overgrown. And I guess the gardeners don't want to bother with it if no one's going to see it."

We stepped inside the courtyard. On all sides the eight-foot-tall hedges acted as walls, enclosing it perfectly from the rest of the yard. If it hadn't been for the bright moon shining down on us, it would have been completely dark inside. We walked farther in, along the same pale, gravel path that now curved through the courtyard, and the party all but disappeared. Through the wrought iron gate I could only catch a glimpse of the white tent flaming up the hill, and the sounds of the party disappeared, replaced instead by the sound of crickets and the wind blowing through the leaves.

"I guess it's kind of a mess," Penn said. "Sometimes I wonder who built it. My mom and dad had the rest of the grounds redone when we moved in, but this stuff has to be really old." He ran his foot along the patio in the center of the garden. "You can tell from how worn the stones are."

Penn kept talking, and I turned in a slow circle, taking it all in. Thick weeds sprouted up through the cracks in the pavers and drowned out the flowerbeds that must have lined the edges of the garden long ago. In the moonlight, a spattering of scraggly weeds with tiny blue flowers surrounded a gigantic overgrown rose bush, which spilled petals across an old stone bench. And next to the bench, water bugs scooted across a long, rectangular pond. The whole garden was a messy tangle of vines and leaves, but there was beauty in the chaos, a wild abandon.

"This is my favorite part of the whole garden." Penn took my hand and led me to the far wall. "You can tell it's been here for ages. The house was built in the thirties and I'm guessing it's probably been here since then."

He pushed aside a clump of vines and uncovered a small cavity in the hedge. Standing inside was a stone statue of a woman. Her face was tilted up to the sky, eyes closed, with an almost invisible smile on her lips.

"She looks like she's waiting for something beautiful to happen," I whispered, reaching out to stroke the rough stone.

"I think she looks a little bit like you."

I swallowed, suddenly more aware of my own heartbeat than I'd ever been before. If I raised my hand to my throat I'd be able to feel it there, fluttering like a thing with wings trying to escape.

"I found her when I was ten. I lost one of my toy cars back in the shrubs and when I went to look for it, she was just standing there waiting for me. I've never shown her to anyone else. I've thought about telling my sisters, but I don't know… I kind of like keeping her a secret. I guess I kind of like being the only one who knows about her." He smiled. "Well now with you, I guess there are two of us."

"I won't tell."

We sat down on a small bench near one of the walls. "So, what do you think?" he asked.

I breathed in deeply, savoring the dank and woody smell of the garden. It was so different than anywhere else on the property. "It's so beautiful. It's like the plants are celebrating."

Penn raised one of his eyebrows. "Celebrating?"

"Never mind." I shrugged, flustered. "It was a silly thing to say."

"No, tell me," he insisted.

I took a deep breath. Maybe here in the dark I could say things that would sound strange anywhere else. "It just seems like they're happy not to be contained," I said. "People might try to force them to be something different for a little while, but in the end, their true nature still comes through."

"Yeah." Penn smiled. "It's *just* like that. Sometimes it's nice to have a little bit of imperfection, isn't it?"

Twelve

*O*utside Penn's garden, the music and the lights brought me back into the real world. At the top of the hill we both paused and stared at the gleaming tent.

Neither of us noticed his mother, but all of a sudden there she was, standing next to us.

"I've been looking all over for you."

Penn's reaction was immediate. His hand flew from the spot where it rested at the base of my spine and he stepped away from me. "Oh, hey Mom. How's the party going?"

She dismissed his question with a wave of her hand. "Your father has been looking for both of you and I'm not sure I can hold him off much longer. I told him you were introducing Ella to the Dibellas, but there's not very much longer—" She stopped talking midsentence and tucked a piece of hair behind her ear, composing herself. "Hello, dear," she said, smiling as the congressman walked up behind us.

He took a long sip from his glass and let his gaze travel

over us. "The Dargers and Mortensons are here with their
kids. I thought you'd be entertaining them," he said to Penn.
"When I saw them a minute ago, they were actually looking
bored." He stopped talking, his gaze darting between the
three of us. "What are you doing out here anyway?"

When none of us responded, he nudged Penn in the
direction of the tent. "You certainly don't need to be out
here keeping Ella company."

Penn glowered, but he let his mother lead him toward
a group of people his age who were sipping drinks and
laughing near the buffet table.

After they were gone he turned his attention to me.
"I hope you're enjoying yourself," he said. "I've got some
friends who are dying to meet you."

He took me by the elbow, leading me in the direction of
the tent, but before we entered, he pulled me close, leaning
down to speak in my ear. "Try not to distract Penn anymore
tonight, all right? There are plenty of other people here
who'd enjoy your company."

The congressman's colleagues were all packed together
on the far end of the tent, laughing loudly and puffing on
thick brown cigars. The air was thick with smoke, but none
of them seemed to mind.

"Not to worry. I found her!" he announced, patting a
few of the men on the back as we wove through the crowd.

There was an empty seat at a table in the corner and the
congressman sank down into it, smiling.

I stood uncomfortably at his side.

"So you weren't lying," a tall man with a mustache said.
He placed his hand on my shoulder and twisted me around
so that he could get a better look. "And this one's even

prettier than the last."

"What did I tell you?" The congressman grinned and took another sip of his drink. "Come on, Charlie," he called across the table to a man with blond hair. "You've got to admit that you're curious. This doesn't make you change your mind about the funding?"

The man gave a consolatory smile. "You always have to be right, don't you, John? How do you expect a man to argue with a face like that? It's unfair."

The congressman threw his head back and laughed, clearly enjoying himself.

"Come here, love," he said, pulling me down onto his lap. His breath was hot against my neck, pungent with the smell of his drink. I wanted to turn my head away, but I couldn't. I took shallow breaths and forced a serene smile onto my face. They didn't need to know the level of concentration it took to look this way, to keep myself looking pleasant instead of puckering with disgust.

It was a skill to silent my body. If I hadn't been trained by Miss Gellner, I never could have sat perched on the congressman's knee without squirming. And oh, how I wanted to. I wanted to peel his hand from my waist. I wanted to scoot forward so I couldn't feel the way his belly pressed against me with each breath that he took.

I'd always been told that a pet was meant to be a showpiece, but this wasn't what I'd imagined. I always assumed that I'd be admired, displayed even, but not handled like an object, like a toy.

By the time the congressman was done showing me off, the dewy turquoise sky had turned black, dotted with an abundance of stars. And still the band played and the people laughed and ate and drank. I watched Penn from where I sat on the low stonewall that ran behind the party tent. He didn't seem to have any trouble entertaining the large group of friends clustered around him. I would have loved to know what they were talking about, but even though I could see their lips move and their heads tip back with laughter, I couldn't make out their words.

After a while I stood and made my way back up to the lounge chairs by the pool. They were familiar and comfortable, the place I spent so much time lately, and I settled down on one. I wrapped my arms tightly around my body. Already, I missed the heat of Penn's body so close to mine.

"Do you mind if I sit?"

I jumped a little, surprised to see one of the young men Penn had been talking to earlier standing next to the foot of my chair. He smiled broadly, bringing two deep dimples to his cheeks. He was dressed in the same sort of black tuxedo Penn was wearing.

"Please." I gestured to the chair next to me.

"Thanks." Ignoring my gesture, he brushed my feet to the side and sat down near my legs. "I've been looking at you all night. Have you not noticed?"

I shook my head.

"I'm Collin," he said, sticking out his hand for me to shake. I took it lightly, surprised when he brought it up to his lips.

"I'm Ella." I didn't know how much Penn had told him about me, but I didn't want to make the congressman's wife angry by saying too much.

"It was kind of rude of Penn not to bring you over to

meet us," he said, resting his hand on the cushion near my leg.

I was suddenly very aware of how short this dress was compared to the other gowns I was used to wearing and I tugged at the bottom of it, trying to get it to cover my knees.

"But I can see how he'd like to keep you to himself," Collin went on, scooting a little closer. "So, is it true what they say about pets?"

I fumbled to pick up my drink, which still sat on the small table by my chair, and took a small sip, but with the bubbles gone it didn't taste good at all. I swallowed. "I don't know what you mean."

"Sure you do," Collin said, reaching out to put a hand on my thigh. "I've always wondered what they taught you at those kennels. It can't just be how to sit there and look pretty."

"I...well...there's etiquette..." I stumbled.

"Not that I have a problem with you just sitting there looking pretty," he said. "Has anyone told you how gorgeous you look?"

"That's very kind of you." I swung my legs over the side of the chaise lounge to give myself some distance. I needed to get out of here, somewhere where I wouldn't be such a distraction. I was afraid this was exactly what the congress-man's wife had been talking about. "I'm sorry, but if you'll excuse me."

"Wait," he said, tightening the grip on my leg. "We were just getting to know each other."

My stomach knotted and I tried to scoot farther away from his grasp. "It really has been a pleasure meeting you, but I think Mrs. Kimball is expecting me."

Collin laughed softly. "No, she's not. Come on, we both

know she's trying to hide you. I mean, look at this dress." He rubbed the fabric between his fingers. "When has a pet ever worn anything like this?"

I shook my head, trying to find my voice. "I don't...I don't know what you're talking about."

"It's all right," he said, stretching his hand more fully across my thigh.

I swallowed back the embarrassment that burned the back of my throat. "I...I shouldn't be talking to you. Mrs. Kimball asked me to keep my distance from the guests."

"How about we keep our distance from the other guests together?" He nodded his head at the dark house. "I bet it's nice and private in there."

My gaze traveled up the shadowed brick to Penn's room on the second floor. My heart stuttered, imagining how different it would feel if he had been the one to invite me inside. I remembered the way he'd kissed me. Is that what this boy wanted to do? I didn't want to kiss him.

"That sounds lovely," I said, pushing down the fear in my voice. "I just need a minute to freshen up. If you want to head inside, I'll meet you in the conservatory in just a few minutes."

Collin grinned. "Don't keep me waiting." He traced a finger along the collar of my dress. "I've been imagining what's under here all night. I don't know how much longer I can stand it."

"I won't," I choked out. As soon as he closed the door behind him, I slid out past the pool house and onto the cool lawn. A swarm of tiny bugs hovered in front of me like a cloud and I batted them away.

Never. I would never let him touch me.

My legs wobbled as I broke into a run. A dark under-current surged beneath the congressman's picture-perfect world, threatening to pull me down and it frightened me... almost as much as what waited for me at the kennel if I was to make a mistake.

Thirteen

$\mathcal{N}$o one called after me as I ran. I headed for Penn's garden, taking the long way past the carriage house. Maybe he'd look up and notice I was gone. If he did, I hoped that he would think to look for me there. It was the only safe place I could think to hide.

I turned onto the Kimballs' gravel driveway well out of reach of the light from the front porch. The wind rustled softly through the trees and I picked up my pace. Being out on this part of the road at night made the hairs on my neck stand on end. The shadows were so dark inside the trees that almost anything could be hiding there, but I'd take my chances with the shadows before I would go back to Collin.

At the end of the driveway a dark car sat idling in front of Ms. Harper's lane.

"Hello?" a voice called from inside the car.

I stopped short. In front of me, the car door opened and the light from the dash illuminated Ms. Harper's surprised face.

"Ella, is that you?" She peered past me toward the Kimballs' driveway.

I started to turn back to the house before I reconsidered. Ms. Harper was peculiar, but she didn't frighten me the way that Collin did.

"It's so nice to see you again, dear," she said, climbing out and slamming the door behind her. "I've been wanting to apologize about the last time I saw you. I can be kind of abrupt. It's not my best quality."

She smiled apologetically. Out here in the dark, she seemed so much older and smaller than I remembered.

"Thank you. It's nice to see you as well," I squeaked, trying to compose my voice. Ms. Harper certainly wasn't someone I'd choose to talk to on a normal occasion, but at the moment her presence almost calmed me.

"Taking a break from the party?" she asked. "I don't blame you one bit. All that merriment can be a bit overwhelming, can't it?"

I nodded.

"I'm more of a homebody myself, but then again, I'm an old lady." She paused. "Speaking of being an old lady, can I ask a favor of you, dear? My nephew was supposed to help me unload something from my car, but he's hasn't arrived yet, and I just can't do it by myself. Would you mind climbing in the backseat and grabbing it for me?"

I glanced down at my dress. I wasn't used to people asking this sort of favor of me, but it seemed rude to refuse.

"I can't thank you enough," she said, opening the back door. "It's back there on the floor, below the passenger seat."

The backseat of the car was dark. I slid across the cold

leather, reaching out blindly with my hands along the floor.

"I don't feel anything," I called. "What is—"

The door slammed behind me and I sat up, fumbling for the doorknob.

"Ms. Harper, it's locked." My voice came out shrill and small. A moment later she slid into the front seat and slammed the door.

"It's locked," I said again, louder this time.

The car roared to life and we started to roll forward out of the driveway. My stomach sank. Something bad was happening.

"Wait!" I yelled. "What are you doing?"

She pressed on the gas and the car peeled out onto the dark road. "For God's sake. Don't scream," she said, glancing back at me in the rearview mirror. "I don't react well to distractions while I'm driving. *Please,* don't do that again."

My hand fumbled once more for the door. "Where are you going? I can't just leave."

"Of course you can leave. They're all so busy with their rich friends and their champagne, they won't notice for hours. We'll be long gone."

Long gone? Surely someone would notice that I was missing before then. But who? The congressman had already showed me off to his friends, and his wife certainly wasn't going to seek me out. That only left Penn, and he would probably just think I was hiding from his father somewhere.

"Please," I begged. "I don't want to go."

"I'm sorry, but this is for your own good. You might not understand now, but you will. I promise."

The car careened around a bend, sending me sliding against the far door.

"You're making a mistake."

"Don't be ridiculous," she snapped. "Do you know how long I've been protesting this law? It's been almost twenty years. And now...to have the chance to finally *do* something about it instead of just holding a picket sign..."

She adjusted her mirror and tightened her grip on the wheel.

"I've opposed this thing since they started letting those breeders in Nevada mess around with genetic engineering. And that was when they were claiming that they were only going to use it to make companions for the elderly and people with disabilities, but I saw this whole thing coming. Every last sick bit of it." She hit her hands against the steering wheel with each word.

"You can't just steal me," I said. But my voice was not nearly as forceful as I wanted it to be.

She fumbled with the radio until she found the station she was looking for. A bit of light jazz filled the car. The sound confused me, so different from the discordant babbling in my mind. "I'm not stealing you, my dear. I'm *freeing* you. Our country decided decades ago that it's immoral for one human to own another, but apparently some people have chosen to forget it."

Immoral? Wasn't it immoral to steal someone's property? Wasn't it immoral to take a person away from the life they'd been raised to lead? I turned around in my seat, climbing up on my knees as the entrance to the Kimballs' driveway faded away behind me, leaving only a dark tunnel of trees.

My fingers fumbled for the door handle, but I didn't pull it. What good would it do? I already knew it was locked.

I propped my head against the glass, wiping at the tears that slid down my cheeks. They blurred the shadows of the trees and fields whipping past in the dark, and my mind moved to other shadows, an image of another girl, another pet. "Did you try to steal her, too?"

"What?"

My heart pounded. "The other pet? Did you try to steal her, too?"

The car slowed just a bit and she turned to look at me for just a moment. "They told you about her?"

"Yes." It wasn't a lie, but it wasn't really the truth, either. Yes, I knew she existed, or that she *had* existed, but that was almost all. What else did I know? That she was good at coloring pictures. That she'd gotten sick.

"I was under the impression that she'd been swept under the table. Out of sight, out of mind," Ms. Harper said.

I was silent. What was that supposed to mean? Swept under the table?

"Clearly they realized that keeping her while she was in that condition was a mistake," she went on. "But I would have taken her. I would have made sure she had a real life afterward. Instead of…" Her voice trailed off.

Instead of what? Instead of what they'd done to her at the kennel? A tight ache crept up through my chest and I clamped my hands over of my heart, trying to push away the pain.

"So, to answer your question, no, I didn't try to take her." Her voice changed. It sounded softer, sad even. "I didn't, but I should have."

The tires hummed against the pavement, moving me farther and farther away from the Kimballs' house. Every

once in a while a light would cut through the trees, reminding me that there were homes back there, with people asleep
in their beds. But after a while the combination of the hum
of the tires against the pavement and the drone of Ms.
Harper's music made my eyes close and I drifted off into
sleep.

*W*hen I woke, my eyes were tight and swollen from
crying. Even the soft light of dawn was too bright, and I
blinked, trying to stop the pounding that thrummed against
my temples. I rubbed my eyes and stared out at the sunrise
peeking from behind the edges of the buildings that sat on
the horizon.

We were driving along a huge road. On either side of us
the city rose up, a giant sea of cement and windows. I didn't
recognize anything. My shoulders ached from the awkward
position I'd been in, pressed against the door with my hands
curled up near my cheek. I moaned and rubbed at the sore
muscles that ran down my back.

Ms. Harper must have seen me moving. "We're almost
there. Twenty minutes, tops."

In the rearview mirror, the dark circles stood out underneath her eyes. Her normally wild hair stuck out in an even
more radical mass.

"Where are we going?" I asked.

"A safe house," Ms. Harper replied. "They'll be able to help
you. There are whole organizations of people who have found
ways to smuggle pets out of the country. It's an underground

movement, but it's been picking up steam for a while."

"Underground?"

"Not literally under the ground," she said. "It means secret. These people are putting their lives at risk. It's illegal to free a pet, you know."

She sounded proud, but it didn't make any sense. Why would someone put themselves at risk just so that they could free a pet who didn't want saving?

"I guess I could try calling them again to let them know we're almost there. I didn't get a hold of them last night and I called about fifteen times. What sort of person doesn't have voicemail?" She sighed.

The thumping of my heart picked up pace as Ms. Harper exited the main road and pulled on to a side street. She stopped the car in front of a long strip of run-down buildings and rooted around in her purse.

"I printed off the instructions." She came up with a crumpled piece of paper and slouched over the steering wheel, running her finger down the words and muttering to herself. "You'd think they'd make it easier to find," she said, pulling back out into the street.

For an hour we snaked through the neighborhoods. I stared out the window at the people who were starting to emerge from the buildings. You could tell from looking at them that they didn't have much. Their clothes were ill fitting and dingy. Even our cotton dresses from the kennel had a sort of simple, clean elegance compared to what they wore. They must have been the kind of working-class people that Miss Gellner had told us about. They weren't like the rich. These people worked hard all day just to make enough money to live in one of these shabby old buildings.

I waited for the buildings to change, to turn back into the elegant estates that we'd left behind, but they didn't. What would I do if Ms. Harper was taking me here, to one of these buildings? I didn't fit in here. I was bred for refinement, not this.

Finally we pulled up in front of a three-story, red brick building surrounded by cracked cement and old cars. The small metal balconies that lined the front of the building were full of old plastic chairs and dead plants. Ms. Harper gazed up at the building and then back down at her paper.

"This is it?" She shook her head. "It might not be very nice on the outside, but that's probably just a cover. I'm sure they don't want people to suspect they're helping runaway pets."

She stepped out of the car and motioned for me to follow. Outside, the air was heavy and humid. Without the relief of trees and grass it was sweltering even this early in the morning. As we walked up a short set of stairs to the door at the front of the building, I tried not to stare at the old man sleeping in the alleyway between the buildings. His face was covered in a dirty beard, crusted with something brownish around his lips. A few sheets of newspaper covered him like a blanket, but his legs stuck out the bottom and his bare feet were black with grime.

Ms. Harper pressed a button beside the door and a bell buzzed. A moment later the little intercom beside the door crackled. "Who is it?"

Ms. Harper glanced over at me and shrugged. "Yes, hello," she said. "My name is Rhonda Harper. I'm a member of the N.R.P.A. I have a rescued pet and a source told me that this is a safe house."

The speaker crackled again. "Who told you that?"

Ms. Harper cleared her throat. "Beth Reynolds. She was speaking at a meeting in Connecticut and mentioned your name."

There was a muffled curse. "Connecticut?"

A moment later the door buzzed open and an over-weight woman in sweatpants and a stained T-shirt stared out at us. "That her?" she said, pointing at me.

"Yes, this is Ella." Ms. Harper pushed me forward.

"Why'd you come all the way from Connecticut?" the woman asked. "We only take pets moving north toward Canada. What are you doing bringing her farther south? That doesn't make any sense."

"I believe there's been a mistake," I said, stepping for-ward. Ms. Harper wouldn't listen to me, but maybe this woman would. "I didn't ask to come. So if you'll just—"

"This was the contact I was given," Ms. Harper inter-rupted, flapping her arms, flustered. "I've driven all night long and my nerves are shot. I'm sorry if I didn't do things to your liking, but I was a bit more concerned with this girl's freedom than with which direction I was headed."

She started to back down the steps, leaving me standing alone on the landing in front of the strange woman.

"Please, I—" I started again, but neither of them even glanced at me.

"Well we can't take her," the woman said. "You can't just show up here without an appointment and expect me to take her."

"I tried calling last night." Ms. Harper's voice was a high squeak, almost breathless with annoyance.

"Did you talk to anyone?"

Ms. Harper huffed back up the stairs, her knotted finger pointed angrily in the woman's direction. "I can't believe this. We're fighting for the same thing here. You can't possibly be telling me that you're unwilling to help, simply because I didn't make an appointment. This isn't the DMV. This is a girl's freedom we're talking about."

"Listen lady—"

"No, you listen," Ms. Harper said. "We can't keep letting these corrupt bastards rule our lives. Besides." She sighed. "I can't take her back now. They'll know I stole her. And believe me, these people will press charges."

The woman put her hands on her hips, clearly unsympathetic. "That's hardly my problem."

"Well, I'm sorry. I can't afford to take her back," Ms. Harper said and tromped back down the stairs. She opened the door to her car and slammed it behind her.

"Please, Ms. Harper, don't go," I called after her. "I'm sure if we just tell the congressman that this was all a mistake, he'll…"

The sound of the car's motor drowned out my words.

"Crazy old woman," the lady muttered, watching Ms. Harper pull out into traffic and speed away. "Well." She shrugged. "I guess you can come inside. Follow me."

Fourteen

$\mathcal{E}$ven though it was light outside, the inside of the woman's apartment was dark and dingy. A little bit of light trickled in through a window above the couch that looked out onto the brick exterior of the building next door.

"You can sit down while I go talk to my husband about this," the woman said, pointing to the couch.

I lowered myself down onto the scratchy brown fabric while the woman sauntered off into a back room, leaving me alone except for a brown striped cat that slunk over, rubbing its body against my legs. It meowed. I tried pushing it away with the tip of my foot.

I'd never been in a room like this before. Even our tiny rooms at the kennel didn't feel like this, cluttered and dark, with a strange smell that radiated out of the furniture. In the corner near the television, a small folding table was stacked with empty bottles and food containers. A few had spilled onto the floor, but obviously nobody had thought to pick them up. On the other side of the room, a windowsill near the kitchen held a row of wilted-looking plants that stretched their gangly stems toward the window.

The whole place filled me with a hopeless sadness.

"You okay?"

I nodded, quickly wiping away a stray tear from my cheek. "Can you help me? I'm not really supposed to be here."

In front of me, the woman stood with her hands on her hips.

"Well, no kidding! I just talked to Doug and he's not so happy about that lady dropping you off like this. Usually things get planned out a little bit more. We don't even have transport arranged and even if we did, we're not just going to send one girl."

"But I don't even want to—"

As if she'd summoned him, the man stepped out of the back room, pulling a white tank top over his head. He stood in the doorway and folded his arm across his chest. "Did you ask her how much the lady sent with her?"

"God, Doug, I just walked back out here," the woman said, clearly annoyed. "You think I had time to ask her anything yet? If you want to know then ask her yourself."

He scratched his oversized stomach and ambled farther into the room. "How much money did she send with you?" he asked me.

My gaze darted between their faces. "Ms. Harper? She didn't send me with any money."

They turned and looked at each other.

Finally the man spoke. "We don't take pets that haven't been sponsored," he said. "Usually it's fifteen hundred dollars.

That'll get you to the Canadian border. But if you didn't come with anything…" He shrugged. "We're not one of those activists that do this for free. This is a business. We're taking a risk here."

"I can give you a little something to eat before you leave, but that's all I can do for you," the woman said. "I'm sorry. It's not like we can afford to keep you here. If we helped you for free then we'd have to help everyone for free. How could we do that?" She folded her arms, waiting, as if she was expecting me to answer her question.

"I wouldn't have come at all, but Ms. Harper took me," I said. I could hear the panic boiling up in my voice. "Can't you just help me get back to my owners?"

The man rolled his eyes. "Oh yeah. Let's just call the police for you and arrange that." He turned and walked back into the other room, not bothering to say good-bye.

The woman sighed, glancing over her shoulder in the direction of the room the man had disappeared into. "He's right, you know. It's not like you can just go back now. There'd be all sorts of problems for you. And not just with the police. I've heard stories about what happens when they catch a girl who tried to escape." She shuddered.

My stomach dropped. "Did they send her through the door?"

"What door?"

A bit of bile rose in my throat. "The red one."

She shook her head, clearly annoyed. "What I'm trying to tell you is that these rich people do *not* like it when their pets run away. They'll make you pay."

"But I didn't run away," I said.

She shrugged. "I'm not sure it makes a difference to

them." She paused. "I'll tell you what. I'll give you fifty dollars for your dress, okay? That way you'll at least have a little something to get you going. And I guess I can give you the address of someone who might be able to help you pro bono, or whatever they call it."

"Pro bono?"

"Yeah. We don't usually work with those people. They've got a group that moves you people from safe house to safe house. It's slow. They can't get you out in one day like we do, but it won't cost you. I can't guarantee anything."

I rubbed the soft fabric of my dress between my fingers. "But I don't have anything else to wear," I said. "This is all I have."

"You'll get eaten alive if you wear that out onto the streets." She scoffed. "The police will pick you up in a second and if not them, it'll be someone worse."

She left me sitting on the couch and went back into the other room. It didn't take her long to dig something up, and in a minute she came back with a pair of shorts and a T-shirt that she threw down next to me on the sofa. "Here. We keep stuff around the house for the pets we transfer. At least you'll blend in a little bit better."

I picked them up and turned them over in my hands. They looked a little bit like clothes that Ruby might wear, except the fabric wasn't nearly as nice. I was pretty sure the shorts used to be blue jeans before someone cut off the legs right below the pockets. They were a little dirty, but I guessed they would fit me. The shirt, pink with a sparkly heart stitched onto the chest, was close enough to my size, too.

"Is there somewhere I can change?" My voice caught, threatening tears.

She pointed to a little bathroom off the kitchen.

"I'll fix you a sandwich," she called after me as I shut the door.

The clothes fit fine, but as I stared at myself in the grimy mirror over the bathroom sink, I couldn't fight the nausea that flooded my stomach. I fell to my knees in front of the toilet, breathing fast and hard, and fingered the pendant that hung around my neck. It was my only link to my life at the congressman's house. Why couldn't these people just use the numbers etched into the back? That's what they were there for, in case I got lost. The congressman would come and get me. And if he didn't, Penn would.

But then I imagined the look on their faces when they found out I'd been taken, the way the congressman's eyes would narrow and Penn's jaw would clench. What if they blamed me? Maybe it *was* my fault. If I hadn't run off, none of this would have happened.

A darker thought started to form in the back of my mind. What if I went back and the congressman chose to send me back to the kennel and pick out a new pet, one that would stay where it was supposed to stay? He'd done it before, hadn't he? I wasn't sick, but I'd most definitely misbehaved.

"They look like they fit okay," the woman said when I walked back out of the bathroom. She handed me a sandwich wrapped up in a paper towel, eyeing the new clothes before she took the dress from me. She stroked her hand over the soft fabric, then led me to the door.

"Do you think it would be possible for me to stay a little bit longer?" I asked. The apartment might have been dark and uninviting, but where else was I supposed to go?

She shook her head. "You've got to understand, we're just barely making it. We aren't like those rich people. We don't have a couple thousand to throw away on you."

"I won't take anything," I said. "I promise I won't be any trouble. You won't even know I'm here."

The woman snorted and opened the door. "Yeah, you pets are a real piece of cake to have around."

"Please," I tried again.

Her lips clenched into a straight line. "Listen, we're the good guys, but there's only so much we can do. Try calling the number I gave you. I'm sure they'll be able to do something for you." She gave me one last shrug before closing the door behind me.

$\mathcal{B}$y midafternoon it was so hot outside that it was difficult to breathe. I sat in a little park down the street from the apartment where Ms. Harper had dropped me off, unsure about where to go. In my pocket I had a wad of cash that the woman had pushed reluctantly into my hand before I left her house, and a rumpled piece of paper with the numbers to the other safe house.

But the numbers and letters on the little scrap of paper meant about as much to me as the ones on the pendant around my neck. I rubbed the necklace between my fingers and sat in the shade of a tall tree near an abandoned playground. It reminded me a little bit of the park Ruby took me to once, except the swings that hung from the swing set were mostly broken and the slide was boarded off at the top.

It was a sad park. The grass was patchy, with large chunks of dirt that showed through, so that I sat mostly on the dry compact ground. There weren't any flowers, only a row of woodchips bordering the chain-link fence that ran the length of the yard. How could one patch of land be so drastically different from another? This soil couldn't be that different from the soil at the congressman's house. The same sun shone down on them both. The same rain wet the ground. So why did it feel as though I'd walked into a different world, one in which all the beauty had been sucked dry?

My stomach rumbled. I'd eaten the sandwich the woman had given to me hours ago. The sticky brown paste in the center had stuck to the top of my mouth, but it had been tasty and I wished I'd saved some of it instead of eating it all at once.

Across the street, a restaurant let off a delicious smell whenever the door opened. For the past half hour I'd watched as people came out with white bags full of food.

Maybe it was courage that drove me, or maybe it was just hunger, but finally I got up and crossed the street. Inside the restaurant, the smell was both intoxicating and sickening, oily and rich. I followed the line of people up to the front where a girl in a yellow shirt and a matching hat stood behind a counter taking people's money.

"What can I get you?" she asked.

I rested my hands on the counter. "Do you have anything with lentils?"

The girl raised one eyebrow. "Are you trying to be funny?"

"How about leeks?"

She shook her head, looking at me like I was an idiot.

"It's fast food." She pointed to the sign above her head. "Read the menu."

I scanned the sign, flustered. Some of the letters looked familiar. Ruby and I had gotten all the way to the end of the alphabet with uppercase letters, but I didn't know what to do with them when they were put together.

"Listen, if you're not ready to order yet, do you mind moving off to the side? There's a huge line behind you."

Behind me, the line of people stared at me impatiently. A man near the front of the line shook his head and grumbled.

"I'm sorry," I muttered, moving out of the way.

Everywhere I turned there was writing—on the green signs posted at the street corners, in large block letters above the stores, even on the scraps of newspaper that blew down the sidewalk. Everywhere. The letters taunted me. Even the scrap of paper in my pocket with the new address seemed to tease me.

I ran back toward the park, but halfway across the street a car horn blared. "Get out of the road," a man shouted from his car window.

On the sidewalk I bumped into a man pushing a cart. He swerved out of the way. "Hey, watch where you're going, crazy bitch."

I ducked underneath the slide. The rusted metal frame bit into my back as I tucked my knees against my chest, but at least I was hidden. I never wanted to go out there again. It felt like something was breaking inside my chest and I laid my head against my knees, trying to remember how to breathe.

Fifteen

*B*y the time the sun had set and the park was dark, I'd almost forgotten about the empty nagging in my stomach. I'd spent the day with my face pressed against the cool dirt underneath the slide, watching birds peck at the patches of grass and listening to the rush of the city around me.

I wanted to be home, back in the big four-poster bed with its mounds of pillows and clean white sheets. I didn't care about Collin or the congressman's argument with his wife or what Ms. Harper had said about being free. Their words were empty. I sat up and rubbed the dirt from the side of my face. I didn't care about freedom. That's not what I wanted. I just wanted Penn to look at me again under the silver moon while we danced, to take my hand in his and walk me through his magical garden once again. I wanted to share more of his beautiful music and give him mine in return. I wanted another chance to learn what it was to be kissed.

I was sick of feeling sorry for myself. I had spent the last ten hours being angry at Ms. Harper for taking me away, but I hadn't done anything to make things better.

I climbed out from underneath the slide and glanced around the dark playground. On a bench by the fence, a couple sat holding hands and talking quietly. The placement of their bodies, so comfortably close to one another, made my limbs tingle. The thought of never feeling the heat of Penn's body near mine made my heart ache.

Out on the street the flashing blue and red lights of a patrol car pulled up alongside the park and I froze. What if the woman at the apartment had been right about the police? I scanned the park, looking for an exit besides the one next to the fence where the patrol car sat, but there was no other way out. Without drawing too much attention to myself, I walked quickly back to my spot underneath the slide and crouched low against the smooth ground.

My heart hammered uncontrollably as I strained to listen. Across the park, the soft mumble of voices droned in and out with the sound of traffic driving by. It was probably just the couple on the bench, I told myself. They were probably saying how much they loved each other. But the thought did little to console me.

I grasped my knees tight against my chest. My breath was ragged in my throat, so loud and gasping that the officers could probably hear it from the other end of the park. As I covered my mouth with a hand to try to quiet myself, the beam of a flashlight cut across the lawn in front of me. It bumped over the uneven grass and slid through the gangly bushes that grew along the edge of the fence, illuminating old food wrappers and soda cans.

"Check the playground," a deep voice called from the other side of the park.

"There's nobody here, Phil," the man holding the flashlight said. "They've probably got us running around for nothing. Those microchips aren't the best technology. We could be off by a hundred yards."

"I don't care what you think about the technology. I said check the playground," the deep voice said. "There's a bunch of rich folks that are going to throw a fit if we don't find her."

A pair of heavy boots crunched closer and a light swept across the ground at my feet. I drew my legs in closer, tried to make myself a ball, as small as I could possibly be, but it was too late. The light moved up my legs, shining like the sun directly into my eyes.

"Holy crap. She's here. I found her."

The lights in the police station were cold and unforgiving. I sat in a chair by Officer Robert's desk, waiting. I'd already been waiting for hours. I guess that's what you did when they brought you in to the police station.

But the officers were kind. It didn't take me long to realize that they weren't the ones I should be afraid of. If I could have stayed with them indefinitely then maybe things would be all right. It was after the congressman arrived that I needed to worry about.

I pulled a blanket tighter around my shoulders. It was cold in the police station, even though it had been so hot outside, even this late at night, and Officer Roberts had seen the way I sat shivering in the chair and had gotten me a blanket from the back room. It was thick and scratchy, but warm. I pulled it over my legs.

"You don't think it's weird?" Officer Roberts said to his partner. "It feels wrong giving her back, you know? Like, I'm supposed to be protecting her."

"It's a property dispute case," his partner said.

Officer Roberts shrugged. "I know, but I don't like it. I've heard people talking about it, but I guess I never really thought about it before. She's the first one I've seen in person."

Simultaneously, they turned to stare in my direction.

"She kind of reminds me of my niece."

"Yeah?"

"Yeah," Officer Roberts said. "She's in eighth grade. Tell me there's not something wrong about this whole thing."

Just then the doors on the other side of the station swung open and the congressman strode in. He was dressed in one of his expensive gray suits, but underneath the luxurious clothes was a haggard man. His eyes were rimmed in red and a bit of stubble grew along his jaw.

"You must be Mr. Kimball," Officer Roberts said, walking across the room to shake his hand.

The congressman held out his hand. "*Congressman* Kimball. It's nice to meet you."

Officer Roberts caught the correction. "Yes, Congressman. If you'll follow me, we've got your…" He paused, obviously deciding how to word it. "We've got Ella right back here."

"Thank God," the congressman said, coming to a stop in front of me. He shook his head. "I still don't get how she got down here. It's over a five-hour drive from New Canaan.

Has she told you anything?"

"She hasn't spoken since we picked her up," the officer said. "There's a lot of fanatics all worked up about that law, though. Probably one of them got wind you had a pet and thought they'd try to set her free. We'll let you know if we find out anything. We've got officers following up on a few leads. It's just a good thing she had the microchip, otherwise you might not have gotten her back."

Microchip? I frowned at the word. The only things I had with me were the clothes on my back that the lady at the safe house had given me. There was no way she would have given me something that the police could have used to find me.

The congressman frowned, shaking his head at the same time. "Yes, well, apparently they come in handy," he said, before he turned back to me. "Come on, love. Let's get you home."

He pulled me to my feet and held me close to his side.

The congressman hardly spoke during the ride home. For five hours we sat in silence as he stared out the window, clutching the wheel so tight between his hands that his knuckles turned white. Every so often he'd glance in my direction before he turned back to the road.

It wasn't until we pulled into the driveway, the gravel crunching familiarly under the tires, that he finally turned to me.

"You need to tell me who it was. Was it that man from the catering company?"

I shook my head, afraid that if I opened my mouth, I would start to cry.

The congressman sighed. "You didn't want to run away, did you?"

"No." My voice cracked and the tears that I'd been saving during the long drive home spilled out. "I didn't want to leave. I begged her not to take me, but she said it was for the best."

"Shh, it's all right. It's all right. You don't need to cry," the congressman said, stroking my hair. I leaned my head against his shoulder until my tears stopped falling. His hand was warm and heavy on my back. Maybe he wasn't mad at me. Maybe if I told him who had taken me he wouldn't send me back to the kennel.

I hiccupped once and took one last shuddering breath before I looked back up into his eyes. "It was Ms. Harper," I said.

The congressman's jaw tightened and he nodded once, but he didn't yell at me. "We'll worry about her later. Right now I just want to get you out of these terrible clothes."

The house was completely quiet as we came inside. I knew it was still the middle of the night, but for some reason I'd imagined people waiting up for us. I'd expected Ruby to come running for me, arms open wide.

The congressman led me back to my room. I'd only been gone for a little more than a day, but somehow I'd expected everything to look different.

"Hurry and get into some pajamas," the congressman said. "I'll wait right here until you're done."

He sat down tiredly on the couch and I quickly grabbed a nightgown from the closet. As much as I wanted to take a long hot shower, I didn't want to keep the congressman waiting. He'd already done so much for me. Obviously he wanted to see me safely to bed before he left.

I quickly changed out of the dirty clothes. I didn't know

what to do with them. Rosa would probably throw them away, but it felt wrong to stick them in the garbage. I folded them, thinking I could just set them in a pile on the counter and Rosa could do whatever she wanted with them. In the pocket was the piece of paper that the woman had given me, crinkled. I fished it out, suddenly worried about what Rosa would say if she found it. I scanned the bathroom for a place to hide it, finally tucking it behind the mirror before I washed my face.

The congressman smiled at me as I emerged from the bathroom. "That's better," he said. "You're back to yourself."

I sighed, moving toward the mound of blankets on the bed, knowing just how wonderful it would feel to sink down into them. He was right. This was the girl I was supposed to be. Even if I didn't feel the way I knew I should.

My heavy eyelids could barely stay open as I lowered my head into the soft pillow. The congressman sat down next to me, resting his heavy hand on my shoulder. It felt as if it was holding me down, keeping me from floating away.

I couldn't keep my eyes open any longer.

"There you go," he whispered as I began to drift to sleep. "Safe in bed. I won't ever let anyone take you from me again."

Sixteen

*W*hen I woke the house was still quiet. Ruby wasn't bouncing through the rooms the way she normally did. She and Penn sat somberly at the dining room table, slowly chomping their cereal.

I wavered in the doorway, hesitant to break the silence, but as soon as she looked up, Ruby let out a little yelp of joy and pushed back her chair. She rushed to me, throwing her arms around my shoulders in a strangling hug. "I'm so glad you're back," she said into my hair. "Everybody was really, really worried about you. Especially me."

I swallowed back the lump in my throat. How could I have dreamed this child up? Her little body warmed mine and I smiled, letting myself relax for the first time that morning.

"Are you okay?" Penn asked, coming to stand close to my side when Ruby finally let me go.

"Yes, I'm fine." Flustered, I pulled out my chair. If I looked

up into his concerned face I might break down, so I stared out
the window instead. The backyard looked the same as it always
did. Every trace of the party had been boxed up or swept away.
Besides a few large holes in the grass where the tent had been,
it was like it had all just disappeared.

Penn's hand hovered at his side, like he wanted to reach
out and touch me. "They didn't hurt you, did they?"

"No," I said.

The congressman's wife appeared in the doorway. "Penn,
Ruby," she said. "Would you mind giving me and Ella a
moment alone?"

Penn's jaw clenched but he didn't argue as he led Ruby
out of the room.

She pulled a chair up next to me and perched herself on
the edge. "John's certainly relieved to have you back," she
said coldly. "Everyone was in quite the uproar when they
found out you were gone. So much fuss."

She stared at me for a minute, perhaps waiting for me
to begin eating, and even though I didn't have an appetite, I
brought my spoon to my mouth.

Her eyes narrowed just a bit. "Of course once the
kennel informed us about the microchip John was convinced
they'd find you. And look, you were gone for less than a day.
Weren't we lucky?" She paused. "I didn't even realize they'd
given you one."

"What is it?" I asked.

"The microchip?" She shook her head dismissively. "It's
a little device that they implant under the skin. You wouldn't
be able to see it. They use it to track things…although those
things are usually animals." Her voice sounded bitter. "I
would have assumed that you'd remember getting it, unless

you were too young. *Do* you remember?"

With trembling fingers I brought my hand slowly to my neck, tracing my thumb along the thin skin directly behind my left ear. Finally my shaking fingers stopped, settling on a bump the size of a pea beneath my skin. The kennel put it there when I was twelve, right before they transferred us to the training center. I hadn't realized what they were, or even what they were called for that matter. It hadn't hurt to put it in, a quick prick and then the pain receded. It used to be that I'd touch the lump whenever I was bored, my fingers drifting to the spot almost subconsciously. But it had been too long since I'd thought about it.

"Is that where they put it?" she asked.

"I didn't realize what it was."

"No matter," she said, sighing. "That whole Harper woman incident was just a big mess. I don't suppose there's anything you could have done about it."

I set down my spoon and folded my napkin, setting it delicately on the table. The congressman's wife's gaze flittered to the leftover food in my bowl. She opened her mouth as if she was about to speak, but something stopped her. Instead, she gave me a quick pat on the hand before she stood to go.

"We were invited to brunch at one of my friend's houses this afternoon," she said. "John isn't happy about leaving you alone after what happened, but there's really nothing I can do. It would be very rude to cancel now."

"I'll be fine," I told her.

"I know," she said. "Rosa has the day off, but I had her prepare your lunch. It's in the fridge. Do you think you can manage to heat it up?"

I had no idea how to go about using the stove to heat up food, but I nodded anyway. "Yes, thank you."

*N*ormally I would have been excited by the prospect of having the house to myself so I could play the piano without being invited, but I wasn't in the mood for making music. Needing to feel some of the happiness I'd found before Ms. Harper took me away, I headed for Penn's garden.

I slipped out of my gown and into my bathing suit. The tiny little patch of fabric had frightened me before, but now it seemed so much more natural than my other clothes. Those dresses, with their yards and yards of fabric that twisted and bunched around my legs whenever I tried to sit, were an impediment. I could actually move in this.

I sat down at the pond's edge, staring out at the length of water stretching in front of me. It seemed endless. Even though I knew the other end couldn't be more than twenty feet away, it might as well have stretched on infinitely. No matter how hard I tried, I'd never be able to get to the other side.

"I was hoping you'd be here."

I turned to see Penn walking through the garden gate.

My throat tightened. "I thought you went with your family to brunch."

He sat down on the side of the pond but he didn't put his feet in. If I stretched my arm out, I'd be able to touch his knee.

"I didn't feel like going," he said. He leaned forward and

scooped a layer of soggy leaves out of the water beside my legs. "It's not so bad underneath the leaves, but you probably shouldn't get in. I don't think this thing has been cleaned in forever."

I could feel him looking at the side of my face, but I kept staring forward toward the other side of the pond. What would it be like to dive headfirst into the water?

"Listen," Penn said, his voice wobbling slightly. "About the other night. I can't stop thinking that if I'd stayed with you instead of caring what my mom thought, none of that stuff with Ms. Harper would have happened." He sighed loudly. "I'm really sorry."

I couldn't meet his eyes.

"Please don't apologize to me," I said. "There's no need, really."

Penn leaned back on his hands and stared up at the sky. I was tempted to look up, too, but I held still.

"Okay, listen," Penn said after a minute. "I suck at apologies. I do. How about we forget about all that and start over? You could come up to my room, I could fix you one of my killer banana splits, and I could play my guitar for you." He scooted forward now, splashing his legs into the water beside me. "What do you say?"

The sun was hot on my face and my neck. I couldn't stay out much longer without turning pink. "I don't know what a banana split is," I finally said. "But I'm guessing it's probably not one of my approved foods."

Penn laughed, taking my acceptance to his apology for what it was. "If you don't tell anyone, I won't tell anyone," he said. "Believe me, you don't want to go another day without tasting one."

*P*enn spent almost fifteen minutes preparing his famous banana split. I watched with a mix of horror and delight as he transformed a plain banana—a food I actually was allowed to eat—into a volcano of goo. He carefully explained each step, as if he was one of those men Ruby liked to watch on the food channel.

"First we take an almost ripe banana filleted lengthwise and arranged at the bottom of a deep dish," he said. "Next, three scoops of ice cream. One vanilla, one chocolate, and one strawberry, for color, of course." He took his time arranging them in the bowl. "Now, on top of the ice cream, we'll add a generous layer of hot fudge."

My eyes widened while he poured on the thick, dark goo. "You eat that stuff?"

"Hot fudge?" Penn asked. "It's chocolate. Of course I eat it."

When my expression didn't change, he groaned. "Don't tell me you haven't eaten chocolate?"

I shook my head.

"That's unacceptable," he said, dipping his finger down into the brown sticky syrup and bringing it up to my lips. Hesitantly, I licked off a tiny bit, almost dizzy with the warm, sweet rush that filled my mouth.

"It's good, isn't it?" Penn smiled, licking the rest from his finger.

The next few steps blurred together as he began dumping spoonful after spoonful of toppings over the chocolate: yellow pineapple, red strawberries, crushed brown nuts. Finally he sprayed on a mountain of white cream out of a can and topped it off with a bright red cherry.

"Maraschino," he said, smiling wickedly.

Upstairs, Penn's room was dark and cool. He'd tidied up a bit since last time and I took a seat on a wide, leather chair beside his desk, cradling the massive bowl that held my banana split.

Penn sprawled out across his bed, facing me and propped his head up on his hands. "Aren't you going to try it?"

I stared down at the concoction, not knowing where to begin.

"Always start with the cherry," Penn said, acting out how I should pick it off the top and plop it into my mouth.

I grabbed the stem and copied him.

Penn stared, watching my face as I chewed the overly sweet cherry. I took a small bite, my spoon dripping with pineapple and chocolate. "You usually eat this whole thing?"

"I won't hold it against you if you can't finish it all on your first try," he said.

"It would take me a month to finish this." I took another bite, scooping up a bit of strawberry ice cream and the rich chocolate syrup.

"Well, yeah, if you eat it that way." Penn scooted to the end of the bed and grabbed the bowl from off my lap. "Let me show you how it's done. You can't be timid. No teeny tiny mouse bites. You've got to attack this thing."

He dug the spoon down into the middle of the bowl, scooping out a giant, dripping bite that he shoved into his open mouth. A bit of chocolate drizzled out the side of his lip onto his chin. For just a second I imagined myself reaching out to wipe the chocolate off his face with my finger, then slowly bringing it to my own lips.

Penn scooped another gigantic bite. "Now it's your turn."

He hopped off the bed and stood over me with the heaping spoon. A bit of melted ice cream dripped down onto my bare leg, but he didn't seem to notice. "Open wide."

I shook my head, trying to shrink away from him. "No. That's too big."

"Get over here."

Penn tackled me, then shoved the giant bite into my mouth. Only half of it made it in as we fell to the floor. I could feel the sticky mess running down my neck, but I didn't care about how I must look or that it wasn't proper etiquette to speak with food in your mouth. I wrestled the spoon from his hand and dove for the bowl, digging out a bite so absurdly huge that Penn cowered on the floor at my feet.

"No, please," he begged, grinning. "I surrender. I surrender. Have mercy on me."

I pounced, shoving the spoon toward him.

We rolled onto our backs, laughing. Both of us clutched our stomachs until we could finally breathe again.

"This is a mess," I said, looking around at the smears of ice cream, bananas, and chocolate smudged across the carpet and across the front of the chair. "Rosa's not going to be pleased with you."

"It's fine." Penn shrugged. "I'll clean it up."

I raised my eyebrows.

"You don't believe me?" Penn smiled. He grabbed a towel off the floor. "Here, I'll start with this."

He wrapped the corner of the towel around his finger and drew it gently along my chin and down my neck. He stopped at my collarbone and paused, looking into my eyes.

My breath stuttered in my throat. I leaned closer to him,

and he dropped the towel, brushing the tips of his fingers along the bare skin of my shoulder and down my arm. My head buzzed. The sensation zinged down into my hands, through my stomach, into my shaking legs. Every inch of me had come alive with a mad, whirring hum.

Penn's hand moved up to my cheek, cradling my face in his hand as he moved over me.

"I want to kiss you again," he whispered.

I froze. Longing welled up inside me, pressing against the inside of my ribs so that it felt like I might explode if I didn't kiss him. But I couldn't. I was lucky that I hadn't been sent back to the kennel after what happened with Ms. Harper. I couldn't tempt fate again, no matter how much I wanted to.

"You shouldn't," I whispered back.

I scooted out from under him and leaned back against the chair. The side of my cheek was still warm from his touch, but the rest of my body felt cold. My stomach ached from the sugary sweet food. This must have been the reason pets weren't allowed to eat this sort of thing. This must have been the reason pets weren't allowed to do a lot of things. "Maybe I better go," I said as I got to my feet.

"Wait, don't go yet." Penn jumped up. "I didn't even get a chance to play something for you."

His face was open, sincere, and I stopped at the door, reconsidering.

"Just one song," I told him. "And then I need to go down and wash up before your family returns."

Penn grabbed his guitar and sat down on his bed, tucking one leg up under his body and dangling the other off of the edge. His eyes caught mine as he strummed a few light chords, deciding what to play.

"Did you know you share your name with another Ella?"

"I do?"

He plucked lightly at the strings. "Ella Fitzgerald." He nodded. "My dad probably wouldn't have agreed to name you that if he knew that she's the reason I suggested it."

"Why not?" I asked.

"My dad's kind of a jerk about anything that has to do with music," Penn said. "And he certainly isn't a fan of jazz. He says it just sounds like noise. It's too free. There's too much improvisation and my dad only likes things he can control. Here, let me play you one of her songs."

His face changed, his eyes grew serious, and his jaw relaxed as he looked back down at his instrument. His fingers moved across the strings the way I'd seen a harpist play, plucking the notes tenderly with the tips of his fingers so the sound floated out, crisp and pure.

Penn started to sing.

His voice moved gently over the words, singing about stars shining and the hush of love being whispered on the breeze. He sang about the way it felt to miss someone, an ache, a longing. He sang about dreaming of the one you love, about how even if you can't be together, at least you can still dream.

I stood rooted in place. His voice was raspy and vulnerable and sweeter than I ever would have imagined. I sank down onto the floor, staring up at him as he sang, his eyes closed, his head tipped slightly away from me. I could almost see myself reflected in his face, the joy and the pain that moved through the center of me when I played, like a knife cutting me open—not to injure, only to expand, to make more room inside for the music.

When the song was over his fingers lingered on the strings and his eyes stayed closed. Finally he opened them and lowered the guitar down onto the bed.

The room was silent, except for our breathing.

"And that, ladies and gentlemen, is a wrap," Penn said. His eyes glistened and he looked away.

I stood. At the door, I turned to look at him one more time, wishing there was some way I could tell him that I knew how he felt, wishing I could tell him not to let his father bully him into giving up his music. Quickly, before I lost my nerve, I darted back to the bed and placed a soft kiss at the side of his mouth. His lips opened ever so slightly and I stepped away, hoping he couldn't see the fear and hope in my eyes before I left the room, shutting the door quietly behind me.

Seventeen

T lay in bed a few nights later, staring up at the dark ceiling. In my mouth I still held the taste of one of Ruby's butterscotch candies. She must have been sneaking them into my room when I was out, because every night since the congressman had brought me back, I'd found one waiting for me on my pillow, the sweetest little gift wrapped in shiny gold foil.

I licked the last bit of sugar from my lips and I tried to stop thinking about Penn. But I couldn't. He'd infested my thoughts.

The cool cement of my patio was familiar beneath my feet. I hadn't gotten out of bed at night since I got back, but it felt good to be out again, roaming the house with the lights all turned off.

Maybe what Miss Gellner had said was true. Maybe we were so much luckier than all those people that had to slave away, working so hard to buy themselves homes, and cars, and food. They certainly hadn't looked happy, out there in the real world. Any one of them would have been grateful to get to enjoy all this beauty piled before me.

Penn appeared at the kitchen door. I hadn't seen him much since the afternoon in his room, and my heart skipped a beat seeing him now.

"I was up, too," he said. "I saw you out my window." He pointed up to his room as if I'd still be able to see him there with the curtains pulled wide, looking out.

The courtyard was quiet. This hushed time of night, after all the lights in the house finally went out, was the only time during my day when I didn't worry whether I was doing things the right way—the way Miss Gellner taught me to do them.

"Don't get too comfortable," he said, coming to stand beside me. "I have something I want to show you." He grabbed my hand and pulled me to my feet.

"What is it?"

He didn't speak at first, just pulled me down the hill toward the orchard. "I really wanted to do something for you. To make you feel better after...you know." He stopped talking for a second, glancing at me out of the corner of his eye. "Anyway, I guess I just wanted to give you something."

"You don't need to get me anything," I said.

"Good." He laughed. "Because I didn't."

"Then what—"

We reached the gate to the garden and he swung it open. "You'll see," he said, leading me inside. His teen glowed white in the moonlight as a wide grin spread across his face. It was such a beautiful smile. I stared up at him a moment longer before I followed his gaze past the tangle of weeds toward the far end of the garden where the round face of the moon rippled across the pond.

"I cleaned it out," Penn said, turning his smile on me. "Now you don't have to put your feet in pond scum."

I opened my mouth to speak, but I couldn't find the words to thank him. I stepped closer to the ebony stretch of water, kneeling down on one of the smooth slabs of stone that surrounded the pond. It was beautiful. Even in the dark I could see how different it looked. The debris that had lined the surface of the water was completely gone. Now the still water shone like glass. The moss that had coated the walls was wiped clean, revealing the same pale stonework that edged the pond.

I drew my nightgown up around my knees and sat down, dipping my feet in the water.

"So I take it you like it?" Penn asked, lowering himself down next to me.

"Yes." I nodded. "Penn… It's so… I don't know how to—"

He shrugged. "Don't worry about it."

It was the perfect gift, made even more wonderful by the mere fact that he was sitting beside me. He clasped his hands in his lap for a minute while we both stared out across the water. A long-legged bug danced across the surface, sending a few small ripples dancing in our direction. When the water was still again, he moved his hands from his lap, letting them rest by his side.

"Why don't you want to study political science the way your father wants you to?" I asked.

Penn slid his hand closer to mine until our fingers brushed. "It doesn't interest me. If I'm going to spend my whole life doing something, I want it to be something I love, not just something I tolerate. My dad thinks that just because he loves something, everyone else should feel the same way about it."

"Maybe he just wants to see you doing something important," I said. "Something that matters."

"Maybe."

"Do you think it's more important to make yourself happy, or to make other people happy?" I asked. I'd never imagined that the two didn't go hand in hand, but maybe I was wrong. Maybe sometimes it was one or the other.

Penn glanced at me sideways. "What's with all the deep questions?"

Now it was my turn to shrug. I couldn't tell him that I'd always thought my happiness depended on how well I served my masters. Their happiness was supposed to be my own. But no one had ever told me that I might want something all for myself.

He turned his face up to the night sky and then down into the pond. "Do you want to get in?" he asked, nodding his head toward the dark water.

"I will if you answer my question."

"Promise?"

I nodded.

He peeled off his shirt, sliding down into the water, and I swallowed back the thrill that bubbled up inside me, trying not to stare at the way his muscles moved as he swept his arms across the surface.

"What was the question again?" Penn asked, pushing off of the wall into the center of the pond.

"Is it more important to—"

"To make yourself happy or to make other people happy," Penn said, finishing my sentence. "I remember. I was just kidding."

He stood silently, and I thought he might not answer me after all. When he did speak his words were quiet, nearly lost in the water surrounding him. "I'd like to believe my dad really is interested in making other people happy," he said. "Maybe when he first got into politics that's what he was thinking about. I don't know. It was when I was really little, so it's not like I really remember."

He waded back over to the edge, propping his elbows on the stone next to my legs.

"So maybe I'm jaded or something," he went on. "Like I haven't really seen anyone who does something to help someone else without expecting to get something in return. With my dad, it's all about the constituents. What's going to make them vote for him again, you know? It's not really about what's best, or right."

I rested my hand on his wet arm. "You're talking about your father, not you."

He shook his head but he didn't respond. After taking a deep breath, he dove underneath the water. In the dark I could hardly see him. I counted to ten, to twenty, to thirty, but still he stayed beneath the surface. Finally, after the blood had started pounding in my ears, he popped up and wiped his face.

"I thought I might find the answer down there," he said, smiling. "But I didn't."

"It doesn't matter," I told him. "If you don't answer, then I guess I don't have to get in."

He stroked smoothly across the length of the pond on his back until he reached the other side.

"Why can't it be both?" he asked. "Why can't I make other people happy and be happy myself? Why does it have to be a sacrifice? You can't tell me music doesn't make people happy. Maybe not people like my dad."

A warm breeze blew over the water, whipping my hair around my face and bringing goose bumps to my arms. Penn was right. Why did it have to be a sacrifice? For him. For me. Why did we have to choose? Maybe we just needed to find the right people to make happy.

"Besides," he went on. "Just one more year and I won't have to worry about pleasing him anymore. He can't control me my entire life. The second I'm an adult, I'm out of here."

He dove back down, streaking beneath the surface like a silver fish. When he popped up next to me, he was smiling.

"That's my answer, like it or not." The water dripped down his face, but he didn't make a move to wipe it away. "Now you have to keep your promise. You're coming in."

"I'd get in, but I'm not wearing a swimsuit," I told him, scooting back from the edge of the pond. "I guess I could run back to the house…"

"Don't use those lame excuses with me," Penn said. "You can swim in your underwear for all I care. Just get in."

My stomach gave a little flip. I could tell he didn't really think I'd do it. Fear and excitement tied themselves together inside me. I'd never imagined that every move I made didn't have to revolve around someone else's notion of what I should do. If it was all right for Penn to choose his own happiness over his father's, maybe I could choose my own happiness, too.

My arms and legs shook as I got to my feet and pulled my nightgown over my head and dropped it down in a pile at my feet.

"Wait. What are you doing?" Penn asked, his eyes wide. "I wasn't serious."

The thin satin camisole and panties that I wore underneath my nightgown did little to hide my body, but I didn't feel like worrying. If I was going to get in the water, it was going to be now, not five minutes from now, not ten minutes from now.

Now.

The cold night air settled across my skin and I wrapped my arms around my body. "I still don't know how to swim." I said, looking down at him. My knees were already knocking together, but it was too late to try to steady them.

Penn grabbed onto the side with one hand and with the other reached up to me. His face was serious when he spoke. "Don't worry," he said. "I won't let anything happen to you."

I stepped closer to the edge and sat back down so my feet hung into the pond. The water was cool, but the chill that ran up my spine had nothing to do with the cold. Penn moved closer to me. He reached for my waist and I was reminded of the last time his wet hands had touched my skin this way, in the pool with Ruby that first day when he'd pulled me from the water. I'd been so scared then, but now a strange sense of calm settled over me.

"Hold onto me," he said, pulling me into the water.

I wrapped my arms around his slippery neck as my whole body slid along his. Beneath the water, his legs felt warm against mine. In the quiet, each one of his breaths was a tiny puff against my face.

I thought back to that first night I'd seen him in the pool, swimming with his friend. And now here I was, the lucky one, the girl who got to wrap her arms around him in the water.

"All right, I'm going to swim to the other side, okay? Just keep your arms around my neck and your head up."

With a few powerful strokes he pulled us across the water. When he stopped, I straightened my legs beneath me. As soon as I felt the smooth stone press against my feet, I let go of his neck, already missing the feel of his skin.

He stood, looking down at me, and I wondered if I saw a bit of regret in his eyes as well.

"That was good." He smiled. "You didn't panic at all. Now the first thing we're going to teach you how to do is float on your back. Have you ever done that before?"

I shook my head. It was too hard to find my breath.

Penn wiped the water from his face. "All right, I want you to lean back into me. I'm going to hold you up, so don't worry." I could tell he was trying to sound confident, but his voice shook slightly.

"You aren't nervous, are you?"

He smiled. "Well, yeah, maybe I am."

"But you're the one who knows how to swim."

He smiled softly. "It's not the water that's making me nervous, Ella. It's you."

It's you. His words reverberated through my head, ringing from ear to ear. I turned around, hoping the moonlight hid my blush.

"Okay, now lean back and kick off the bottom. Try to bring your hips up to the surface," he said again, guiding me down into the water.

I let go. My arms and legs floated up to the surface.

"Relax. I've got you."

His gaze roamed my body. Maybe I should have been worried about the way my camisole clung to my figure, hardly even fabric anymore as much as a second skin, but I couldn't bother to care. All I could think about was the way Penn's hand cupped the back of my head while the other brushed along the length of my spine, finally stopping in the middle of my back. The water sloshed around my ears, making the world seem lost, and far away, as if the only things that existed were Penn, the night, and me.

He leaned his face closer to mine. "Okay, I'm going to slowly let go. You just stay relaxed. See if you can stay afloat."

I waited for his face to recede, for his hands to move off my body, but if anything he seemed to come closer, those beautiful eyes swimming above me, staring down into my own. My body lifted, weightless, as if I was floating high above the world, Penn's touch the only thing holding me there amidst the stars.

"Ella…" His voice trailed off, his breath hot against my cheek.

I wanted him to lean closer so there wasn't any air separating us. I wanted to close my eyes and breathe him in.

I wanted it so badly the *want* scared me.

His lips brushed mine and my body stiffened. My arms beat the water at my sides, reaching out for something to grab onto as my feet searched for solid ground.

"I'm sorry," I said, standing. "I…I have to go."

I waded to the other side and climbed out, leaving Penn standing alone in the dark water behind me.

Eighteen

*T*he next evening both the congressman and his wife were actually home at the same time for dinner, something that didn't seem to happen all that often. The congressman had been in Washington for the past few days and had already exhausted his family by talking incessantly for the past fifteen minutes about the Domestic Energy and Jobs Act.

They stared at him with glazed eyes while I nibbled my food. If it were me who was sitting up at the table with them, I would look the congressman in the eye, nodding when he paused, and asking questions here and there about spending and committees. I could see he was craving some sort of response from his family, but I didn't dare speak up from my spot across the room.

"Penn, are you even listening to what I'm saying?" the congressman asked, setting his fork down with a loud bang.

"Dad, I've been listening to this same conversation for

the last ten years. There's only so many times a person can pretend to be interested in budget committees."

The congressman's wife set down her fork as well and dabbed her mouth with her napkin, casting a disparaging look at her son.

"Well you'd think after ten years you'd finally have something to say on the matter," the congressman said.

"I'm sorry." Penn sighed. "I guess I'm just distracted."

"Distracted?"

He shrugged and rolled a cherry tomato across his plate. "The owner of Bayou Grill called me yesterday. He wants to hire me for a show next Saturday."

"A show? We are talking about playing your guitar, aren't we?"

Penn nodded.

"Well, I can't imagine what would make them call you out of the blue and ask you that?"

"I applied for the show, okay? Is that what you want me to say?"

The congressman shook his head. "No, I want you to say you'll stop wasting all your free time dreaming about being a rock star and start thinking practically. What about the internship I lined up for you? Have you even called the commissioner back yet?"

"No, I—" Penn began.

"Elise, why haven't you reminded him to call?"

"Don't you think you're being a little pig headed? It's not my—"

He didn't wait for her to finish her sentence. "How is he going to get a degree in political science if he doesn't do the internship? He can't even carry on a conversation about a legislative session for heaven's sake."

Penn stabbed at a large piece of meat on his plate. "Well maybe I should consider getting a degree in something that actually interests me."

Ruby's hand was paused above her dish in midair, staring intently between her family members.

The congressman snorted. "Yes, a degree you're interested in. That's a smart move. I'm happy to see you're really thinking about the future. Because heaven knows what the world is lacking now is more starving musicians playing music for change at the subway station."

"Do we really have to do this again?" the congressman's wife asked.

"Yes. Yes, we do. He's got a year to turn things around. One year. I don't think now's the time to start pampering him and feeding him false hope about following his dreams." He drew a hand over his face. "What's so wrong with wanting your son to do something that really matters, to try to help people?"

"Well maybe I'll just marry money the way you did, and then I won't have to worry about it. God, you're such a hypocrite," Penn said. He stood up, his chair skidding away from the table as he threw down his napkin.

The congressman and his wife stared at each other for one long moment before they picked up their knives again.

I wanted to get up and follow after Penn, but I stayed seated. Even though I didn't have an appetite, I continued taking small bites of my food. For a few minutes the sound of our forks scraping against our plates was the only sound in the room. Finally, the congressman's wife looked up at Ruby as if she was noticing her daughter sitting there for the first time all night.

"Ruby, take smaller bites, honey. It's not polite to chew like that."

"If I eat all my salad can I have dessert?" Ruby asked, her mouth still full of food.

The congressman's wife grimaced. "Ruby, what did I just say? It's impolite to have that much food in your mouth, let alone to talk while it's still full."

Ruby swallowed. "Can I?"

If I'd been sitting next to her I would have kicked her under the table, but there was nothing I could do from where I sat. I'd never considered myself lucky for being trained by Miss Gellner before, but now I realized it was a gift. How could Ruby and Penn not know how to have a conversation with their own parents? I could see their mistakes so clearly; how they should have answered their parents politely instead of sticking so forcefully to their own opinions.

"No dessert," the congressman's wife said before turning to her husband. "A little help here?"

He shrugged, crunching loudly on his salad.

She threw up her hands. "Oh, so this only goes one way? You expect me to read your mind about internships, but when your daughter wants to spend all day eating brownies and cupcakes you suddenly don't want anything to do with it."

The congressman lifted his hands in surrender. "Calm down, Elise. I don't see what the big deal is. She's not hurting anyone."

"She's hurting herself. Do you know what size pants she's wearing these days?"

Ruby's face crumpled. "Never mind," she said. "I'm not hungry anymore."

"Oh, Ruby," her mom said, patting her hand. "I'm sorry. I shouldn't have said that. Maybe if you just got a little bit more exercise. Tomorrow morning you could take Ella for a walk. I bet she'd like that."

Suddenly everyone's heads turned in my direction. I smiled politely, unsure whether to agree or to act as if I hadn't been listening to their conversation all evening.

Ruby's face brightened a little bit as she met my eye. "Okay," she said. "I didn't know I was allowed to take Ella for walks. Does she have to wear a leash?"

The congressman and his wife laughed, their faces finally warming. "No, she doesn't have to wear a leash."

*T*he next morning I stepped outside carrying a pair of soft leather sandals by their straps. Ruby had said to wait for her by the pool after breakfast so we could go for our walk. I'd dressed in one of the few short dresses that I could find in my closet. The soft coral sundress hung right below my knees and the simple bodice wasn't embroidered with any beads or lace. It was just the right dress for a walk on a summer morning.

Near the pool house, Penn sat on one of the lounge chairs, gnawing on the end of a pencil while he stared down at the notebook in his lap. I sank down onto one of the lawn chairs next to him.

He glanced up, startled. "Oh, hey." He smiled, setting down

his pencil.

"How's your writing going?

He sighed, tapping his pencil against the page. "My dad keeps bugging me about this internship essay, but it's the last thing I want to do. Why waste time on this crap when I could be writing lyrics instead?"

He went back to his paper, but I could tell he was still looking at me out of the corner of his eye.

"Ruby is taking me for a walk this morning," I told him, leaning forward with my elbows on my knees. It wasn't a proper way to sit, but being around Penn made me feel like I didn't have to try so hard to be perfect all the time.

"A walk? It's about time. You've got to be getting bored being stuck here all the time." I couldn't tell if there was a touch of anger or annoyance behind his voice, but a moment later it was gone. "But then again, how could you get tired of looking at this." He gestured toward the yard. "Or this." He pointed at himself, grinning.

A hot blush sprang to my cheeks and I made myself busy strapping on my sandals. When I raised my gaze he was still staring at me, a bit of hair had fallen down over one of his eyes, but he didn't move to brush it away.

"Ella?" he said, his voice soft.

I froze with my hand on the strap of my shoe. "Yes?" I swallowed, fumbling with my shoe again. My trembling fingers wouldn't cooperate and the clasp suddenly seemed so small.

"I thought maybe you'd come out again last night."

"Oh, I was kind of tired," I lied.

"Did I do something wrong?" he asked. "Because I didn't mean to. If it's about the—"

"No," I interrupted. "I mean yes...maybe." I lowered my head into my hands.

"What's the matter?" he asked

"This," I whispered.

"What?"

"You and me. I'm not supposed to feel this way."

Why hadn't they taught me how to deal with something like *this* at the training center? Who cares about small talk or politics? What could I do to steer us in another direction, away from want, and need, and all this danger?

Penn knelt in front of me and grabbed my hand. He leaned so close that our heads were only a whisper apart.

"Why does this have to be wrong?" he asked.

Behind us, Ruby skipped out of the kitchen door, hollering my name. I pulled away from him.

"Are you ready?" Ruby asked, stopping next to me.

As we walked away, I turned Penn's words over in my mind. *Why does this have to be wrong?* Why?

*R*uby and I rounded the corner out of the driveway onto the stretch of Smith Ridge Road. She grabbed my hand, swinging it back and forth as we sauntered along the side of the street, being sure to stay on the right side of the solid white line.

Already things looked different, and we were only a couple hundred yards away from the house. I had assumed I would remember the world away from the congressman's house, considering it hadn't been very long since I'd driven down this very stretch of road. But it felt like I was seeing it for the first time.

We walked past Ms. Harper's long driveway and I squeezed Ruby's hand a little tighter. What if she was down there right now, watching for me? The congressman hadn't mentioned her since the night that I told him she was the one who had taken me.

"It's okay, the cars always slow down if they see a person on the side of the road," Ruby said, probably assuming I was nervous about the walk.

I relaxed the grip on her fingers, daring to look back over my shoulder at the wooded stretch of land that bordered Ms. Harper's lane, but there was no one there.

"So, where should we walk?" Ruby asked, looking around at the woods and bushes that lined either side of the road. "There's not really anywhere to go. We could try to make it to the country club, but it's pretty far."

"It's just nice walking," I told her. "We don't have to go anywhere."

"Maybe if there was something fun to look at, but it's all like this." She turned in a complete circle. "Trees and grass. That's it."

We wandered on. It was true there were trees and grass, but there were also beautiful low stone walls that followed the rise and fall of the land, and every once in a while we'd catch a glimpse of the front of a house through the trees.

"So, do you have a crush on any boys?" Ruby asked a little shyly. "Like from the school you used to go to?"

"I don't know what a crush is, but I didn't really go to school," I told her. "And at the training center there were only other girls."

"Oh, an all-girls school," Ruby said. "My dad wanted to send me to one of those. But I'm glad he didn't. Not that any of the boys in my school like me."

The tall trees on either side of the road cast the street in shade, but every once in a while we stepped out into the hot sun. The heat seemed to surprise us both and we'd stop simultaneously and look up at the sky.

Up ahead a long white fence ran along the edge of the road and Ruby picked up the pace, dragging me toward it.

"Let's go see the Davenports' horses," she said, climbing up onto the first slat of the fence and leaning against the top with her belly. "Come on, Ella. Grab some grass. Let's see if they'll come over."

I tugged on a clump of feathery grass growing at the base of the fence. It came up easily, dangling a chunk of moist dirt from the bottom.

"Not the dirt," Ruby said, laughing. She snatched it out of my hand, banging the clump against the fence so that bits of soil flew in every direction. "See, if we hold it out, they'll come over."

Already, three horses were clomping across the field in our direction. I stepped away from the fence as they drew closer. Their footsteps thudded against the dirt and they puffed air out of their noses, shaking their heads as they came over to us.

"Are you sure it's all right?" I asked.

Ruby leaned over the fence, waving the grass like a flag. "Horses love grass," she said just as a black horse took the grass from her hand.

It chomped loudly, moving its jaw in a wide circle as it chewed. I'd never seen such a huge creature. If I stepped out and reached my hand through the slats in the fence I would probably be able to lay my hand against its side. The idea was both terrifying and thrilling and without really thinking it through, I moved closer to the fence, reaching my hand out as I went.

My fingertips brushed its fur, and then, before I knew it, my whole palm was pressed against its hot belly. My hand moved with the rise and fall of its breath.

"Do you want to try feeding one?" Ruby asked as she climbed off of the fence, tearing out huge chunks of grass.

She handed over a clump and I grabbed onto the fence, hoisting myself up the way Ruby had. With one hand I gripped the rough wooden slat, while I leaned forward with the other, offering the grass to the nearest taker.

A light-colored horse with a pale white mane and fur the color of dried grass took a step closer to me. It stood still for a second before sniffing my offering with one wet puff. I steadied my hand as it reached out with twitching lips and snatched the grass out of my fingers, happily chomping it up. It switched its tail and lifted its head, looking me right in the eye.

"She likes you," Ruby said. "I think she wants to be friends with you."

Behind us, the sound of voices made us turn just in time to see two girls on bikes rounding the corner. Ruby hopped down off of the fence and came to stand next to me, crossing her arms over her chest.

"Look, it's Ruby," one of the girls said, pulling over to the side of the road and straddling her bike. She had brown hair in a high ponytail that swung as she turned back to face her friend. She waited, as if she needed permission for what to do next. Finally she turned back to face us, raising her hand in a wave. "Hi, Ruby."

Ruby waved back timidly. "Hi, Sarah. Hi, Jayne."

"What are you doing?" the girl asked.

"Just feeding the horses," Ruby said quietly, not bothering to move closer to them.

The other girl shielded her eyes and looked up the little hill toward where we stood. I guessed both of the girls were probably close to Ruby's age, but this one seemed to carry herself differently, as if she was already trying to be grownup. Her long blond hair was loose, and even though it was a little mussed from being blown in the wind, I could tell she'd spent a long time curling it earlier.

"Who's that with you?" the girl asked, tossing her hair back over her shoulder and jutting her chin in my direction.

Ruby turned to me. Obviously this girl made her nervous.

"This is Ella," Ruby finally said. And then drawing a deep breath, she added, "She's my pet. My dad got her right after school got out."

The girls turned to one another, deciding whether or not to believe her.

"I didn't hear you got another pet," the blond girl said, her voice challenging. "I thought Gretta Holmes and I were the only ones in our grade that had pets anymore."

Ruby stood up a little taller. "No, we got another one. My dad's one of the ones that helped pass the law so we kind of have to have one."

"What law?"

Suddenly Ruby looked a little flustered. "The Freedom of Pets Act, or whatever. I don't remember what it's called. It's the law that says we can have pets."

"I didn't know there was a law," the girl in the ponytail said.

"Well there is," her friend snapped. "You probably just don't know about it because your family doesn't have a pet." She turned back to Ruby, smiling as if she'd defended her. "Do you want to come over to my house? We could play and do hair."

"We were actually out for a walk," Ruby said.

"That's okay, I can walk my bike. My house isn't that far anyway." She kicked at her bike stand and grabbed the handlebars before throwing a large smile at Ruby.

"Come on, Ella." Ruby grabbed my hand and skipped down the hill back to the road.

As we started walking, the blond girl turned to her friend. "I totally understand if you want to go home, Sarah. You probably don't want to hang out with me and Ruby since you don't have a pet."

The girl with the ponytail stopped walking. "Oh, that's okay. I'll just watch."

"Well, it probably makes more sense for you to go home now," she said, swinging her hair over her shoulder. "I don't want you to feel left out or anything and I'd feel really bad if you got bored."

As the girl with the ponytail turned her bike around and rode off, Ruby smiled uncomfortably at her friend. "I don't mind if Sarah stays," she said. "Ella won't mind if she wants to do her hair or something."

"No," Jayne said, shaking her head decisively. "It's better if it's just us."

Nineteen

ayne's house wasn't any bigger than Ruby's, but it had a different feeling to it. Maybe it was all the gold furniture and picture frames, all the elaborate moldings and marble statues, but something made the house feel cold and unfriendly. Of course I didn't really know her, but her house seemed to give off the same impression that Jayne did, as if people noticing how lovely it looked was the most important thing.

"Mom," Jayne yelled as soon as we entered the foyer. "Where's Missy?"

From the other room, high heels clicked across a marble floor and a moment later a grown-up version of Jayne appeared in the foyer.

She stopped in front of us. "Don't yell, Jaynie," she said, smoothing her daughter's hair.

"Where's Missy?" Jayne asked again. "Ruby brought her pet over to play."

Jayne's mom's gaze moved over me slowly. "She's in the den with your father."

We followed Jayne to the back of the house where her father sat behind a large mahogany desk, reading the paper and sipping a drink. In the corner, on a fur-lined chaise lounge, Missy lay back, nibbling dark red raspberries.

It was strange to see another pet that wasn't one of the girls I'd grown up with. I hadn't expected to be so excited, but here I was, my legs shaking, my hands sweating. She wasn't exactly like a Greenwich girl. Her lips were fuller than mine. Her nose was different, too, rounded on the end with a broader bridge that made her look almost feline.

She looked quite a bit older than me, though. I'd never seen a pet who was more than a couple years older than me. She was still beautiful, but there was no doubt that the years had left a mark.

She glanced up at us and popped another raspberry in her mouth.

"Daddy?" Jayne asked. "Can we steal Missy?"

He hardly looked up from his paper. "Of course, dear."

Jayne clapped her hands and pulled Missy from the couch. The pet sighed heavily, gathering up her wide skirts as Jayne ushered us all out of the room and down a hallway to a large bedroom. Missy draped herself across the bed, the folds of her dress puffing up like an elaborate dessert, and closed her eyes as if we weren't there.

Jayne slapped her lightly on the hand. "Don't go to sleep. This is Ruby and her pet, Ella. We're going to do hair and stuff."

Missy remained unsmiling. She raised herself up onto one of her elbows and stared at the rest of us in a way that brought goose bumps to my skin. It wasn't the meek look that a pet was supposed to give. It was forceful, almost aggressive.

"Why don't you play with that pet," she finally said, pointing a lazy finger in my direction. "I'm not in the mood for your games."

Jayne narrowed her eyes and folded her arms. "Missy, if you don't play with us I'm going to tell my dad. And he's obviously home this time so you can't use that as an excuse."

Missy sighed loudly and dragged herself into a sitting position, but it was obvious that even though she was doing as Jayne had asked, she wasn't going to be happy about it.

Ruby nudged me. *What's her problem,* she mouthed, her eyes wide.

Jayne, however, didn't seem to mind how Missy was acting as long as she was finally doing as she was told.

"Come on, Ruby," she said, pulling her by the hand. "Let's go pick out outfits for them."

They disappeared down a small hallway and into a large walk-in closet.

Missy turned to look at me. "You have a very heart-shaped face," she said, as if this statement was telling of something more.

"Uh, thank you," I said.

"I didn't mean it as a compliment. I thought thinner faces were more desirable."

I stood in stunned silence, unsure how to respond.

"Where were you bred?" she asked, running her hands through her long blond hair. It was hair very much like Jayne's only a bit thicker, a bit more brilliant.

"Greenwich."

She snorted. "I should have known."

A moment later Ruby and Jayne came back in, each carrying an armful of clothes and started laying them out across the couch. They didn't look a thing like my everyday gowns.

"My dad lets me pick them out of a catalogue," Jayne said, continuing the conversation she must have been having with Ruby in the closet. "Each one costs over a thousand dollars, but that's because they're exact replicas. This one is a Marie Antoinette gown, and this one is Scarlett O'Hara."

Ruby's eyes were big as Jayne held up the dresses. "I read a book about Marie Antoinette," she said. "Did you know she was tried and convicted of treason and then had her head cut off in the guillotine?"

Jayne wrinkled her nose as if she said something disgusting. "Why don't you put yours in the Marie Antoinette then, since you know so much about it? Missy doesn't like it anyway because the corset is hard to get on."

Ruby nodded obediently.

For the next hour and a half Jayne made us put on costume after costume. Then she had us walk down the long hallway, turning to pose in front of the mirror before we walked back again in what she called our "mini fashion show." But after a while even that grew old. It was clear she'd done this many times before and even with another pet in the show she became bored, slumping back on the couch with a frown.

"Let's go watch TV," Jayne said and ran from the room with Ruby in tow, leaving me and Missy to stare at one another, still clothed in our elaborate costumes.

Missy unclasped the buttons on her gown and slipped

out of it. She stepped over the mountain of fabric at her feet and lounged back on the bed once more, seemingly unbothered by the fact she was only in her underwear.

I turned away from her and climbed out of the Chinese kimono I was wearing, pulling on my own sundress as quickly as I could. I could feel her gaze on my back and knew that when I turned around she wouldn't even pretend to be looking in the other direction.

"I don't usually play these games," Missy said. "But when her father's home I can't really say no."

I kept my back to her.

"It isn't much fun," I said by way of agreement.

She huffed. "No, it's not."

"You don't really like me, do you?"

My straightforwardness startled both of us and Missy raised her chin and turned her head away from me. "No," she said. "I don't."

Her honesty stung, and my eyes burned. Even though I didn't want to care about her, I couldn't ignore the peculiar bond that tied us together. She was more like me than anyone else I'd met since I moved to the congressman's house. It didn't matter that she didn't look exactly like one of the Greenwich girls. There was an invisible thread that bound us.

"Why not?" I finally asked.

She shifted on the bed, leaning up on one elbow with her head resting in her hand as she stared at me. "Because you're so naïve I can practically smell it," she said. "It turns my stomach just looking at you. You have no clue, do you? You're like some poor little baby deer with those wide open eyes."

I sank down onto the bed. "I'm not as naïve as you think

I am." My voice was small. It didn't fool either of us and she raised one of her eyebrows, not even wasting words to argue with me.

"I'm not," I insisted. "I was kidnapped. The Kimballs' neighbor tried to set me free."

Missy rolled her eyes. "Oh, I'm sure it was *terrible* for you."

"It was! I saw how horrible the world is out there."

"Then you know exactly how lucky we are." She gazed around the room as if she was seeing it for the first time: the gigantic bed, the plush carpet, the velvet drapes. "I've never understood why anyone would want to leave a life like this. I can have anything that I want. All I have to do is ask for it. My master spoils me more than he does his own *family*. All I have to do is let their little brat pull my hair out and dress me up like a doll every once in a while."

She picked up a little silver bell that sat on the bedside table. "If I ring this, they'll come running to see what I want. If I want more pillows, they'll get them. If I want lotion rubbed on my back, they'll stop what they're doing and help me. If I want to sit by the pool in the sun, I'll do it. I don't have to worry about making money or impressing people."

I nodded, but there was a seed of worry burning in the pit of my stomach.

She stood up languidly and went to stand in front of the full-length mirror that stood opposite the bed. She picked up a brush from a small table beside the mirror and ran it slowly through her hair.

"It seems like a perfect life, doesn't it?" she asked. When I didn't answer she swung around to face me, her eyes fierce. "Doesn't it?"

"Yes," I squeaked.

"Well, enjoy it while you can because it won't last forever."

I froze. "What?"

"Have you ever wondered what happens when you get old?" she asked. "When they get tired of their shiny new toy and decide to move on?"

"We're lifetime companions," I said, repeating Greenwich's slogan.

Missy snorted. "Sure we are. Have you ever even considered what happens if you get sick?" She didn't wait for me to reply. "No, of course not. Why would you? You're healthy. You're young. Never in your wildest dreams would you imagine that you could drink from the wrong glass, or touch the wrong doorknob, and suddenly wake up in the hospital with tubes hooked up to your arms."

"The kennel will take me back." But even as I said it, I knew the congressman's story about the kennel offering to give their previous pet the special care she needed might not really be true. I pictured the needles and Miss Gellner's stern expression when she told us about the girls they'd had to put to sleep. Is that what had happened to the Kimballs' previous pet?

"Have you thought about what happens when you come of age? When you're a *woman* rather than a child's plaything?"

I opened my mouth to respond, but all I could see, all I could *feel*, was the congressman's lips on my cheek, his hot breath against my ear while he held me on his lap in front of his friends. The vision shifted abruptly to Penn. His warm body sliding against mine in the cool water. The press of his lips against mine. How badly I wanted to feel both again...

Missy tossed her head back and laughed. "You're thinking about it now, aren't you? I can see it on your face. It's already started, hasn't it?" She leaned forward, her expression suddenly serious. "They will tire of you. They always do. And when it happens, the people who were supposed to be your 'lifetime companions' will sell you off to the highest bidder."

"But pets can't just be sold to anyone," I blurted out. My head spun, tiny dots of black crowding into my vision like I might pass out. "There's the selection process...and the background check...they have to come from the top one percent..."

"Grow up!" Missy yelled, loud enough that I cringed, waiting for someone to appear at the door. But no one came. "They couldn't care less what the kennel says about who they can and can't sell their pet to. They own us. They can do whatever they want." Her voice cracked.

"But they're the ones that wanted us," I said. "It's what we were made for—to make them happy."

Missy sank back onto the bed, stretching her smooth legs across the blankets. "Powerful men tire of their toys easily. And the novelty of a pet doesn't last forever. After a while even the prettiest things become ordinary."

"Then why—"

"We're expendable, get it? You think you're safe because you're pretty and young, well, don't get used to it. That's all I'm saying. I let myself believe it once, but I won't let myself do that again."

"Missy, I didn't realize—"

"No, you didn't," she snapped and grabbed a magazine from the side table. She flipped through the pages, obviously done with our conversation and done with me.

"You know how to read?" I asked.

Missy rolled her eyes. "Of course I can't read," she said. "Nobody reads magazines. I look at the pictures." She grabbed another magazine off of the stack by her bed and tossed one to me. "Here, you can keep this one. I've already looked at it."

The room stayed quiet, the only sound the shush of the pages as they turned.

"I get all the fashion magazines," Missy said without look-ing up. "None of these girls are ever as beautiful as we are."

*T*he tapping pulled me from sleep.

I opened my eyes and stared up at the covers that still hid my face, holding completely still as I waited for the sound to come again. Had I imagined it? *Tap tap. Tap tap.* There it was, something knocking against the windowpane.

I pushed the covers off of my face. The teal-colored sky outside my window cast enough light to see by. It was colored with only the tiniest hint of pink along the horizon, as if the idea of morning was only the smallest suggestion of things to come. I sat up in bed. Through the glass, Penn's smile shone white in the early light.

I tied the belt of a silk robe around my waist and opened the door. "Is everything okay?"

"Oh yeah, everything's fine," he said, pushing his hair back away from his eyes. "I'm sorry to wake you so early, but I wanted to show you something and I didn't know if there'd be a chance after everyone else was up."

"Do you want to come in?" I asked, opening the door a little wider.

"No. I didn't bring it here. I need to take you."

The look on his face was so hopeful that I couldn't say no.

"Let me put on some slippers," I said, grabbing a pair from beneath the bed.

We stepped out together into the cool morning. The air was still, almost silent except for the occasional frilly song of a robin. Penn took my hand lightly in his as we made our way down the path to the orchard. It was the first time he'd really touched me since the night we'd gone swimming and even after Missy's warnings, the feel of his skin against mine made every inch of me come alive.

"What is it you want to show me?" I asked, even though I suspected from where we were headed that it had something to do with his secret garden.

Penn wagged a finger at me. "Uh uh, I'm not telling. Haven't you ever heard of a surprise?"

"Okay, no more questions from me." I pretended to zip my mouth shut, trying to cover up the smile that hid there.

As we drew nearer to the hedge that hid his garden, Penn cast a sideways glance at me, pulling me to a stop beside a tree hanging low with small green fruit. He pulled a piece of fabric from his pocket. It looked like a strip cut off of one of his old T-shirts. But the cloth was clean and soft.

"Sorry, no more peeking. From here it's strictly confidential."

He took me by the elbows and turned me around so my back was to him. Then, reaching around me, he covered my eyes with the cloth and tied it snuggly at the back of my head.

"You can't see, can you?" he asked.

He leaned closer and I felt his arm moving, like maybe he was waving his hand in front of my face. I caught the scent of soap mixed with the sweet smell of cut grass drifting just below the surface. The smell confused me. It filled my whole head, making me dizzy and perfectly happy all at once, and I reached out to grab his arm.

"No, it's completely dark," I said, hoping he wouldn't detect the tremble in my voice.

"Now hold on to me," he said, turning me back around and marching me forward.

The wrought iron gate squealed ever so slightly as he swung it open. We took a few more steps and I knew we were inside. Even with my eyes covered I could picture the wild tangle of plants and the pond stretched out beyond them.

"Okay, now to throw you off your game, we'll just give you a little spin," Penn said, twirling me in a circle before he yanked off the blindfold, pointing me in the right direction with two strong hands.

I blinked, my eyes adjusting to the light, but I was seeing double. In front of me, two stone statues floated across my vision, mirror images of one another. I blinked again and they were still there, two woman dreaming secret thoughts behind those closed stone eyes.

"Do you like it?" Penn asked, his voice suddenly shy. "After I cleaned out the pond I decided that it wasn't fair to keep her hidden anymore. Besides, the pond reflects her perfectly."

I took a better look at the long, thin pond. The last

time I'd seen it was in the dark and even though it had
been beautiful in the moonlight, I hadn't really been able
to appreciate how gorgeous it was. It was simple, a narrow
rectangle of stone the exact same color as the statue, which
lay flush with the ground, as if it was part of the earth.
Without all the leaves and muck, the water inside it was
perfectly clear and as still as glass, reflecting the stone girl,
the green hedge, and the pale sky.

"It's perfect."

Penn's face reddened. "No, this is perfect," he said,
laying his hand over my heart. He stared at me for a long
moment before taking my chin lightly in his hand and
turning my face so that I looked up at him.

My heart raced, and my stomach dropped out from
under me. I couldn't allow myself to feel this way, but no
matter how hard I tried to convince myself not to, I wanted
this feeling. Maybe there was something wrong with me. A
part of my brain that couldn't be made to understand that I
wasn't one of them. The thoughts that had hijacked my mind
recently belonged to someone else, someone who would be
allowed to eat dinner at the same table as a boy. Someone
who could move slowly on a dance floor under sparkling
lights in his arms in front of everyone. Someone who could
let him kiss her and allow herself to kiss him back.

I wasn't that girl, but I wanted to be.

"I should really be getting back," I said softly, but I
didn't step away from him.

He tucked a strand of my hair behind my ear. "You
don't have to go yet."

"What if someone is looking for me?"

"They won't be looking for you. It isn't even six yet."

He took my hands in both of his and held them to his chest. "Ella, I can't stop thinking about you. All day. Every day. I try to write, but the only words I can find are about you. I can't ignore it anymore."

I felt the same, but it was wrong. So very wrong. "Penn…"

"I don't care about my dad. He doesn't own your heart."

He pulled me down onto the bench and leaned in, so close that our noses whispered against one another. "I want to be with you. I don't want to feel guilty about it anymore."

I shook my head. "We can't."

"We *can*. We can be together here. This can be our spot."

The feel of his breath on my face made me dizzy and I exhaled. I hadn't realized that I'd been holding my breath. His hands pressed tightly against my back, and his lips brushed against mine. They were so warm. So soft. And I melted into them. My own lips parted, letting the heat from Penn's body fill me up.

When I closed my eyes, the image of his face lingered there.

Our lips moved together. Gently at first, then desperate. Greedy for one another. *This* was what it meant to be kissed, only this time I didn't need to be taught. Kissing him felt natural, as essential as air. I breathed him in, filled my mouth with the taste of him.

Penn's hands traveled down my back, drawing a line along my spine. They stopped at my waist and his fingers spread out, feeling the soft curve of my hips. His grip tightened, pulling me into him and a spark moved through me, catching like kindling that flamed in the darkest corners of my body.

Missy's words nudged their way forward in mind, trying

to push out this feeling, this heat. But I wouldn't listen. I didn't even care if I *was* just a toy that the congressman would tire of. It didn't matter. Not in this moment.

The only thing that mattered was the way Penn's skin felt against mine. Touching him was like music, a strong clear note that drowned out everything else. And I wanted more. I wanted to move my fingers across his skin the way they moved across the keys, stringing together one perfect note after another until we'd made a symphony.

I opened my eyes, coming up for air.

This was what I wanted, to be with him, and maybe here, within these secret walls, it was actually possible. He was right. This spot could be ours.

"Yes," I whispered, smiling up into his face. "I want us to be together, too."

Twenty

$\mathscr{I}$ lived for the stolen hours between midnight and sunrise. It was the only time Penn and I could truly be together. Sure, I saw him during the day while he and Ruby fixed cookies in the kitchen or swam in the pool, but I didn't dare let my gaze linger on him for too long, especially when the congressman was in the room.

Sometimes, if I simply thought of him, a rush of heat would flood my cheeks and I would look up to make sure the congressman hadn't seen. If he did, I was certain he would know my secret, my longing like a hot brand seared across my face.

I was so distracted that I almost forgot that Claire was bringing her new fiancé home to visit. It was easy to forget that the congressman and his wife actually had three kids, but I had to face the fact that there would be two more people in the house for a while. And it worried me, not only because I was intimidated to meet her, but because her presence might interrupt the only time I had to spend with Penn.

Ruby ran around the house in a frenzy. The congress-man's wife had asked me to take her up to her room to play, but we only lasted fifteen minutes before she was back downstairs again, pulling on her mom's sleeve and asking for the four hundredth time when her sister would arrive.

"Come on, Ella. Let's go sit on the front steps. That way we'll be the first ones Claire sees when she gets here," she finally said, after her mother pushed her away with the threat of hard labor if she couldn't settle down and wait like a normal human.

Ruby had been talking about Claire since the first day I arrived, and up until now she'd seemed more like a myth than a real person. She was an idea, a fairy tale, a lovely face that floated behind the glass on mantels and side tables.

"You look pretty today," Ruby said, scooting closer to me on the wide stone steps and smoothing out the folds in my dress. "I bet Claire's going to love you. I bet she'll wish she could take you home with her."

These were the things I knew about Claire: she went to Cornell, which was where the congressman had met his wife; she was studying law; she had just gotten engaged to Grant Wentwood, who had graduated from Harvard last fall, and would make his soon-to-be-father-in-law very proud some day; and last but not least, she would make the most lovely bride ever to walk the face of the earth. That was it. At least, that was all I'd learned about her from listening to the congressman and his wife.

The rest of what I'd learned about her was what I'd picked up listening to Ruby, like the fact that she was an expert at fixing her hair in fancy chignons, could spell any word out of the dictionary, and hated mashed potatoes. Ruby also liked to tell the story about the time when Claire was little and had beaten her dad in a hot-dog-eating contest, which seemed hard for me to believe since I'd never seen the congressman eat a hot dog. Although Ruby assured me it was a common kind of food, and was not, in fact, made from the animal of the same name.

I wasn't really sure any of these things were going to be helpful in understanding who Claire really was. All I knew was that she must have been someone special to have the whole house it such a tumult of anticipation. Even Penn seemed distracted, more distant, lost in thought. Today, instead of going on our usual walk down to the garden before the others woke up, he'd spent the morning on the patio, scribbling in his notebook. Now he was downstairs waiting for her to arrive the way everyone else was.

"Look, look, someone's pulling into the driveway!" Ruby yelled. She dragged me to my feet and ran down the steps and out onto the driveway. She flopped up and down, waving her hands above her head as the car crunched over the gravel and came to a stop in front of us.

The dark windows made it hard to see inside, but a second later the door opened and a woman stepped out, smoothing down the wrinkles in her skirt before she lifted her head. She looked very much like the girl I'd seen in the pictures—a thin face and high forehead, bright blue eyes and dark hair like her mother, but there was something in person that the film hadn't been able to capture. It was that same regal presence I found so intimidating in the congressman's wife.

"Claire! Claire! Claire!" Ruby yelled, jumping on her sister as soon as she was standing.

"Settle down, Miss Ruby Roo," Claire said as she patted her sister on the head. "Let me get my legs working first. We've been driving forever."

Ruby stepped back and grabbed my hand, still smiling even though the disappointment on her face was clear. Claire's gaze skimmed over me before they turned back to the car, where her fiancé, Grant, was shutting the door behind him. He was tall and thin, with fair hair and light hazel eyes.

Just then the door to the house swung open and everyone else spilled into the driveway.

"Hello, sweetheart," the congressman's wife said, kissing her daughter on the forehead. "I'm so glad you made it. How was the drive?"

The two women wrapped their arms around each other and began walking toward the house. "Can you get the bags, Grant?" Claire called back over her shoulder. "And bring in that wine we brought for my parents. And those packages on the back seat."

The congressman clapped his future son-in-law on the shoulder. "Penn and I will get the bags," he said. "It looks like you've got your hands full."

Ruby and I stood off to the side of the car as the bags were unloaded. It was difficult to stand so close to Penn, to feel the brush of air as he moved past me to grab the suitcases and not be able to reach out and touch him.

Grant nodded at me over the top of the car. He had a knowing smile on his face, as if he'd been able to see inside of my head and knew exactly what I'd been thinking about Penn. He caught my gaze and held it before he bent back into the car and pulled out two large shopping bags.

"So Miss Ruby," he said, coming around to where we stood. "Will you and your lovely assistant be so kind as to escort me inside?"

He held his free hand out to her and she giggled happily. "Ella's not my assistant. She's our new pet."

Grant winked at me before Ruby dragged the three of us inside.

Claire and her parents were standing at the kitchen counter, already drinking tall glasses of iced tea. "Mother, you remember Grant?" Claire asked, grabbing her fiancé around the arm and walking him into the room where she handed him his own drink. He brought the sweating glass to his lips and took a long sip.

"It's a pleasure to see you again, Mrs. Kimball. Your house is lovely."

"It looks like you've made some changes since I was here last," Claire said, looking directly at me as she spoke.

"Well, we got new furniture for the living room," the congressman's wife said. "But I'm not crazy about the draperies."

The congressman came and stood next to me, resting his big hand against my shoulder. "And of course there's Ella."

Claire's face puckered slightly. "Yes, that does seem like a rather big change. When you mentioned getting a pet at the beginning of summer, this isn't exactly what I'd envisioned. I thought you already had one and it didn't work out."

The congressman laughed, waving off her comment. "After working so hard on the legislation, it seems absurd not to have one ourselves. She's beautiful, isn't she?"

The congressman had already started talking again, telling Grant all about the trip to pick me up at the training center, so he didn't notice Claire's resentful stare.

"Sorry to interrupt you, Daddy," she said, butting into his story right as he was starting off on a tangent about isolating DNA. "Would you mind very much telling us the rest of your story at dinner tonight? I'm exhausted from the drive and I'd really love to go upstairs and lie down for a little bit, especially if we're going to a show later. Wouldn't you like to join me, darling?" she asked, turning to Grant.

He patted her hand. "You go up without me. I'm going to have your father and your brother show me around the house."

The congressman grinned, completely ignoring the frown on his daughter's face.

"I'll take you up and get you settled," the congressman's wife said.

As the others left the kitchen, Ruby chased after her mother and her sister. "Can I come up, too?" she asked. "I promise I'll be really quiet."

From what I'd seen of Claire I expected her to give Ruby an annoyed roll of the eyes and tell her that she wanted to be alone, but she surprised me, placing her arm tenderly around her sister's shoulder and pulling her along up the stairs. It was a nice gesture, but it didn't change the way she made me feel, like I was something dirty that needed to be wiped away.

*I*t turned out Grant only wanted a brief tour of the house and before long they'd settled down in the conservatory. I hadn't strayed from the kitchen. I sat at the counter, staring out past the pool.

"Ella," the congressman called from the other room. "Come play Grant one of your pieces on the piano."

I emerged in the doorway and all three men turned to look at me. The congressman smiled and then turned to look at Penn as he spoke. "Ella plays the piano exquisitely, doesn't she, Penn?"

Grant squinted ever so slightly and smiled, looking between the father and the son as if it was all too easy to guess what was passing between them. "Claire has actually mentioned that Penn's the family musician. Are you all right with the new pet stealing a bit of the thunder?" he asked.

Penn didn't take his eyes off of his father as he responded. "Quite all right," he said. "I'm not really the type to get jealous."

The congressman chuckled before he turned his attention back to Grant. "Are you a big fan of classical music? She can play pretty much anything."

I sat down at the piano and arranged my hands delicately across the keys.

"Oh anything," Grant said dismissively. "To be quite honest I could only name a handful of composers and I'd probably come up blank if you asked me to name one of their songs. Is there such thing as a 'Moonlight Sonata'?"

The congressman chuckled. "Don't worry. I'm pretty sure none of your colleagues will hold it against you if you can't produce a list of Bach's concertos. I'm definitely more impressed with Claire's news that you've been hired at Dunford and Gray. I don't even live in Boston and I know what a great firm they are."

It sounded as if they could go right on talking while I

sat there all day, my hands poised above the keys, waiting for them to choose a song. I risked a quick glance over my shoulder to where Penn sat in the wingback chair by the wall.

"Play some Schubert," he mouthed and I smiled, turning back around to face the piano.

The music was soft, the sonata in B flat major. It was a beautiful choice, made even lovelier by the fact that Penn had been the one to make me think of it. I didn't even mind that Grant and the congressman kept talking as I played. They didn't even realize what they'd given us, this moment that now belonged to only Penn and me. I could feel his stare against my back, my arms, my fingers, and suddenly it was like we were back in our pond again, only this time I was the one that held him, suspended from the music as if we were floating.

I stopped playing and bowed my head over the keys, breathing hard. Behind me I knew Penn had felt something special, too.

The congressman and Grant stopped talking and clapped politely, as if they'd only now noticed that the room had grown silent, that I had been playing at all.

Twenty One

I don't know whose idea it was to take me along to the opera—maybe the congressman's wife, thinking that I'd be a good distraction for Ruby in case she became bored during the show—but somehow I ended up sitting between Ruby and Penn on the first mezzanine in the Metropolitan Opera House.

I'd never imagined a ceiling so high, or so grand. The golden gleam of it was lit below by the most enormous chandeliers. An elaborate velvet curtain hung almost four stories high in front of the stage like the gown of some beautiful, monstrous woman. If it had lifted up, I wouldn't have been surprised to see two enormous feet perched on the stage.

Every nerve in my body was buzzing like a piano string that had been struck long and hard. I could almost hear the note hanging in the air around me.

I wanted so badly to lean against Penn, pulling him forward

with me as I stared out over the audience, but I could hardly enjoy being this close to him, not because I was worried about the congressman seeing us together—he was still out in the lobby happily talking to a group of constituents—but because ever since we'd found our seats Claire had kept him wrapped in conversation, talking relentlessly about all the things she'd seen since she'd been away at college. And every time Penn would make even the slightest move to turn away from her, she'd launch in again about a favorite professor she couldn't wait to introduce him to, or all the wonderful little coffee houses she'd discovered near campus. I wondered if she was purposefully distracting him from me.

From where we sat, right above the stage, I stared down at the musicians lined up in front. It seemed crazy to think this was their job, to sit in this beautiful auditorium night after night and play music.

"Are you okay?" Ruby asked, raising her eyebrows.

She'd been trying to talk to me ever since we sat down. She was leaning over the balcony and pointing out all the men with bald spots. It was a game she'd made up. She'd point out all the bald-headed men and I was supposed point out all the women with cleavage. But I could tell I was disappointing her. I'd only pointed out two people since we sat down.

"I'm fine," I said, patting her hand. How could I explain to her the feeling I had in my chest? Fear and desire all knotted together inside of me. How, if I could, I would leap from the balcony and take my place at that piano.

Just then the lights flickered and the audience quieted. Once more and they dimmed completely. As if on cue, a hum rose from the orchestra, the sound of their instruments rising up to make one beautiful resonant sound. And for the first time since we'd taken our seats Penn turned to look at me. It was only one brief glance, but even in the dim light I knew what it meant—that he wished it was just the two of us here tonight.

"I've seen this one before," Ruby whispered to me as the curtains opened to reveal a foggy stage "The girl dies and her boyfriend has to go to the underworld to get her back. It's an old Greek myth, but they turned it into an opera with all the singing and stuff."

The music built slowly and then, as if it was growing out of the fog, a chorus of voices rose from the stage. The pure beauty of the sound startled me and I gasped.

"Don't be scared," Ruby said, patting my leg. "They're just the mourners. See? It's Euridice's tomb."

I nodded, too distracted by the music to tell Ruby that it wasn't the opera that frightened me.

We'd learned plenty of operas at the training center. I'd sung bits myself, but they never sounded like this before. The realization struck me; we'd been singing empty words all those years. Without emotion, the words had been useless. But as soon as the curtain lifted and the actors opened their mouths, I realized for the first time what those words were really made of—pain and heartache, so strong that you could see it stamped on their faces as they sang.

I leaned forward, watching as Orfeo vowed to rescue his love from the land of death. Around me, the whole world disappeared. I forgot all about the auditorium filled with thousands of red velvet seats. I forgot about the fancy chandeliers and the gilded railings.

Every muscle in my body strained forward as Orfeo

approached the Gate of Hades. He was allowed to bring Euridice home, but only if he promised not to look back at her as he led her out of the dark labyrinth of the underworld. My fingers dug into the seat beside me and I struggled not to call out to him. *Don't look back. Don't look back.* But nothing I could do could stop him from turning back around to face his love. I was powerless to stop the tears that rolled down my cheeks as Euridice crumpled to the ground.

Penn's hand brushed mine. I grabbed onto it, shivering as goose bumps spread up my arms. "How could someone write a story that ended this way?"

His eyes reflected a bit of the light from the stage. "It isn't over yet."

I held on tighter.

Out of the corner of my eye I saw Claire glance at where our hands were clasped. Quickly, I pulled mine away.

For the rest of the show I kept my hands clutched tightly in my lap. My heart was beating fast, a nervous hammer that distracted me from the joyful sound rising from the stage. I could hardly appreciate seeing Euridice rise again and reunite with Orfeo. All I could think about was the look on Claire's face when she'd glanced in our direction.

Had she seen? If she had, it would ruin everything. I'd taken the touch that Penn and I shared inside our secret garden and brought it into the light. And now Claire might know. What if she was angry? Or worse, what if she told her father?

As the lights came up, I wiped at my wet cheeks. Around us, the rest of the audience was getting to their feet, *ooh*ing and *ahh*ing about what a fantastic show it had been. They'd never seen such a delightful Orfeo, such a compelling Euridice they said, as they shuffled to find their purses and their jackets.

"How did you like the show, Ruby?" Claire asked, leaning across Penn.

"It seemed pretty much the same as the last time we saw it." Ruby shrugged.

"And what about you?" Claire shifted her gaze to me. "Did you enjoy the show?"

My voice trembled. "Yes, very much."

"It wasn't too intense for you?" she asked. "Especially toward the end there?"

The congressman rose from his seat, looking pleased. "You know, they say you can tell a true opera lover by the look on her face after a show. I didn't doubt Ella would love it. Look at her face. She looks like she's been to hell and back right along with Orfeo."

Claire cast an irritated look at her father, but she stayed quiet and I let out a relieved breath. We left the theater, walking down the gigantic curved staircase and out into the bustling crowd that milled about in front of the fountain in the courtyard. It had been a beautiful evening and I wished I could savor it all without the fear that I'd messed it up.

The sky had grown dark while we were inside, and now as we climbed back into the car waiting to take us back home, I stared transfixed at the lights of the city sprawled out before us. It seemed impossible that there could be so many lights, so many people. With Ruby's warm body pressed up against me, my eyes grew heavy and as the wheels of the tires hummed beneath us, I closed my eyes and drifted off.

I woke to the sound of my name and the brush of a hand against my cheek.

"Ella, we're home, love," the congressman said, lightly stroking the hair back away from my face.

I sat up, surprised to see that everyone else was gone. The car was empty, save for the congressman in the seat beside me.

"You were exhausted," he said. "At first I thought you'd get up by yourself, but I'm starting to think you could stay out here all night if I didn't wake you."

"I'm sorry," I said, rubbing my eyes. My cheek was cool from leaning against the glass. "The show must have worn me out."

He reached across me to unfasten my seatbelt. "Yes, the theater can be draining," he said. "But at least I know who to take with me the next time I have tickets."

I swallowed. "I'd be happy to accompany you. It was beautiful."

"Good." He nodded.

The car was too quiet. His body was hot against my side, the smell of his cologne almost overpowering in the small space.

"It must be late," I whispered. "Has everyone else already gone to bed?"

He turned and looked out the window at the quiet house. "Yes, it is late," he said. "Too late for an old man like me."

In the glow cast by the porch light the congressman's face did look old and tired as he turned back to me. After a moment he lifted his hand to my face. His palm was hot against my cheek, but I didn't move. He leaned imperceptibly closer to me and inhaled deeply, closing his eyes as he breathed me in. A small smile plucked at the corner of his lips. I couldn't help the tremor that moved up my legs and through my arms and I took a shuddering breath, trying to still the shaking.

After a minute he dropped his hand back to his lap and opened the car door. The fresh night air wafted across my face and I scrambled across the seat and up the front steps.

"Good night," I called behind me, walking quickly back through the study to my bedroom. When his footsteps faded down the hallway in the other direction, I stopped, leaning back against the wall in relief.

Missy's words played through my mind as I walked the rest of the way back to my room. But nothing I told myself could erase the uneasiness I felt. If I really was safe, why did I feel so afraid?

I closed my door behind me.

Across the room Penn sat on my couch, quietly waiting for me to return. A bit of moonlight shone through the window, lighting the side of his face. My heart leapt. I loved that face.

"Finally…" In a heartbeat, he crossed the room and was standing in front of me. "I was starting to think you'd never come."

Almost delicately, he lifted his hand to my forehead and brushed a strand of hair from my eyes. The touch was so light, almost invisible, but it sent a quiver down through my toes.

His body seemed so large, so solid in front of me, an anchor to hold on to. Unbreakable. I reached out for him in the dark, desperate to feel him, as if his presence could keep me from being swept away.

My touch was like a lit match, igniting him. He pulled me to his chest, just as frantic to hold me as I was to hold him. We stumbled back toward the bed, landing on the soft mattress with a *whoosh*, our mouths crashing together, our hands hungry for the feel of each other's skin. It had only been a couple days since we'd been together, but I felt starved. I craved the taste of his mouth the way I craved Ruby's candies, the memories never enough to fill me.

"We can't stay here," I panted.

He moaned. "Please, Ella."

"No." I shook my head, scooting back. "Your father's still awake. We can't."

His face looked pained as he let go of me.

"I'm sorry."

He shook his head and climbed off the bed, pulling me after him.

"What are you doing?"

"If we can't stay here, we'll go to the garden."

He headed for the door, a little smile tipping the corners of his mouth upward. "It's time for another swimming lesson anyway, isn't it?"

*I*t wasn't any wonder I dreamed of Penn. But even in my dreams there was always that little breath of distance between us, so small, yet insurmountable. No matter how much I wanted to feel the press of his body against mine, there was always something holding us apart.

I stood inside one of these dreams, balanced one inch away from that kiss, when a hand touched my arm, pulling me up into the real world.

When I opened my eyes, it was morning. Not the dim blush of dawn I was in the habit of waking up to, but the bright, full light of day, yellow and streaming. I blinked twice, letting my eyes adjust.

"Rise and shine."

I rubbed my eyes and moved my head to see the congressman standing beside my bed. He was already dressed in the casual clothes that meant he wasn't going into work today: a crisp blue shirt, unbuttoned around the collar and rolled at the sleeves, and soft, tailored slacks.

I sat up in bed and pulled the covers up across my chest. "I must have overslept."

"Yes, it's getting late," he said. "A person could stand here all day watching you sleep, but we've got places to go and people to see."

"We do?"

He chuckled, but there was no humor in his eyes. "Well maybe we don't have people to see, but you *will* be accompanying me on a little outing this afternoon."

"Of course." I pulled off the covers and hopped out of bed, overly conscious of the way his gaze followed me across the floor to the closet. "Is there something special I need to wear?"

"I don't particularly care what you wear, as long as you don't take too long getting ready." He crossed his arms over his chest, sitting down on my couch as I sorted through my gowns.

I pulled down a simple, lilac colored dress and turned to hold it up for the congressman, who nodded his approval.

"Is there time for me to bathe before we go?" I asked, standing in the bathroom doorway. I could still smell Penn and the lingering scent of the pond on my skin.

The congressman must have noticed the way my face flushed, and he stood, perhaps assuming it was my embarrassment of having him in the room as I showered that made my cheeks color this way. "I have some business to take care of anyway," he said, walking to the door. "We'll leave after lunch."

The hot water washed away all the traces of the night before. When I was finished bathing, I pulled on the clean gown, noticing the way the color turned my eyes greener than usual.

Maybe it was the nervousness of not knowing where he intended to take me, but I pulled my hair up in a braid around the crown of my head. It wasn't much of a comfort, but at least it was one small things I could control.

*T*he congressman didn't join us for lunch and even though I wasn't eager to see him, I started to get more and more nervous as the day grew late. He had seemed irritated when he woke me and I didn't want to do anything else to aggravate him. Finally, right before dinner, he popped his head into the kitchen where I sat at the counter with Ruby watching Rosa cut potatoes.

"Shall we go?" he said impatiently, as if it had been me who'd kept him waiting the whole day.

He placed his hand on my back, steering me out the door.

The beautiful little turquoise car we'd driven home from the training center was already parked outside waiting for us, and he opened the door, ushering me inside in one fluid sweep.

"I put the top down," he said, climbing in beside me. "There's nothing quite like driving a convertible to the beach."

"I've never been to the beach," I said as we pulled out of the driveway, leaving the house and all its inhabitants behind us. The beach sounded pleasant. Not at all like somewhere a person would take another if they were angry.

The congressman adjusted his mirrors. "No, I assumed as much. That's the reason I'm taking you." He reached over and squeezed my leg just above the knee. "You can't imagine all the things I'm going to show you, all the wonders you never even dreamed existed. There's so much I'm going to give you, my pet."

The wind whipped across my face, stinging my eyes as we sped past stands of deep green trees and fields of summer grass. Already we'd left the house in the dust. Within minutes we'd sped past the few landmarks that seemed familiar and now everything was new again. Even the light that flickered sideways through the trees seemed like something I'd never seen before, as if light wasn't something shared across the world, but something specific to each location, as distinct and varied as the landscape it fell across.

"I didn't see the ocean for the first time until I was twenty," he said. "I didn't move to the coast until I was in college. I grew up in Wichita." He glanced at me out of the corner of his eye. "I don't expect you to know where that is. It's in Kansas, the middle of the country. Also close enough to the middle of nowhere for someone like me."

He paused and I took the moment to look at him fully, trying to imagine what he must have been like when he was a young man. He would have looked like Penn, I expected. Fresh and handsome.

"I moved away from home as soon as I got the chance. Lucky for me I made it into Cornell. That's where I met Elise. We were both so pleased when Claire decided to follow in our footsteps."

"Did you always want to be a congressman?"

"No." He smiled. After the stern expression he'd worn most of the morning, it was a welcome change. I wondered if he was pleased his pet wanted to know more about him. "I wanted to be a businessman. I wanted to build things, to make things, to own things. Politics didn't come along until later."

"But at some point you realized that you wanted to help people?"

"You mean, is that why I got into politics? Yes, I guess that's a noble way to look at it."

The sun was already starting its decent into evening, but it still warmed my shoulders. After a while, the air began to change. I lifted my head and drank in the smell, closing my eyes so I could sense it more clearly. It carried something pungent and briny on the moist breeze.

The car bumped to a stop and I opened my eyes.

"Here we are." The congressman swept his arm toward

the view but I could feel his gaze on me, watching, waiting.

I took in a deep breath and held it. In front of me a deep blue slash was cut across the horizon. Earlier in the day it had probably been cheerful, but now, with the sun fading behind us, the ocean looked dark and ominous. Above it, a few clouds smeared the sky, reflecting the pinkish glow of the setting sun, while a group of white birds dove in and out of the small waves. Along the beach a spattering of people lounged on the sand, but to me they were inconsequential.

"Do you want to get out?" he asked.

The wind whipped my dress around my legs as I made my way across the small strip of grass that led to the beach. My feet sank as I stepped onto the sand. It was warm around my ankles, gritty but soft, a perfect contradiction.

The congressman followed me out to the edge of the water. The sand was harder here, packed down and moist. I slipped off my sandals and let my toes sink down into it.

"It's not like the pool, is it," he said, looking out across the water.

"It's so…big." It sounded stupid, but what else could I say?

"You'll really need to know how to swim if you want to get in that water." He stepped closer, until his mouth was right next to my ear. His words were clear, unmarred by the wind. "Next time you need a swimming lesson, why don't you come to me?"

He moved his hand to my neck, brushing aside the stray hairs that had come loose from my braids, and wrapped a finger around a strand of hair.

My words stuck in my throat as I looked up at him. His jaw was set, his eyes stern, angry even. Had he followed us last night? Watched as we shed our clothes and slipped into the dark water?

Had he been following us all along?

His eyes softened slightly. "I can't really blame Penn," he said. "And I hate to chastise you, but you must realize that it's impossible, this thing between you and my son. It isn't real. He's terrible at controlling his emotions, even if he must realize that they're absurd. So please, love, stay away from him. Don't make it any harder on the poor boy." He smiled, twirling the lock of my hair around his finger. "Or any harder on this old man."

I nodded once and lowered my head. I couldn't bring myself to look back out at that grand vista before me. It felt spoiled now.

Twenty Two

The house was dark when we finally returned home.

The congressman opened the door for me, smiling contentedly as if we'd actually just spent a lovely day at the beach. His words were still a cold knot in my chest, but I smiled sweetly and reached out my hand, letting him help me from the car.

"Thank you for taking me to the beach." My voice was small, but I hoped the fear stayed hidden.

"I'll take you again soon," he promised. He placed his hand on my back and walked me up the front steps. "Although, I hope we have nicer things to talk about next time.

I paused stiffly by the front door as he unlocked it. "Well…good night," I called as the door swung open, ready to sprint to my room.

Before I could leave, he grabbed my arm. "Make sure you get your rest tonight."

I nodded. He didn't need to elaborate. I knew exactly what he meant. As if he hadn't been clear enough at the beach. No more nights out in the garden. No more Penn.

As I moved through the conservatory I noticed a light coming from the kitchen. I turned the corner expecting to find Penn standing in front of the refrigerator drinking a cold glass of water the way he sometimes did right before bed.

But before I could step into the kitchen, the soft sound of voices made me duck back into the shadows. Claire sat across from Penn in one of the bar stools with her back to me. A bit of hair had come loose from her chignon and had fallen down her back.

"I mean, really," she said. "Why not get a golden retriever or a pony? What was Dad thinking?"

I shrank farther back into the hallway, my pulse thumping wildly. I knew they were talking about me. I also knew that I shouldn't stay and listen. It was wrong to eavesdrop, but I couldn't help myself. Miss Gellner would be mortified if she could see me here, holding my breath as I slipped my shoes from my feet and tiptoed closer to the kitchen, pressing my ear against the wall.

"It's not really what you think." Penn's voice was soft. "She's not bad. You'll like her after you get to know her." His words brought a little smile to my lips.

"I don't plan on getting to know her," Claire said. "And neither should you."

From where I stood in the shadows of the hallway I could only make out part of Penn's face on the other side of the kitchen. He frowned. "I mean it, Claire. You should give her a chance."

"I never even wanted a pet dog. What makes you think I'll like some little princess of a girl who's obviously got her claws set in my brother?"

"What's that supposed to mean?"

"It means that I can tell what she's doing to you and it's a bad idea. Seriously, Penn. So stop thinking about it now before you get in any more trouble."

Penn shook his head and stepped away from the counter, putting distance between himself and his sister.

"Come on. I see the way you look at her. You and Dad both. It's disgusting. And don't tell me I'm making it up. I saw you holding hands with her at the opera, like she was some sweet little waif so touched by the music that she could hardly stand it. Nobody actually cries at the opera. She just knows how to work you."

My stomach dropped even further than it had already fallen.

"It's not like that," Penn said. "You don't know her."

"You can't lie to me. I've known you your whole life, remember?" Claire said, "You do that stupid thing with your eyebrows when you're lying."

She sighed and placed her hands flat against the marble countertop, spreading her fingers wide as if she was laying it all out for him to see. "What do you imagine is going to happen, anyway? You think the two of you are going to go off to college together, maybe share an apartment, grow up and have some kids? She's a *pet*, Penn. Our *father's* pet. You're kidding yourself if you think she's anything else to you."

"I know what she is." Penn's voice wasn't soft anymore.

"Do you?" Claire asked.

"Yes."

"Then start acting like it," Claire said. "How can you even stand to have her here? Did you forget about what happened the last time? How she ruined our family?"

"No," Penn mumbled.

"Because it sure seems like you have."

"She's not the same as the other one," Penn said.

Claire snorted. "Oh, I'm sure."

"She isn't—"

"She might not be the same one, but she'll do the same thing," Claire snapped. "She's still one of them. She's still a pet."

Penn groaned. "You don't have to keep reminding me that she's a goddamn pet. I know it, all right. I *know*."

He turned away from her and his full profile came into view. The hurt and anger in his voice was written clearly on his face.

"Then stop treating her like she's one of us. I don't know what you've let happen between the two of you, but it has to stop and it has to stop now. Dad will *kill* you, Penn! This isn't like the thing with your school. This is serious. He'll make your life hell."

"I'm not afraid of him," Penn said.

"You should be." Her voice cracked and she leaned forward. "Please, Penn. I'm worried about you. And I'm not just saying that. You *know* Dad. He's relentless. When he wants something, he has to have it—no matter the cost. I don't want you to get hurt."

Penn's jaw clenched. "I won't."

"Yes, you will," she said, slumping back in her chair. "And none of us will be able to save you if you make him your enemy."

I stumbled away from the doorway. I didn't know what the other pet had done to their family, but I didn't want to be like her. I didn't want to hurt anyone. Especially not Penn. He wasn't the one Claire should be chastising for dreaming that there was a future between us. It was me. I was the one who'd started to hope that things could be different.

What a fool I was.

I turned away from the kitchen, away from Penn and the false hope that I'd ever be anything more than a pet. My bare feet slapped against the shiny wooden floor as I ran down the hallway, through the French doors, and into the empty yard. To my right, the black water of the pool reflected the full moon, a cold white face, mocking me.

The gravel bit into my feet as I ran past the carriage house and down the lane, out to the long stretch of road leading away from the Kimballs' house. On any other night, the dark driveway that led to Ms. Harper's house would have stopped me short, but I kept running.

By the time I reached Missy's house, my feet were raw and scraped, but I hardly noticed. That invisible cord binding the two of us together pulled me to her.

The house was dark, but I found her window easily enough. I climbed through the bushes that bordered the flowerbeds and pressed my face close to the cool glass. Next to the window a honeysuckle perfumed the night, making me dizzy with memories of Penn's secret garden. But I couldn't think about that now. If I didn't do this, he'd lose everything.

I rapped my knuckles against the window, three quick taps before I pressed my back against the brick and held my breath. Nothing. No lights, no alarm, no barking dogs. I tapped again, a bit louder this time, until the soft, yellow light of a lamp spilled out into the night.

A moment later the window cracked open and Missy peered out, bleary eyed and beautiful.

"Who's there?"

"It's me, Ella. I'm so sorry for waking you, but I didn't know where else to go."

The sleepy look disappeared from Missy's face. "What are you doing here?"

"Please, can I come in?" I squeaked. "I need to talk to you."

Missy calmly slid open the window, plucking off the screen as if she'd done it a million times before and I scrambled through, falling into a pile on the floor at her feet.

"I've had plenty of people knock at my window at night wanting to be let in," she said, "but this is a new one."

I leaned back against the wall. A sob worked its way up through my chest and I covered my face with my hands, surprised to find that my cheeks were already wet with tears.

"So…it's a boy." Missy said.

She lowered herself down onto the edge of her bed and stared at me. The soft ticking of a bedside clock counted out the seconds, but neither of us moved.

"I didn't mean for it to happen."

Missy closed her eyes and a sad smile pricked at the corners of her mouth. "We never do. But it's not like it matters. Not really. Him loving you was never going to change anything."

"I can't go back. It isn't safe for him with me there."

"Well you can't stay here. Believe me, one pet is enough."

"Come with me," I blurted. "We can leave…the two of us."

Missy's lip trembled, but the rest of her face was as still as porcelain. "We can't just leave."

"I have a piece of paper that has the name of a safe house on it. We could go there. There are people that can help us."

"No one can help us," Missy said. "Those people want you to think they can because it makes them feel important. Finally, they can be the powerful ones. But it isn't true. Our owners would find us. You know they would. They would find us and then they'd put us to sleep, or worse. I was lucky last time, but I'm older now."

"Not if we—"

"*No,*" Missy said, her eyes shining. "I've met girls that have been sold two, three times. And it isn't to homes like this. You can't imagine the things they've seen…the things they have to do for their owners." Her face went white. "No. I…I can't. I've still got a few good years here. I can't risk that for a silly dream."

"But what if it's not a dream?"

"It's all just a dream," she whispered.

We stared at each other in silence until, finally, a tear streaked down her cheek. Her jaw clenched. "I'm sorry, Ella."

Before I realized what she was doing, she grabbed the silver bell at her bedside and shook it. "Help!" she screamed. "Help! Master!"

The sound of her voice mixed with the clear, high chime of the bell. Down the hall there was the sound of doors opening. I scrambled to my feet, desperate to make it to the open window, but before I could climb out, a strong hand clamped down on my arm, dragging me back inside.

Twenty Three

The room was bright now. The mean, overhead lights glared down at me accusingly.

"What's the meaning of this?" Missy's owner growled, spinning me around to face him. "Who are you?" Bits of spittle flew out of his mouth as he talked. "Wait a second. Are you a pet?"

"She tried to take me," Missy cried, cowering so convincingly on her bed that I almost believed for a moment I'd truly frightened her.

I shook my head. "Missy, please…don't."

"She wanted me to run away with her," she went on. Her eyes were wide and wet with tears.

"It's all right now," Missy's owner said, tightening his grasp around my arm. "You're safe. You just go back to bed now, darling. You, too," he said, turning to the door where his wife and daughter stared in, openmouthed. "I'll take care of it."

"That's Ruby's pet," Jayne said, backing away from me as her dad pulled me down the hall. "Daddy, that's the Kimballs' pet."

"I said get back to bed," he snapped.

Inside his office, he finally let go of my arm, throwing me down onto the chaise lounge where I'd first seen Missy.

"You sit right there," he said, poking his finger into my chest. "And don't you dare think about moving."

He switched the light on over his desk and picked up the phone, fumbling through a thick leather bound notebook until he found what he was looking for. "Yes, I'm terribly sorry to bother you in the middle of the night, Congressman, but it appears your pet has ended up at my house." He paused. "Yes, quite sure. Thank you."

He slammed the phone down and folded his thick arms across his chest.

"You better hope your master is a better man than I am. Because if I caught my pet trying to run away, she wouldn't get a second chance."

A second chance. The congressman had already given me a second chance.

In my mind, the kennel's red door yawned open. The screams of pets echoed in my ears until my knees went weak.

When the congressman arrived, he nodded solemnly at Missy's master, refusing to even glance in my direction. "I'm so sorry about the trouble, Craig," he said, pulling him in for a tight handshake. "I hope there's some way I can make it up to you."

"Nonsense," Mr. Miller said. "It's no trouble, really. I'm sure you'd do the same for me."

Even though it was well past midnight, the congressman

was dressed in a pressed shirt and slacks, but his hair was mussed and the exhaustion in his eyes was unmistakable.

Without being asked, I rose from the chair and went to stand next to my owner. I bowed my head, staring at the floor. I couldn't bear to see the disappointment in his eyes.

"I don't know what sort of training program her kennel had, but quite a few of them offer special programs for situations like this. Even the least subservient can be made to obey," Missy's master said. "If we do it with our Dobermans we can do it with them, right?"

The congressman chuckled softly. "Yes, I suppose so," he said. "Now if you'll excuse me. I won't take up a moment more of your time."

"Oh, it's been no trouble, really. Can I interest you in a nightcap?"

The congressman waved away the offer. "Thank you, but maybe another time." Finally he turned to look down at me. "Ella, come. Good night, Craig."

Back home, the house was silent. The congressman didn't touch me as he lead me through the dark halls and into my bedroom, but I could feel his gaze against my back, as sharp as Miss Gellner's training stick.

In my room, I paused for just a moment, afraid to look through the window for fear that I'd see Penn sitting at the edge of the pool with his feet dipped in the water, the bare skin of his back shining ever so slightly in the light from the moon. But the pool was empty. The yard was a dark blanket, smooth and desolate.

"I'm sorry to have to do this, Ella, but you've really left me no choice," the congressman said as I neared the bed.

I turned to him, confused. "What are you…?" I stopped

midsentence, noticing the key that he held in his hand.

He reached out to stroke my hair, running his fingers through it like a comb. It was an intimate gesture. If the anger in his eyes hadn't been so intense, it might have reminded me of the way Ruby played with my hair while we watched television. But it wasn't meant to be kind and it wasn't meant to be comforting. His grip tightened as he knotted his fingers through the hair at the back of my neck. "I trusted you once," he whispered. "I believed that there were crazy people out there, and I only wanted to keep you safe. But I don't know what to believe now."

His grip was strong. He didn't let go as he pushed me forward.

At the front of the bed, a wide metal band had been attached snuggly around the wooden post and then bolted to an anchor in the wall. Welded to the metal band, a long chain sat coiled on the floor. It rattled as he wrapped the chain around my wrist, fastening the end with a lock. He turned the key once and gave it a tug, testing it.

"It might be uncomfortable, but it's going to have to do for now."

My legs gave out beneath me and I sank down onto the mattress, staring down at the chain that held me.

There was a tap at the French door and the congressman and I both turned as it cracked open. Penn's gaze trailed from my face down to my wrist, confusion settling over his features. "What's going on?" He pushed the door open and stepped into the room. "You're chaining her up?"

"What would you have me do? She ran away again," the congressman said, holding up his hand to stop his son from coming any closer. "I thought it would be best to make sure she was secure. The kennel had this installed in case we ever needed to use it, which I never dreamed of, but I won't be able to rest imagining that she's going to sneak off."

His eyes narrowed as he spat out the last two words.

Penn took a small step back. "But…how can you even know that's what happened?"

"Oh, I know," the congressman said bitterly.

Penn stared at me, his eyes full of hurt before he focused on his father. "What if she needs to get up? You can't leave her chained there like an animal."

"You can cut the melodrama," the congressman snapped. "It's plenty long for her to move about the room. It'll stretch all the way to the bathroom, so settle down. It's not like it's cruel and unusual punishment."

"Dad, you can't just keep—"

"I said *enough*!" the congressman bellowed. "It's late, and I've already had to deal with Mr. Miller tonight. I don't need to deal with you, too." He looked at me. His hand wavered at his side, but I couldn't tell whether he wanted to reach out and brush my cheek or slap me.

"I suggest you get back to bed," he said to Penn.

Penn clenched his jaw, but he didn't argue. His gaze met mine before he turned and walked back out into the night.

The congressman locked the patio door behind him. "This door is to remained locked at all times. Understand?"

I nodded as he strode back across my room, flipping off the light before he shut the bedroom door, leaving me alone in the darkness. Weariness seeped over me, weighing me down so that I didn't even have the energy to care about the chain, or Penn, or the congressman. I only wanted to lie down in the heap of blankets and forget.

I woke up to the feeling of someone crawling onto the bed and pulling back the covers. I opened my eyes to see Ruby's freckly face right in front of my own. She cuddled up to me as the bright light shone in through all my windows, reminding me of how tired I must have been to have slept so late.

"What time is it?" I asked.

"You're always up before me, but when I came downstairs it was just Claire and Grant. My mom told me you weren't even up yet," Ruby said, not answering my question. "And then when I came in here I thought maybe you were dead or something. Like Euridice, and I was going to have to go searching for you in the underworld."

I stretched out, letting my feet drift closer to hers beneath the covers. "I'm not dead," I said. "See?" I wiggled my fingers in front of her face.

"I'm glad you're not dead," she said, burying her face in my neck.

I swallowed back the lump forming in my throat and held onto one of Ruby's little hands. Last night, I hadn't considered what it would be like to leave Ruby behind. I'd only thought about myself and Penn. It wasn't fair of me to forget about this little girl that obviously needed me.

"Are you going to ask Claire to put your hair up in a chignon today?" I asked.

She shrugged, not moving her face out from where it was hidden. "My mom was talking about taking Claire and Grant into town for a celebratory lunch, but I don't think she's planning on taking me. It's a grown-up restaurant. And my dad is grumpy about something so I can't ask him."

I studied the almond shape of Ruby's dark eyes and the impish ways her lips turned up at the corners even when she wasn't smiling. I wanted to memorize her face so I could keep it with me forever.

"Why are you looking at me funny?" she asked.

I shook my head, the lump in my throat threatening to turn into something more. "I was thinking that I always want to remember your beautiful face...how you look right this minute."

A perfect smile broke across her face. That smile really did transform her into someone beautiful and for a moment I could see the woman she would turn into.

"I love you, Ella," she said, wrapping her arms around my neck in a tight hug.

The chain wasn't only for sleeping.

By breakfast time I realized that the congressman had arranged it so that no matter where I was in the house, the chain could always be attached to my wrist on one end and something unbreakable on the other. I didn't know who he thought I was—someone with superhuman strength?—because I'd never felt smaller or weaker in my whole life.

I sat at my little table picking at the food in my bowl. The congressman, who must have been feeling guilty about pulling me around the house on a leash, had asked Rosa to fix me a bowl of pitted red cherries topped with fresh cream. It was a treat I wouldn't normally be allowed.

The cherries sat in the bowl, uneaten, as the cream slowly turned pink.

Across the room, Claire and Grant walked in arm in arm, each pulling out a chair across from Penn, who sat silently pushing his eggs across his plate. I didn't want to stare at him sitting there, but I couldn't keep my gaze off of him. Each time I looked away it would stray back, the way my finger had become accustomed to searching out my microchip's tiny lump beside my ear, an unconscious movement.

I had secretly been hoping that Claire and Grant would have cut their visit short. But obviously I hadn't been so lucky. The fact that Claire knew I'd run away made my stomach clench, and I set down my spoon, unable to even pretend that I could eat anymore.

With Claire around, Penn wouldn't even look at me. But I couldn't ignore him. The need to be with him was a sickness. All I wanted was to be back in the garden with him.

I imagined the two of us alone, the rest of the world melting away into the dark the way it seemed to do when he looked at me. I could spend the rest of my life wishing things could have been different, but it was useless to wish for something that couldn't come true. It was better to be grateful for the little mercies I'd been given. I'd choose to remember the way my arms had felt around his neck, the slick feeling of our skin touching underneath the water and the way he'd lifted me weightless in his hands. I'd remember the soft press of his mouth on mine and the way my body prickled with heat whenever our skin touched.

"Well this has certainly been an eventful weekend," Claire said, pecking her father on the cheek as she sat down next to him. "You must be exhausted, Daddy. After being up half the night."

She cast an angry look in my direction and my face burned with shame.

Penn met my gaze. My stomach knotted as his gaze moved down to my wrist, then followed the length of the chain down to the floor where it disappeared beneath the tablecloth.

He pushed his plate away and stood. "You know, I actually just lost my appetite."

"Come on, Penn," Claire begged. "We hardly ever get to see you."

"I can't keep sitting here while he has her chained up like that," he said, backing out of the door.

Grant chuckled, reaching for a plate of toast. "It looks like that little pet of yours is more trouble than you bargained for."

"Don't be silly," the congressman said dismissively. "Penn's just being melodramatic."

Claire spooned a heaping pile of sliced melon onto her plate before she turned back to her father. "You know, it's probably not too late to take her back."

"She's got a point," Grant said as he bit into a piece of buttered toast, sending crumbs skidding across the polished table. "With all the work you did for them, these breeders must be mortified. Is there another kennel you could consider next time? Maybe one of the West Coast ones?"

The congressman set down his fork with a thump and turned to his wife for help, but she was busily peppering her eggs. "I don't want to take her back," he finally said. "At this point we don't even know she ran away for certain."

Claire raised her eyebrows, but she didn't comment as she delicately cut into a piece of melon.

"Besides," the congressman went on. "The people at Greenwich are completely on top of things. They've assured me that they have measures to deal with this sort of situation."

"I don't know," the congressman's wife said, finally looking up. "Chaining her up...is that the way they expect us to deal with things? God, I feel like we've relapsed to the Middle Ages. I can hardly stand to look at her."

"It's only for a little while." The congressman sighed. "It's hardly corporal punishment."

"A little while?" She didn't sound convinced.

"The director at Greenwich said it's probably just her hormones. Sometimes these pets are a little too much like their teenage counterparts. I guess they can't control genetics as much as they'd hoped." The congressman sighed again and leaned back, folding his arms across his chest. "She probably ran away because she was in heat."

"I thought you said we didn't know whether she ran away or not," Claire said.

The congressman picked his napkin off of his lap and threw it down across his plate, still half full of food. "We don't. For all I know it could have been one of those crazy civil rights nuts again. The point is, we don't know. That being the case, the breeders thought that to be on the safe side I should bring her in to be spayed. We scheduled an appointment for tomorrow afternoon."

"Spayed?" Grant asked. "They do that?"

The congressman ignored him, speaking instead to his wife. "And they're waving the fee of course. The way I look at it, it's the least they could do after something like this happened. After that, we won't need the leash."

I turned my head away from them, bile rising in my

throat. How could they talk about this in front of me? As if I wasn't even there.

"And you're okay with this? Getting her spayed?" The congressman's wife's voice was harsh. "A month ago you were the one complaining about this sort of procedure, and now you're all for it?"

I looked out the window, wishing I could cover my ears with my hands. I didn't want to hear it. How could he think that spaying me would make me want to stay? If they were going to send me back to the kennel, they might as well just send me through the red door and get it over with. I was already tarnished, wasn't I?

*A*fter lunch, the congressman sat in his office, reading over a thick stack of papers on his desk while I sat on the chaise lounge by the window, absently stroking the plush fabric in one direction.

Ruby appeared quietly in the doorway. She looked between her father and me as she scratched nervously behind her ear.

"Hi, Daddy," she finally said.

The congressman glanced up from the pile of papers and smiled. "Hello there, little miss."

"Can Ella come outside and catch butterflies with me?" she asked. It was the first time she'd spoken my name since she realized I was chained up.

"I don't know," the congressman said, looking down at the pile of paperwork on his desk. "I need to catch up on a lot of reading. I don't really have time to come out and watch her."

Ruby stepped farther into the room, coming to stand next to me. "Why can't you take this off?" she asked, running her finger along the chain around my wrist. "She's not going to go anywhere. Just in the backyard."

The congressman sighed. "Sorry Ruby, we can't take it off."

"Can she wear it outside?"

He ran a hand over his eyes. "I don't have time for this right now."

"But she looks sad here," Ruby said. "And it's such a pretty day outside. You and Mom are always saying that we need to get fresh air on a day like this."

"All right. All right," he said. "Why don't you go find Penn and have him rig something up so she can play outside with you?"

Ruby jumped up and down, clapping her hands. Normally her enthusiasm would be contagious, but not this time. My body was frozen, unable to even work up the energy to smile for her.

"I'll go get my net," she called behind her as she ran out of the room. "I'll meet you outside."

*P*enn knelt in front of me, bolting the end of the chain into a newly drilled hole on the side of the pool house. His face was still white from the moment, ten minutes earlier, when he'd glanced up from his notebook to see his father leading me across the patio on the end of the chain.

"Make sure it's nice and tight," the congressman said. "I

don't have time to keep checking on her."

Penn swallowed and gave the wrench another twist. "It's plenty tight," he said. "She's not going to try to go anywhere."

"I'm glad to know you're an authority," the congressman said. "Now stay out here and help your sister keep an eye on her."

Down the hill Ruby squealed, bouncing. "I caught one. I caught one!" She raced up the hill to where I sat and held up the thin white net. "I caught one, Dad."

He ruffled the hair on the top of her head. "Good job, sweetie," he said, before he turned back to the house without really looking at the creature inside.

"Look, Ella," Ruby said, swinging the net around so I could get a better look. "I think it's a monarch. Did you know they're the only butterfly that migrates the way birds do?"

I leaned closer to the flimsy, white netting. Near the mouth of the net, Ruby's hand was clenched tight around the fabric, but right below her clenched fist I could make out the tawny-orange wings of a butterfly. They opened and closed slightly, unable to find the room to move inside the collapsed bag.

"What are you going to do with it?" I asked.

Ruby shrugged. "I could put it in a jar, I guess."

"Why don't you look at it a little more and then let it go," Penn said, rising to stand beside me. "It's going to die if you keep it in there."

Without hesitating Ruby unclenched her fist and shook the butterfly loose. "I'm going to see if I can catch a blue one!"

As Ruby skipped off, happily waving her net above her head, Penn turned to face me.

"You ran away?" The words seemed to pain him.

I lowered my gaze. I never meant to hurt him.

"Why?" he asked. "Why would you want to leave?"

I looked at the house. The windows reflected the mid-morning sun, making it impossible to see inside. Was the congressman inside watching us?

Ours eyes met and I silently pleaded for him to understand. His face hardened and after a moment, he nodded. One nod, but it was enough.

At my side, the soft brush of his fingers grazed my own.

Twenty Four

*I*t was late, well past midnight. Through my window, the empty pool looked like a dark hole in the ground. I was tucked in bed for the night, the chain coiled snake-like at the foot of the bed.

The inside of my wrist ached where the chain weighed heavily against my skin. The congressman had tried to line it with a piece of velvet to keep it from biting into me, but it didn't really help. My wrist was raw and sore, a lot like my heart.

Across the room, the doorknob turned and I sat up against the pillows, pulling the covers up tight around my chest. Without any light in the little alcove it was difficult to make out the figure that lingered in the doorway. There was only bulk, the mass of a large body pushing through the dark. My heart sped up. This stupid chain around my wrist made me feel as vulnerable as one of Ruby's trapped butterflies.

A moment later the figure stepped forward. The small amount of light shining in through the windows lit Penn's worried face as he tiptoed closer to my bed.

"Ella," he whispered. "Are you awake?"

I took a deep breath, trying to still my shaking body. "I hoped you would come."

"How could I not?" he asked, sitting at the foot of my bed. "I've been staring out my window for the past hour. I kept thinking that I'd see you taking the path down to the garden, the way I used to, even though I knew you wouldn't come…that you couldn't."

His gaze traveled down to the chain around my wrist and my free hand drifted unconsciously to the sore spot, rubbing it gently.

"Your dad would be furious if he knew you were here," I said.

"I had to see you." Penn scooted closer to me and picked up the chain. "I can't believe he'd do this." He dropped the metal as if it was something hot. "He has to know it's wrong."

"It's my fault," I said.

Penn's eyes grew bigger. "It's not your fault. None of this is your fault."

I shook my head. "Yes, it is. I should have known my place. I should have remembered what I am. A pet."

Penn cringed, as if the word hurt him.

"They're taking me back to the kennel tomorrow morning. They made an appointment…"

"No." He shook his head. "*No.* This is bad enough, chaining you up like an animal or something, but getting you spayed is wrong. It's *wrong.* My dad won't go through with it."

"They said it would keep me from running away again."

I dropped my face into my hands, unable to hold in the pain and fear anymore.

In a second, Penn was at my side. His warm arms wrapped tightly around my body, but feeling him there did nothing to ease the pain. If anything it deepened the ache inside me. Why did I have to feel this way about him? Why did I have to want him to hold me this way forever?

I sat up, wiping the tears away with the palm of my hand.

"Are you all right?"

I nodded and took one more long, shuddering breath.

"Good," he said. His face was set, as if he'd come to some sort of resolve while I'd been crying. "Now we need to figure out how to get you out of here. I don't know how long the drive is to Canada. Maybe seven hours? But I'm pretty sure if we leave now we can be pretty close before they figure out you're gone. If we can get you to the border they'll have to let you in. It's asylum or something, they—"

"Penn."

"—have to take you in because—"

"*Penn!*"

He stopped talking. Even in the dark I could see his features had come alive.

"You can't help me run away," I said. "It won't work."

"Yes, it will. I can you get away from this."

I looked around the room at the beautiful furniture, the chandelier, the soft, welcoming bed. After what I'd seen in the city with Ms. Harper, did I really want to leave this? Maybe Missy was right, maybe I should make the best of what I had right now. If I could just give up my stupid desire to be one of them, I might actually be happy. We could all be happy. Even if it was for just a little while.

Penn followed my gaze. "It's not worth it," he whispered, holding up the chain that was attached to my wrist. "It's a beautiful cage. But it's still a cage. You deserve more than that." He took a deep breath. "I need to tell you something."

"What?"

He took me by the shoulders. Normally his strong hands would have been a comfort, but the look in his eyes frightened me. "Maybe I should have told you before, but it just didn't seem right." He paused. "But you need to know... You *deserve* to know. Our other pet...she wasn't sick. That's not why my dad sent her back."

"But if she wasn't..."

"She was pregnant, Ella."

"Pregnant?"

"Yes. She was going to have a baby."

No. No, no, no. That couldn't be right. He must have misunderstood. "But—"

"It's the reason my mom wanted to have you spayed."

No. I clamped a hand over my mouth, trying to push back the bile that rose in my throat. Not even Missy's threats could have prepared me for what Penn was saying. How could something like that happen here? How could they *let* it? There would be no special care for a pet carrying a baby, no room at the kennel waiting to make her well. She'd be dragged straight through the red door, and they'd sent her back anyway.

I swallowed, shaking. "Who did it?"

Penn shook his head, his lips tightening, but he didn't answer.

I clenched my hands. "Tell me!"

His eyes clouded. "My dad told us that it was one of

the gardeners, but I don't know. I'm not sure my mom ever really believed him. I'm not sure any of us did."

I buried my face in my hands. This changed everything. *Ruined* everything. "I can't go."

"But you have to get out of here!"

"No. And not with you. Your father won't forgive you for something like this. Who knows what he'll do if he finds out."

"Well, I can't sit here and let him do this…or worse." He ran his hands down my arms. Their warmth soaked deep into my bones. "We have to go. It's not a question of maybe."

My whole body trembled. "But it's not that easy. Even if I got to Canada, I wouldn't know what to do when I got there. I was raised to be a pet. It's all I know how to be. I can't even read." My voice caught. "I can't take care of myself."

"That's why I'm coming with you," Penn said. "I'll teach you. This isn't who you are. It's what they made you."

"But you can't just run away. You can't leave your whole life behind. Everything is here. Please, think of all the things you'd be giving up: your family, your home, your money. If you stay here you can have a future. If you came with me you wouldn't have anything."

"I'd have you."

The words were quiet, but clear. They made my head spin. And suddenly my chest expanded with hope. I wanted to believe it. I wanted to believe he loved me.

"I don't care about those other things," he said. "Let my father keep it all for himself. I don't want it."

And then he was in front of me, so close I could smell the hint of mint on his breath and the soft, clean smell of his soap. He lifted his hands to my face, gently cupping my cheeks in his palms before he kissed me.

I closed my eyes and let go, leaning into the tender press of his mouth. I felt as weightless as a girl in a nighttime pond. Without fear, without question, I let myself float there, suspended as the whole world melted away. This was how it was supposed to be—the two of us.

I opened my eyes.

"Please. Please, go with me."

I nodded. What else could I say but yes? I'd risk anything to feel that way again.

He smiled, pulling me into another kiss and the uncertainty of leaving blurred to a thin haze until all that I could see, or hear, or think, or feel, was him. He eased me back across the bed, his lips moving against mine, softly at first, and then with a desperation that matched my own.

When he finally pulled away, the dizzy world spun slowly back into place.

"Okay, we've got to think this through," Penn said. "First we need to get this thing off of you." He tugged at the chain where it was bolted to the bedpost. "I think we've got bolt cutters in the garage."

Suddenly my stomach dropped. We'd forgotten something important.

"Penn," I said, my hand touching the skin behind my ear. "There's something else."

"What is it?"

"My microchip."

"Damn it." He lifted his hand to my neck, running his thumb over the skin. "It's okay. It's okay," he said, nodding his head like he was trying to convince himself. "We just have to hope we get a good enough head start."

"No," I said. "You go find the bolt cutters. I'm going to

get this out."

"What do you mean 'get it out'?" he whispered.

"It's right below the skin. I can feel it. I'm going to cut it out. I'll use a razor from the bathroom."

Penn shook his head. "You can't cut yourself."

I clenched my hands, a cold wave of fear and power running through me at the same time. "I'm not going to sit here hoping things will work out for me. I have to do something. I want a chance…a chance for us, a chance to be together, a chance to be happy. I can do this."

It was impossible for him to hide the worry on his face, but I could tell he was trying. "Okay. You get the chip out. I'm going to get the bolt cutters. I'll throw a few things into the car and then I'll be back here to get you. I won't be long. I promise."

He stood to go and then turned back around to give me one more quick kiss before he disappeared back into the shadows, pulling my door shut quietly behind him.

*T*he chain reached into the bathroom, but just barely. As I stood in front of the mirror, my left arm was stretched out toward the bedroom, the metal cutting painfully into the already raw skin around my wrist. The razor was just out of reach. In the dark, I could barely make out where it sat on the edge of the claw-foot tub, the dark handle merely a slash against the white enamel.

I strained against the chain and my shoulder threatened to pull out of its socket. I was so close. So close. I could wait for Penn to get back with the bolt cutters, but I was afraid if I waited too long my courage would fail.

Balancing on one foot, I reached out with my other, hoping that if I tapped the razor with my toe it would fall forward onto the floor instead of down into the tub where it would be out of reach. My leg shook as I stretched it, straining as far as it could go. I only needed to reach a little farther. With a grunt, I pulled against the chain. It slipped ever so slightly, catching on the little bone jutting out at my wrist. My vision blurred for a second from the pain, but then my toe brushed against something plastic and the razor clattered to the tile floor. With one little kick I sent it skidding over next to me and I bent down to get it.

It didn't take long to crack the plastic casing surrounding the blade, and in a moment I had it free, squeezed between the fingers of my right hand. I stepped closer to the mirror. My left arm stuck out behind me like a broken wing. It was almost impossible to make out my reflection in the dark, but I was afraid to turn on the light.

My hands shook as I lifted the razor to my neck. Already I felt faint. I had to be quick. Holding the blade between my thumb and second finger, I found the pea-sized bump of the microchip with my pointer finger. The thrumming of my pulse made my fingers bounce and I took a deep breath, trying to steady myself.

One cut, that was all I needed. Just one cut.

I pressed down on the blade, pushing against the microchip as if I was trying to cut it in half. I expected blinding pain, but there was only a sharp sting as the skin peeled apart. I fumbled with my fingers. A wet trickle ran down my arm as the tiny round capsule popped out and rolled across

the counter, finally falling beneath the tub where it skidded to a stop. I couldn't reach it but I didn't care. It could sit
there forever.

I reached for a towel and pressed it against the warm
trickle that ran down my chin and the world started to
spin. I turned around to face the bedroom as the darkness
crowded out my vision, leaving the smallest pinprick of light
before it all went black.

Twenty Five

$\mathcal{T}$he world was moving beneath me, rocking me. I opened my eyes and Penn's face was there above me. He held me cradled in his arms and then leaned forward, setting me down gently on the bed.

"Thank goodness," he said. "I didn't know whether I was going to end up driving you to Canada or to the emergency room."

"It was just the blood," I muttered, stunned by the pain that suddenly sliced through my neck.

"The cut isn't too deep," Penn said, sitting me down on the edge of the bed. "I put a butterfly bandage on it. I think you'll be fine."

He bent down and picked up a large tool resting on the floor by the bed. "Let's hope this works," he said, placing it over the end of the chain next to my wrist. "Otherwise we're going to have a lot of explaining to do."

He pushed down on the handles, straining to move them.

"Damn, they make this stuff hard to cut through." He grunted, bearing down again. He let go and readjusted his hands on the grips. "One, two, three." He pushed down again, his arms shaking from the strain.

"What if it doesn't work?" I asked. The throb of my pulse pounded in my neck, making me flinch with pain at every beat.

He stood up once more and wiped at his forehead. "It'll work. It has to work."

Once more he squeezed. The tendons in his neck stood out as his whole body shook with the effort. Finally, the metal began to give. The teeth of the bolt cutters sank through the chain. *Snap. Snap.* The chain fell from my wrist, clanging against the floor and I cringed. It was loud. Too loud.

"Crap," Penn whispered, whipping around to look out the window at his parents' wing of the house.

The two of us paused, holding our breaths as we waited for the light to come on. Every sound seemed amplified: the *tap* of a stick blowing lightly against the window, the *tick* of the clock down the hallway. Penn and I strained to see across the dark patio, waiting for his parents to awaken. Waiting to be discovered. The seconds dragged by, but nothing happened. The house stayed dark.

"We need to hurry," Penn said. "I pushed the car down to the end of the lane so we wouldn't make so much noise, but now I'm worried about you. Do you think you'll be able to make it?"

The room was still spinning, but my body filled with an odd strength. If he asked me to walk all the way to Canada, I could do it.

"I'm—" Just as I opened my mouth, a sound at the door made both of us turn.

"Penn?" The congressman's wife stood in the doorway. Her silk robe was wrapped tightly around her chest, but still she brought her arms across her body as if she was trying to warm herself.

Penn stood up, openmouthed. "Mom," he said. "It's not what it looks like."

"It's not?"

"He can't keep her chained up like this," Penn said. "You can't treat a person like an animal."

"Your father will never forgive you for this."

Penn closed his eyes, but I could see the pain on his face. He might be angry with his father, but he still loved him. "I'm sorry, but I've got to get her out of here."

"And what? You were just going to run off into the night?"

"I'll figure something out."

"Do you have money? A place to go? Have you thought any of this through?"

He opened his eyes and clenched his jaw.

His mother sighed heavily. "So you're just going to throw everything away? Your future? Just so you can set a pet free?"

"What future?" Penn snapped. "The one Dad has all planned out for me? I don't want that. I don't want any of it and if you make me stay, you'll be chaining me up, too."

"I never said I was going to."

He froze. "What?"

"I never said I was going to make you stay."

Penn took a deep breath, but he stayed silent. The two of them stared at each other for a long moment and even though they didn't speak, it seemed as if they'd come to an understanding. "You only have one chance. Just look at the mess that stupid Harper woman made. If she'd taken my help instead of insisting she do it all herself, it would have worked the first time."

"Wait," Penn said. "If she'd taken your help?"

The congressman's wife smiled. "Oh, don't act so surprised. I never wanted her here." She turned to look at me. "And maybe some little part of me likes that I'm doing something meaningful for once."

*F*ifteen minutes later the three of us were out of the house. I sat in the car while Penn and his mom stood next to my door. In my arms I held a small bundle of clothes stuffed into the case of one of my pillows.

"I wish we could have left a note for Ruby," I said, imagining her asleep in her bed. I wanted to run upstairs and kiss that sweet freckled nose one last time. I didn't want to think about the look she would have on her face when she woke in the morning and realized that Penn and I were gone.

Out of the corner of my eye I saw Penn swipe his eyes with the back of his sleeve, but I pretended not to see.

"Don't worry," his mother said. "I'll make sure she knows."

Simultaneously we turned to face the sleeping house one last time. It really was beautiful, even in the dark. I wanted to picture it this way forever, quiet and elegant, the perfectly trimmed boxwood hedges standing like sentinels beside the front door, protecting all that was beautiful inside.

I closed my eyes, trying to seal the image there. I didn't want to think about what would happen in the morning when the congressman came to get me out of bed, only to find a broken chain and a bathroom full of blood.

"I'll keep him from finding out for as long as I can," the congressman's wife said, handing Penn a thick envelope. "Here's some cash. It's not a lot, but it should get you by for a while. There's an address on top. They'll take care of you." She reached into the pocket of her robe and pulled out a small paper bag. "I know how much you like them."

The paper crinkled as I took that bad and opened it. Inside, the bright yellow wrappers of a couple dozen butterscotch gleamed up at me.

"It was you," I said, thinking back to those bright wrappers on my pillowcase each day.

She nodded once.

"Thank you," I croaked, hoping she knew how grateful I was, not just for the candy, but for all of this.

"Now get going," she said, kissing her son softly on the cheek.

"I love you, Mom."

"I love you, too," she whispered.

Penn pushed the car out of the driveway, waiting to start the ignition until we were out on the lonely stretch of blacktop that would take us away. The car rumbled to life underneath us and Penn sent us speeding into the night.

He sat forward in his seat, both hands clutched around the steering wheel. Every minute or so he glanced in the rearview mirror, but even though the road stayed dark behind us I could feel the anxiety radiating off of him like heat.

"How's your neck feeling? Do I need to change the bandage?" His dark eyebrows knitted together in concern.

"My neck's okay," I said. "It's the rest of me that hurts. My whole body feels like it's tied in a knot."

"Me, too," Penn agreed. "I've never disobeyed my dad like this. He'd kill me if he knew what I was doing. Forget that he's never supported the death penalty. I'm pretty sure this would change his mind."

He was trying to be funny, but I could see the seriousness behind his words.

"My dad spent my whole life telling me what to do. It's like he was trying to turn me into a mini version of himself, but I've never been good enough. Everything I've ever done has been a disappointment to him. So really this shouldn't be anything new, should it?"

"How could you ever be a disappointment?" I asked.

The world continued to rush by. Trees and fields started to make way for houses and shopping centers. It was hard to imagine there were so many lives being lived out there and none of them had anything to do with us.

"Are you sure Ruby will be all right without us? I keep thinking about what she's going to do when she wakes up and we're both gone."

"She'll be all right," Penn said, unable to hide the catch in his voice. "At least she'll have Claire."

I knew how much he loved his little sister, but I wasn't so sure that Claire would be any comfort to Ruby. I hated to think about the perverse sort of happiness our running away would give Claire. Now she'd be justified in believing what she had said about me—that I was just waiting to tear her family apart.

"Maybe this will make Claire happy," I said.

"Why would she be happy?"

"Because she'll be right," I said, turning away from him. I could make out a bit of my face reflected in the glass, a ghostly version of myself speeding along beside us through the trees.

"What are you talking about?"

I swallowed. "Maybe she was right. Maybe I was the worst thing that could happen to your family. Look at how I tore you apart."

Penn sighed. "Claire doesn't understand. And maybe some part of her is jealous of you. You know, she's been my dad's pet since she was a little girl." When my eyes grew wide he shook his head and chuckled. "Not a pet like you. She's always been my dad's favorite. And all his attention didn't help. She does everything he's ever wanted. She got good grades. She went to the same school he went to. She follows his politics. She studied law because she thought it would make him proud. God, she's probably only marrying Grant because she thinks he'd want her to."

I reached out and held onto Penn's hand, hoping what he said about Claire was true and that she wasn't really as bad as I'd believed. His hand was warm and solid in mine and I held on tight while we drove in silence, our headlights cutting a trail through the dark.

"Are you sure you're okay?" Penn asked after a while. "You look so pale."

I nodded. "The farther away we get, the better I feel."

Penn clenched and unclenched his hand around the wheel, glancing over at me uncomfortably. "Can I ask you something?"

"Of course."

"Last night...when you went to the Millers' house. You

weren't *really* going to leave without…" His voice cracked.

"I was."

"Even though you knew how I felt about you?"

"I wanted to tell you," I said. "But after I heard you talking to Claire…"

He shook his head like he didn't understand. "To Claire?"

"I don't need to be reminded what I am," I said. "I know… I know I'm just a 'goddamn pet.'"

Penn sat back, letting the words sink in. "Ella, that's not—"

"I heard what she said to you, about what your father would do if he found out what was going on between us. I was scared. Scared about how I felt about you. Scared of your father. He saw us. At the garden, he *saw* us."

"You're sure?"

I told him about the trip to the beach, the words his father had whispered so close to my ear.

"God, that's just like him," he said. "He wants to control everything and everybody. Well guess what, he can't control how I feel about you. Not anymore." Penn shook his head, looking down at the dashboard. "Damn it," he said, slamming his palm against the steering wheel. "We're almost out of gas."

He slowed the car, pulling off the dark highway toward the glow of a large green sign. As we pulled up in front of the store, he threw the car into park and turned to face me. "You know I don't just think you're a stupid pet, don't you?"

I opened my mouth, but I didn't speak.

"Ella?"

As I turned away from him to look out into the parking lot, he slammed the door behind him, leaving me alone in the car.

Twenty Six

$\mathcal{I}$nside the gas station the bright florescent lights overhead seemed as harsh as the afternoon sun compared to the
dark of the car and I squinted, scanning the store for Penn.
I'd never been inside a building like this. The shelves were
crowded with shiny packages that reminded me of Ruby's
butterscotch candies and along the back wall, behind glass
doors, there were rows and rows of bottled drinks full of
reds and blues and greens and browns; colors you could
hardly dream a drink could be.

"Can I help you?" the woman behind the counter asked,
cocking her head as she stared at where I stood beside the
door.

Penn stood in front of her at the counter. "She's with
me," he said briskly as he opened up his wallet, and then,
turning to me, "Go back and wait in the car." His voice
sounded agitated.

The woman's gaze darted between us. "Were you at a ball

or something? She looks like Cinderella."

Penn glanced over at me as if he was seeing me for the first time. His gaze traveled down over my gown. "Oh...it's nothing."

"I always wanted to wear a big ball gown," the woman said to me. "Only I never had anywhere special to wear it. I guess I could've gotten one of those big gowns when I got married, but I couldn't really stomach spending so much on a dress I'd only wear once."

Penn nodded, pushing the money closer to her. "I need forty dollars on pump number eight."

The woman finally took her eyes off of my dress and I slipped back out through the door. A minute later, Penn followed me out.

"What were you thinking coming inside?" Penn shook his head. "Now she's seen you. What if she can identify you?"

"I'm sorry," I said, "I didn't think. I didn't mean—"

"Why didn't you come to me when you heard what I said to Claire?" he interrupted. "Why run away?"

"I don't know."

He groaned and headed back to the car. "Why did you let me take you away if you thought I didn't care about you?"

"I do believe you. But it's complicated," I said, jogging to catch up to him. "In a way, Ms. Harper cared about me, too."

"This is nothing like what Ms. Harper did. That lady's crazy," he said, stopping in front of the car. "She had an agenda and my mom was trying to get rid of you." Penn placed his warm hands against my arms and pulled me close to him. "This isn't about stupid politics or being a hero. It isn't about anything but you, Ella. I just want to be with you."

He placed his finger beneath my chin. Gently he lifted my face to his. Above us, the light from the sign cast a green halo across our heads. In his eyes I saw so much worry, so much kindness, that for the first time ever I let myself believe this boy standing next to me could be someone I could share my life with.

$\mathscr{B}$ack in the car, Penn's hands finally started to relax their grip on the wheel and his body settled back into the seat. The tension that rode high in his shoulders seemed to melt away. He rolled down the windows and the cool night air washed over us, bringing in the smell of moist earth and summer grass. With a flick of his wrist, he reached down and switched on the radio and the first few soulful notes of a song started to play.

"This one's dedicated to you," he said, turning to smile at me for the first time all night.

I leaned my head back against the seat and took a deep gulp of night air. I was afraid to admit it, but I could almost taste freedom, fresh and sweet on my tongue. A moment later Penn's warm hand settled on top of mine.

I stared at the place our fingers intertwined. They looked the same. Two hands. One big. One small. Looking at them, you'd never know that one of them belonged to a pet. They were just hands. That was all.

For a long time we drove in silence, listening to song after song as we passed roads lined with houses, and then long stretches of emptiness, nothing but trees and fields and telephone poles.

I closed my eyes, too tired to keep them open any longer.

"Do you think I'll ever get to play a piano again?"

I was almost afraid to hear his answer, but I needed to know. Was the piano something I'd left behind forever the way we'd left Ruby?

"Of course you'll play the piano," Penn said. "It's who you are."

"Is it?" I asked, opening my eyes to look at him. "I don't know what parts are *me* and what parts are what Greenwich Kennels says I should be."

Penn shook his head. "I don't know. I guess it all depends on what makes you happy."

I took my hand off of his and turned to stare out the window at the thick stands of trees surrounding us. What made me happy? How should I know? It was a feeling I was used to pushing down, a dangerous emotion that belonged to someone else, not to me.

"Miss Gellner says I'm not supposed to be happy. I was created to tend to other people's happiness, not my own," I said. "How can I suddenly start believing something different?"

The bluish light of early morning illuminated Penn's tired face. "I don't know," he said as he shook his head. "I really don't, but when I hear you play the piano I have to believe it's coming from somewhere deep inside you. It's a place that you created, not Greenwich."

He was right. The piano was my first taste at love, a secret I kept for years. But I didn't have to keep things secret anymore.

"Yes," I finally said. "The piano makes me happy." I smiled at him. "And do you know what else makes me happy?"

"What?" he asked, a smile breaking out across his face.

"You, Penn Kimball. You make me happy."

Twenty Seven

*A*s the sky lightened and buildings and parking lots began to replace the forests and fields rushing past our windows, Penn's hands regained their murderous grip on the wheel. He stiffened at every car that pulled behind us. After a while his nervous energy migrated across the car and into me.

As I glanced in the car's side mirror at the road behind us, I kept imagining the red and blue lights of the police cruiser that had found me before. With every glint of light, every flash reflected off a window or stop sign that gleamed in the sun, my heart beat faster and my stomach worked itself into a tighter knot.

"He's probably awake by now," I said, knowing these were the words Penn must be repeating in his own mind.

"Yeah, probably."

"Do you think he found the microchip yet?"

Penn shrugged. "I don't know. Even without it, he has to

know where we're headed. I guess we're lucky there are lots of places to cross the border. There's no way he can know which one we're going to."

"You're right," I said, even though the knot in my stomach told me the congressman always had ways of knowing things.

"Have you ever heard of Niagara Falls?"

I shook my head.

"I'm pretty sure it's one of the busiest places to cross the border. Hopefully we'll blend in with all those tourists. Luckily, we won't have to show our IDs until we get to the other side. By then we'll be safe on Canadian soil. I don't have my passport, but I know they'll let us in once we ask for asylum. They've been really vocal about how wrong they think our new laws are. My dad complains about it all the time."

Out the window crowds of people strolled hand in hand with large cameras strapped around their necks and huge grins plastered on their lips. Even this early in the morning the streets were packed.

"Look," Penn said, slowing the car. "You can see the falls."

As we came around the bend, a plume of mist rose into the sky. It was magical, a place where clouds were born. The river was churning them out before setting them free into the sky.

"It's amazing," I said. "I didn't know anything like this even existed."

Penn smiled weakly. "I wish we could enjoy it more." He reached down and switched off the radio. "I'm sorry. I need to concentrate."

As the first bridge came into view in front of us, Penn

instinctively hit the brakes. Behind us, a car honked, but Penn hardly seemed to notice. He swerved over to the side of the road, staring ahead at the line of police cars that cordoned off the bridge.

"They're checking the cars," Penn said. "He must have called in a favor. Dammit! I should have known."

"What are we going to do?" I asked.

"They've got all our information. I'm sure he gave them the license plate number."

"Can't we take it off?"

Penn shook his head. "It wouldn't do any good. They'll have the make and model."

"Can we leave the car here and just walk across the bridge?"

Penn sighed loudly. "No, we can't just walk across. Too many people will see you. We can't risk it."

"I'm sorry, I—"

"No, I'm sorry," Penn said. "I shouldn't have snapped at you like that."

"Maybe if we had a different car?"

"We don't—" Penn stopped midsentence. "Yes!" he smiled, leaning over to kiss my cheek before he put the car back into drive.

A few minutes later, we pulled to a stop in front of a squat gray building.

Penn swung his door open. "Here goes nothing."

Inside, we were met with an icy blast of air conditioning. On the other side of the room a man who must have only been a couple years older than Penn leaned against the counter, thumbing through a magazine. He flipped it closed, placing it on top of a stack of papers.

At the other end of the counter, a young couple stood bent over a clipboard filling out paperwork. The man only glanced up at us for a moment before he turned back to the clipboard, but the woman stared at me a little longer, studying me.

"Hey, how's it goin'?" the man behind the counter nodded as the door jangled shut behind us.

"Good." Penn smiled. "Uh, we're kind of thinking about renting something for the day."

"Have you ever rented with us before?" the man asked, seeming to take the two of us in for the first time. A peculiar look crossed his face.

"No, I don't think so," Penn answered.

"Well...I can always check. Let me just see if your name's in our database," the man said.

"Oh, yeah..." Penn faltered. "Actually...um, do you have a brochure or something that we could look at first...to see the prices and stuff?"

The man fiddled with the edge of a piece of paper sticking out from underneath his magazine. "Yeah, we might have something." He stared at me as he spoke, like he hardly even noticed Penn was in the room.

Beside me, Penn fidgeted uncomfortably while the man bent behind the counter and shuffled through the cabinets. "What's the matter?" I whispered.

He put his arm around my shoulder and faced me away from the counter. "I can't give him my name. I'm going to have to try to snag some keys or something. We need to try to get him to go in back."

A second later the man stood back up. "Most people just look things up online," he said. "So we don't really have any brochures up here. I can go check in back."

Penn perked up. "That would be great. Thanks."

At the other end of the counter, the young couple had finished filling out their paperwork and were staring intently at the whole exchange.

"Uh, let me just give these folks their keys and then we'll talk," he said, opening the door to a little cabinet behind him, revealing rows and rows of keys.

He snatched a pair and tossed them to the man, hardly glancing at him. "It's the white Honda out back. It's ready to go," he said, obviously trying to get them out fast.

As the couple walked out, the man behind the counter wiped a bit of sweat from his brow. "So, it might take me just a sec to find one of those brochures," he said. "If you just want to sit down and make yourself comfortable, I'll be right back." He pointed to the seating area behind us.

Penn didn't even glance behind us. "Yeah, sure."

The man waited, watching us as we lowered ourselves down on the chairs. Could he tell how nervous Penn was?

As soon as the man disappeared behind the swinging doors, Penn was on his feet. He slid across the counter, sending the man's magazines flying onto the ground at my feet. He swung open the cabinet and grabbed a set of keys with shaking hands.

"C'mon." He grabbed my hand to pull me out the door, but a paper on the ground made me freeze. I bent down to pick it up and the world around me slowed.

It wasn't a good copy. The photo was grainy and black and white, but still it was obvious that it was a picture of me. I stared at the big, bold letters, wishing they meant something to me.

RUNAWAY PET. $5,000 REWARD.

"What does this say?" I held it up to show Penn and his face blanched.

"Shit," he muttered, grabbing the paper. "It's a reward poster."

"You don't think—" I started to say, just as the man pushed back through the swinging door.

"Hey," he yelled when he saw Penn holding the paper.

"You asshole!" Penn yelled. "You called them, didn't you?"

"I'm sorry, man. It's five thousand dollars."

Penn crumpled the paper in his fist as he turned back to me. "We've got to go. They could be here any second."

He grabbed me by the hand and pulled me out the side door, pausing just long enough to glance back at his car parked out front. Already we could hear the sirens. We raced to the back of the building where row after row of cars lined the parking lot.

Penn glanced down at the key he still clutched in his hand.

"Which car is it for?" I asked.

He shook his head, fear burning in his eyes. "I…I don't know," he croaked. "We're going to have to run."

A long, thin alley ran between a row of buildings in front of us, but even from here it was easy to see there was no place to hide.

Behind the building a white car idled next to the air pump.

"Is everything all right?" the woman inside asked, rolling down the window as we ran toward the car.

"Please," I begged, falling against the car. "Please, will you give us a ride?"

"Of course," she said, reaching back to unlock the door. "Get in."

"What's this—" her husband began.

"Not now, honey. Get in and drive," she ordered.

Flustered, the man threw down the air pump. For a moment it seemed like he might argue with her, but he only opened his mouth once and huffed before he did what his wife asked. Moments later we bumped across the parking lot and out onto the main road.

"Thank you! Thank you so much," I said to the woman before turning around to watch as the flashing lights grew farther and farther away behind us.

"I thought I recognized you from the flyer when you came in, but I didn't want to say anything," the woman said. "The clerk was looking at it when we got there."

"What flyer?" her husband asked. "What are you talking about? You aren't felons or something are you, because—"

"You're the first one I've ever seen," the woman said. Her eyes were locked intently on mine. "To be honest, I didn't really think it was true. I mean, I've seen stories about it on the news and stuff. I'm Jocelyn, by the way," she said, reaching out to shake my hand.

"What stories?"

"God, Howard, would you stop asking stupid questions. She's a pet. That stupid man at the rental place was going to turn her in for a reward. It makes me sick."

"Oh." His eyes went big as he studied me in the rear-view mirror.

"We're here for our anniversary," she said. "I've always wanted to come, but now it just seems absurd to think that our biggest problem was figuring out how to get around and see the scenery while you were trying to make it to freedom."

"We just need to make it across one of the bridges," Penn said, speaking up. "I'm so sorry to ask you to take us."

"The police are checking cars," I explained "They're stopping everyone who's trying to walk across."

"But won't they check our car, too?" Howard asked.

Penn shrugged. "I guess we'll just have to take that chance."

A few minutes later, our car inched forward, following the line of vehicles stretching toward the bridge. "We just have to make it past the tollbooth and then we'll practically be there. It looks like that's where they're stopping cars," Penn said. "The Canadian border starts halfway across the river, but we need to make it to the immigration checkpoint. Can you see it?" He pointed to the line of booths running across the far side of the bridge. "Once we're there, you'll be safe."

Howard drummed his fingers impatiently against the steering wheel and I looked behind us. The line of cars had grown, trapping us in.

My hands started to shake.

"Are you okay?" Penn asked, glancing over at me. "You look pale again."

"I'm fine." I nodded weakly.

"Here, put on my sweater," Jocelyn said, tossing back a soft pink cardigan. "And hold these up when we drive past. It'll cover your face." She handed me a pair of binoculars.

The cars in front of us crept forward and finally we

pulled up in front of the tollbooth. Howard fumbled with the buttons and rolled down the window, smiling up at the attendant.

"Three-fifty," she barked.

He reached into his back pocket for his wallet with the fake smile still plastered to his lips.

"Move forward," the attendant said, waving us on to the uniformed police officer who stood next to his vehicle, checking everyone that passed.

The officer studied the car. His gaze moved over Howard and Jocelyn. "Sorry for the delay, folks," he said, leaning against the window. He peered in the back and I pulled my cardigan closed with one hand and pressed the binoculars to my face with the other, pretending to stare out over the falls.

"We're stopping everyone passing into Canada today," he explained. "Just want to make sure you haven't seen this girl." He held out a photocopy and Howard peered down at it.

He shook his head. "Sorry."

The officer stared into the car a moment longer before he patted his hand against the car door and ushered us forward. "No problem. Enjoy your day at the falls."

Finally our wheels hummed against the bridge. We were almost there.

"That was terrifying." Jocelyn laughed. "I think my heart's going to beat right out of my chest."

I tried to swallow but my throat was completely dry. Past the bridge, the falls gushed gallons and gallons of water into the river.

I set the binoculars down next to me on the seat and took Penn's hand in mine.

"Almost there," he croaked.

Once more I glanced in the rearview mirror at the line of cars behind us and my heart stopped. There, at the back of the line, the red and blue lights of a patrol car winked in and out of sight. I sat up straighter and rubbed my eyes, hoping I was only imagining it. But then Penn glanced back. "No," he moaned. "No. No. No. Please don't be for us."

My ears filled with the sound of rushing water and for a moment I wondered if I'd accidentally rolled down my window. I stared at the glass, confused, realizing that the deafening noise was actually the rush of panic swelling through my head.

"Damn it! Hurry up," Penn yelled, beating the back of Howard's seat.

"I'm going as fast as I can," he said. "We're blocked in."

Behind us the lights grew closer as the cars in line slowly pulled to the side, letting the patrol car pass.

"We should have taken the plate off," Penn said. "That asshole at the rental place must have given them the number."

We pulled forward slowly, but there were still a half-dozen cars between us and the checkpoint.

Penn turned to me, his face slack. "We've got to get out. We've got to run. They'll be here any second."

"But what if we don't—"

"Just run!" he yelled. "As soon as you get to that checkpoint you tell them who you are. Tell them you need asylum. They have to take you." He reached in his pocket and pressed a piece of paper into my palm. "I'll be right behind you. Now go!"

We threw open our doors and ran. Behind us the sound of sirens pierced through the rumble of the falls. My dress billowed out behind me as my feet smacked the pavement.

"Stop!" a voice bellowed behind me. "Stop or we'll fire."

"Keep running!" Penn shouted.

Light glinted off of the cars, so close to me on either side that I could reach out my hands and touch them. Inside the people looked up at me, startled. Their mouths moved in noiseless cadence before they turned around to stare at the police that trailed behind me.

In front of me a group of men in uniforms emerged from out of the shadows, running toward me with their weapons raised. I didn't know if they were the people I was supposed to be running from, or running toward. I turned back to Penn for help, my hair fanning out behind me like the manes of those horses I'd seen with Ruby.

"Penn!" I yelled, frantically searching the sea of cars.

Why don't I see him?

I slammed to a halt. Off to the side of the bridge an officer held Penn's arms behind his back. Penn's face was contorted in pain. He caught my eye for just a moment before the policeman elbowed him in the back, making him crumple forward onto his knees.

"Run, Ella!" he choked out.

The world spun back into focus. A policeman sprinted toward me. His face was red, his mouth opened as he yelled at the other officers running at me with their guns drawn.

I plowed into their arms. "Help me," I gasped, hoping desperately that these were the people I could trust. "I need asylum. Help."

"Stop her!" the policeman yelled. He skidded to a stop in front of me as I grabbed onto the officer's shirts. "She's crossing illegally. That girl is the property of John Kimball."

I held tight to the tall man with reddish hair. "Don't let him take me," I begged. "I'm a pet. I was bred in Greenwich Kennels. I need asylum. Please."

The man stared down at me, confused.

"Did you hear me?" the policeman yelled. "She's owned by Congressman John Kimball. She was stolen late last night."

"I wasn't stolen," I cried. "Please. Don't let them take us."

The red-haired man looked from me to Penn as if he was trying to deduce if what I said was true. His eyes narrowed. Finally he turned back to the policeman.

"I can't let you take her," he said, and in one quick movement he stepped in front of me as if to shield me with his body. "She's on Canadian soil."

The policeman's face was a florid shade of red. On his forehead, a vein stretched taught underneath his skin. "It's my job to return her."

"Are you listening to yourself?" the officer said. He placed a hand protectively against my arm, pushing me even farther behind him. "This girl isn't property."

"Please," I said. My voice was so small it was almost carried away into the great roar of the falls.

"You need to leave her alone," the officer said. "And let the boy go. Unless those rich people own you, too?"

The policeman drew the back of his hand along his mouth, wiping away the spit that had formed at the corner of his lips. "Nobody owns me."

"No?" the officer said. "First they buy the laws, and pretty soon they've bought your soul."

The policeman's eyes narrowed. "It's my job to uphold the law, not to judge it." He turned to the policeman holding Penn's arms behind his back. "Put him in the car!"

"Penn!" I screamed.

I raced forward, but the red-haired man held me back.

"You can't go," he said softly, squeezing my arm. "I can't protect you if you go back there."

"But I can't go without him!"

My knees buckled and I fell to the ground. The soft fabric of my gown ripped against the blacktop and the pavement bit into my knees, but I didn't care.

Through the line of cars I could see Penn. A dark red gash above his eyebrow dripped blood down the side of his face, but his eyes were bright and fierce as he strained toward me. If I'd ever doubted that he loved me, it was clear now. I wasn't just a pet to him. When he looked at me, he saw his future, too.

Our eyes locked and time slowed. Around us there was only light and the fine mist of water that sprayed off the falls. It seemed as if the sky had shattered, raining down tiny pieces of blue on top of our heads.

"I love you, Penn." My mouth moved, but the words stayed trapped somewhere deep inside me.

And then time rushed forward. The policemen pulled him away from me. Down the bridge, the patrol car stood ready, its door swung wide open. With each step they took, Penn moved farther from the border, farther from the future we were supposed to have together.

I waited for them to take him away from me. Penn, my Penn, the boy I'd tried so hard not to fall in love with. What was freedom without him?

I thought that freedom and happiness would be indistinguishable, but now I didn't know. Maybe freedom wasn't a state of being. Maybe it was an act of courage. Maybe freedom was defiance and sacrifice and pain, something that couldn't be won without giving up something else in return.

I don't know how long I stood on the bridge. Next to me the officer with the red hair waited patiently with his hand resting lightly on my shoulder as the cars behind us began moving again.

I leaned against the metal railing and stared out over the rushing water that was almost the same color as the white puffs of the clouds overhead. They were all the same—a ceaseless flow of water to mist to clouds, which finally fell to the earth as water once again.

I clenched my fists, suddenly remembering the paper Penn had given to me. My hand shook as I opened my palm and unfolded the crumpled sheet, damp with sweat.

The paper was covered in letters and numbers, some I recognized, but some looked foreign in the elegant, loopy scrawl. But I didn't need to know how to read to know what they meant. It was the paper that Penn's mom had given him before we left, the one with the name and address of the people waiting here to help me.

I turned toward Canada. I didn't know who I was now. Without Penn, without the congressman, without Ruby, without Miss Gellner…who was I?

Deep in my belly something stirred. I didn't know what it was, maybe hope or courage—maybe just the knowledge that I'd be able to find the answer on my own.

I licked the moisture from my lips, testing the first bittersweet taste of freedom.

BONUS
content
Keep reading for exclusive scenes
from Penn's point of view!

Just a Girl

$\mathcal{E}$lla hadn't made me nervous when she was downstairs playing the piano. Surprised, maybe. Impressed. Not nervous.

Once I had her in my room, though, my palms started to sweat. It was dumb, because it wasn't like I hadn't had girls in my room before. I wasn't a player or anything, but there had been plenty of times when a group of my friends came over to swim or watch a movie and I'd ended up alone in my room with someone.

But it was different with Ella. She didn't bounce down on my bed, throwing her hair over her shoulder and giggling like other girls. She stood timidly in the doorway, her eyes wide, taking it all in. When my dad brought her home, I assumed she must not be very smart, the way she stared at everything with those big, naive eyes, inching their way so slowly over every new thing, like she didn't know what to make of it. But after a while, I realized that she was studying it all, soaking it in, digesting it.

It must have been weird, growing up inside that kennel and then all of a sudden getting thrown into the real world. From the way she stared at the pictures on my dresser, you'd think she'd never heard of a concert before, or a bonfire, or a Halloween party.

She took a few more steps into my room, and her gaze darted across the walls. Granted, there was a ton of stuff to look at. My mom hated it. She said it looked like someone plastered a junkyard to my walls. But it was a hell of a lot better than the room she had the interior designer decorate.

I stopped watching Ella for a second and scrolled through my playlists, trying to figure out what to start her off with. Maybe something classic like Leonard Cohen or Eric Clapton. Or maybe it was better to pick something newer. It was kind of intimidating, like she was a blank canvas or something, and whatever music I introduced her to would paint a huge, bold stroke across everything that came after.

"Do you play those?" Ella asked, pointing to the wall where my collection of instruments hung above my amps.

"Yeah, most of them…at least a little," I said. "But I'm only really good at a few. Mostly I play the guitar."

I was pretty good at the mandolin and the banjo, but the guitar was my love. And not in that cheesy way some guys who don't *really* play like to tell you when they're trying to show off. When I'm playing it, I go somewhere.

Maybe that's why it surprised me so much to walk into the house and hear Ella playing the piano. At first I was just impressed by how well she knew the music, but as soon as I walked into the room, it was clear it was more than that. She went somewhere, too. I saw it. I don't know if that place was deep inside her or if the music took her outside of herself like it did for me, but it transformed her.

Our other pet had never been that way.

"Okay," I finally said. "I'm starting you out with Amos Lee since you liked Ray LaMontagne so much."

I hit play and leaned against the bookcase as the first few notes began to fill the room. I didn't mean to stare at her, but I couldn't help myself. Almost immediately, she closed her eyes and tilted her head ever so slightly toward the ceiling. Her arms rested limply by her sides, but her chest swelled with breath.

She was beautiful. So open. So exposed.

Of course, I'd noticed that she was pretty before, but not like this. Maybe I was just seeing her through my dad's eyes, as an object, a pretty little thing that he could set out on the couch for his friends to admire when they came over. And I didn't want to see her that way. Maybe I even sort of blamed her, too, but I didn't want to anymore.

The song moved into the chorus, and she took a shuddering breath, opening her eyes, and for a second I thought she might start crying.

"Are you okay?" I asked.

She gave the smallest nod and closed her eyes again. I eased myself down onto the bed next to her. The sun shone through my window, lighting the side of her face. It made the delicate, downy hairs that covered her cheek and neck glow golden, and for a second, my hand twitched at my side, wanting to reach out and draw my finger along her skin. Those tiny hairs made her seem more real than she ever had before.

The music faded away and she opened her eyes again.

"That was beautiful," she said. Her voice sounded so small.

"Yeah." I smiled. "It's one of my favorites. Who would have guessed I'd have the same taste in music as a pet from Greenwich Kennels?"

Her face fell, and I felt like an ass. I hadn't meant it to be offensive. At least not about her. I just meant we were so much more alike than I'd realized. When I looked at her now, she hardly seemed like a pet at all. She just looked like a girl, simple and real, sitting next to me.

The Banana Split Incident

◯◡◯

*E*lla held the banana split like it was a bomb or something, like if she made any sudden movements the thing was going to explode, sending ice cream and nuts and hot fudge flying everywhere. She sat down carefully on the edge of my chair and stared down into the bowl with a face so full of nervous wonder that I almost burst out laughing.

It seemed impossible that a person could go through sixteen years of life without tasting chocolate or ice cream, and maybe part of me kind of liked being the one who got to share it with her for the first time. Not like I was corrupting her or anything—more like I got to give her this amazing gift that no one else had ever given her.

I flopped down on my bed. "Aren't you going to try it?"

She stared into the bowl, but she didn't move. It wasn't like she was being one of those girls who wouldn't eat sugar because she was afraid of getting fat. She was looking at it like it was some weird foreign food made out of fish heads and tentacles.

"Always start with the cherry," I said, pretending to plop an invisible cherry in my mouth.

She grabbed the stem and slid it past her lips, and my heart started pounding. How lame was I, turned on by such a simple gesture? But it was hot. The way she tipped her head back, exposing her long neck. God.

She picked up the spoon and took what had to be the smallest bite in the history of the universe. "You usually eat this whole thing?" she asked. I couldn't tell if it was mortification or awe in her voice.

"I won't hold it against you if you can't finish it all on your first try," I said.

"It would take me a month to finish this." She took another tiny nibble.

I laughed. "Well, yeah, if you eat it that way." I grabbed the bowl. "Let me show you how it's done."

I shoveled up a normal-size bite and shoved it in my mouth. Hot fudge drizzled out of the side of my mouth, and I wiped it away with the back of my hand before I dipped my spoon back in the bowl, scooping up another heaping bite.

"Now it's your turn." I tried to sound menacing, but the smile that sprang to my lips probably made it less than convincing. I hopped off the bed.

It was time to teach this girl how to eat a banana split.

She cowered, shaking her head, but that sweet little innocent look wasn't going to work on me. I dove for her. "Get over here."

I grabbed her elbow, pulling her down to the ground with me, and she squirmed, trying to free herself from my grasp. Her body felt so small beneath mine. So warm and soft. I was used to seeing her in the big ball gowns that she usually wore. They were puffy and elaborate and made her look like the showpiece my dad wanted her to be, but in the little black swimsuit she had on, she was just a girl.

The feel of her skin distracted me, and I shoved the bite toward her laughing mouth. I mostly missed, sending cream and chocolate oozing down her neck. She froze, panting. I waited for the smile to slip from her face as she realized what a mess we'd made. Her whole life, she'd been taught to look proper. She'd probably be mortified if she could see herself now.

But instead of wiping it away, she lunged for me, wrestling the spoon from my hand. Like a slow-motion scene from a bad action movie, we both turned to look at the bowl of ice cream that sat at the foot of the bed. Her eyes narrowed and she dove for it. When I saw the enormous scoop of melting ice cream swinging back my way, I dropped to the floor and shielded myself.

"No, please," I said, laughing. "I surrender. I surrender. Have mercy on me."

Her eyes softened, but the look only lasted for a moment, replaced by a devilish grin. What would my dad say if he saw that look? It wasn't meek or subservient or docile.

She pounced, attacking with the agile strength of a wild cat, and wrestled me to the ground. This pet had claws, and she wasn't afraid to use them. Ice cream dripped down my chin, smeared across my shirt, seeped into my hair. Eventually, I gave in and let her have her way with me.

We rolled onto our backs, laughing until we finally caught our breath. Her head listed to the side, and she sighed. "This is a mess."

I followed her gaze to the clumps of bananas and chocolate and cream ground into the carpet. The sign of an epic food fight.

"Rosa's not going to be pleased with you," she said.

It was true. If Rosa actually bothered to come in my room anymore, she'd be pissed, but luckily we'd all come to an unspoken agreement that besides running the vacuum over the carpet once a month, she'd leave my room alone.

"It's fine." I shrugged. "I'll clean it up."

She raised her eyebrows, like she didn't believe me.

I couldn't hide my smile. God, she was cute—and she had no idea. No idea what a look like that could do to a boy.

"You don't believe me?" I grabbed a towel off the floor. "Here, I'll start with this."

I wrapped the corner of the towel around my index finger and drew it gently along her chin and down her neck. I'd never noticed it before, but there was a tiny mole at the base of her neck. It was the smallest imperfection on her otherwise flawless skin, but I couldn't look away. That one little spot was beautiful.

She leaned closer.

My gaze traveled back up to her face. Did she think about that kiss next to the pool? Did the feel of it still linger on her lips like it did mine? Did it make her heart race and her palms sweat whenever we were in the same room?

I let my fingers skate over her bare skin, pausing for a second to rest against that tiny imperfection before continuing over her shoulder and down her arm. Her eyes widened. Those eyes. They were so pretty, like sea glass, like clear water.

I cradled her face in my hand.

"I want to kiss you again," I whispered.

Floating

I hadn't swam in the pond before, but I already liked it better than the pool. The water didn't have the harsh smell of chlorine. It was probably just the bits of moss that still clung to the stones, but it smelled kind of leafy and green. It smelled *real*.

I didn't really think Ella was going to get in with me, but that didn't stop me from asking. Just the thought of her in the water with me had my body way more worked up than it had any business being.

I was thankful for the dark night and the shadowy water.

"I'd get in, but I'm not wearing a swimsuit," she said, scooting back from the edge of the pond. "I guess I could run back to the house…"

"Don't use those lame excuses with me. You can swim in your underwear for all I care." Obviously, I cared. I was alive, wasn't I? I was a guy with a pulse. There wasn't much more I wanted from life in that moment than for her to peel off that nightgown so I could see what was underneath. "Just get in."

She started to stand, and the stupid smile dropped off my face. I'd offended her, and now she was going to go back to her room. I shouldn't have pushed her. No matter what my body wanted, just being near her was enough. I could stay out here all night watching the way her feet swished through the water.

I opened my mouth to tell her not to leave, but she didn't head for the gate. Instead, she pulled her nightgown over her head with one fluid motion, dropping it onto the ground at her feet.

"Wait. What are you doing?" I choked. "I wasn't serious."

My mouth hung open as I watched her step to the water's edge, but I couldn't close it and I couldn't look away. I couldn't even blink. It was like I'd lost all control over my body, and now the only thing it could do was stare at the way the thin fabric clung to her skin in the moonlight.

I didn't know what you called the sort of underwear she was wearing. It was delicate and slightly shiny, kind of like a tank top that fell to just above her belly button so that a few inches of pale white skin showed above her panties. It was way more conservative than anything you'd see on TV or the skimpy bikinis girls wore to the beach, but it was the sexiest thing I'd seen in my whole life.

"I still don't know how to swim," she said, jarring me out of my shock.

I grabbed onto the side and reached up to her. "Don't worry. I won't let anything happen to you."

I hoped she couldn't hear the way my voice shook.

She grabbed my hand and lowered herself back down to

the pond's edge. Her feet brushed against my body, and all of a sudden my heart was beating out of my chest, so loud that it almost drowned out the sound of the crickets.

I clasped my hands around her waist and pulled her down into the water. "Hold onto me."

She nodded, clamping her hands securely around my neck.

I held onto her with one hand as I steadied myself with the other. Every muscle in my body felt tense. Tight. Beneath the water, her tank top inched up, and my hand slid farther up the slippery skin of her sides. I clamped my mouth shut to keep myself from moaning at the feel of it. If I didn't watch it, I was totally going to humiliate myself.

"All right, I'm going to swim to the other side, okay? Just keep your arms around my neck and your head up," I said close to her ear.

She nodded, her breath coming out in puffs, short and fast like she'd been running. Maybe I wasn't the only one who was affected by the way our bodies slid together.

As I swam forward, her body pressed even closer to mine, and my head spun. I was going to go crazy from the feel of her. Man, I was in trouble. So much trouble.

All too soon, we were at the other end, and I stood up, letting her warm body drift away from me.

"That was good. You didn't panic at all." I tried to keep my voice nonchalant but failed miserably. Could she tell what she was doing to me? I tried to shake it off. "Now the first thing we're going to teach you how to do is float on your back. Have you ever done that before?"

She shook her head.

I wiped the water from my face, trying to compose myself.

"All right, I want you to lean back into me. I'm going to hold you up, so don't worry." My voice shook when I spoke, and even though it seemed impossible that her eyes could get any wider, they did.

"You aren't nervous, are you?" she asked.

"Well, yeah, maybe I am."

"But you're the one who knows how to swim."

If it was only that easy. Swimming was nothing. Swimming made *sense*. These feelings did not. If I told my body to do a breaststroke, it would do it, but if I tried telling it to stop lusting over this girl, it shut off. It stopped listening. It was like it didn't even belong to me anymore.

"It's not the water that's making me nervous, Ella," I finally said. "It's you."

She didn't speak.

Maybe I'd embarrassed her, or maybe she didn't know what I meant. I meant to say that I wanted her. I meant to say that she was the most amazing girl I'd ever met.

"Okay, now lean back and kick off the bottom," I said quickly, as if this were actually a swimming lesson, as if my sole intention was teaching her how to float on her back. "Try to bring your hips up to the surface."

I tried guiding her back in the water. She hesitated, but it only lasted a moment before a calm expression settled across her face and she let go, floating back into the water. Her body rose to the surface and her hair fanned out, a golden halo floating around her head. Here in the dim light, she looked like something magical: a nymph rising out of the water.

In the pond's dark surface, the stars wavered. Ella's body seemed to hang there, like she was floating in the night sky, and my gaze traveled down over her body. Maybe I was a jerk to look, but I couldn't help myself. Her top clung to her curves, leaving nothing to the imagination. I managed to keep my eyes above her waist, but only barely.

I cupped the back of her head in my hand, letting the other one trail down her back. She was floating. I could let go if I wanted to, and she would be fine. But I didn't want to.

"Okay, I'm going to slowly let go," I whispered. "You just stay relaxed. See if you can stay afloat."

My hands twitched against her skin, but I didn't pull them away. I couldn't. How was I supposed to let go of something that felt so good?

"Ella…" I started to say.

She looked at me, and I leaned forward. Maybe I shouldn't kiss her. Maybe she didn't want me to, but I couldn't help myself. The wonder in her eyes was too strong. I was as helpless as a magnet pulled by forces so much bigger than myself.

Our lips touched, but before I could let myself fall into it, her body stiffened. Her arms flailed as she fought to hold onto something, and before I knew it, she was out of my arms, wading through the water toward the edge.

As she climbed out, the water slid off her body, collecting in a puddle around her feet. Without turning to look at me, she reached down and snatched up her clothes.

"I'm sorry," she said. "I…I have to go."

I watched as she dashed out of the garden, leaving me behind, the most frustrated, aching, smitten boy in the whole western hemisphere.

Acknowledgments

Thank you to my awesome group of writing cheerleaders—ever ready with pompoms, words of encouragement, and smart criticism: Tyler and Tanya Jarvik, Cathy Birch, Emily Scalley, Ellen Fagg Weist, Elaine Vickers, and Dan Beecher.

Thank you to my agent, Kerry Sparks, for your honesty, hard work and support.

To all the people at Entangled: Sue Winegardner, Stacy Abrams, Liz Pelletier, Kelley York, and Heather Riccio, thank you for helping to make this book a reality.

To Heather Howland, the most amazing editor a girl could dream of having, thank you for sharing your brilliant mind with me. Your knack for finding the true shape of a story is inspiring. Thank you for patiently coaxing this one out of me. But most of all, thank you for being the number one fan of this book from day one.

Thank you to my mom, Elaine Jarvik, for humoring the

pet lover in me since age two when I spotted my first pony at the carnival. Thank you for your enthusiasm for my never-ending projects, for letting me learn to create and imagine without fearing failure.

Most of all, thank you to my family. Thank you to Morgan, Noah, and Rebecca for laughing at me, for loving me, for supporting me, and for inspiring my crazy dreams. And thank you to my Bry Guy for lifting me up, for encouraging me, and—even though it's not the most fun job—for being the practical one who knows that you can't keep a mini horse in our backyard. Thank you for allowing me to be the one who keeps dreaming that everything is possible.

THE BODY INSTITUTE

by Carol Riggs

Thanks to cutting-edge technology, Morgan Dey is a top teen Reducer at The Body Institute. She temporarily lives in someone else's body and gets them in shape so they're slimmer and healthier. But there are a few catches. Morgan can never remember anything while in her "Loaner" body, including flirt-texting with the super-cute Reducer she just met or the uneasy feeling that the director of The Body Institute is hiding something. Still, it's all worth it in the name of science. Until the glitches start. Now she'll have to decide if being a Reducer is worth the cost of her body and soul...

AWAKENING

by Shannon Duffy

The Protectorate supplies its citizens with everything they need for a contented life: career, love, and even death. Then Desiree receives an unexpected visit from her childhood friend, Darian, a Non-Compliant murderer and an escaped convict. Darian insists that the enemy is the very institution Desiree depends on. That she believed in. The government doesn't just protect her life—it controls it. And The Protectorate doesn't doesn't take kindly to those who are Non-Compliant...especially those who would destroy its sole means of control.

IN THE BLOOD

by Sara Hantz

For seventeen years, Jed Franklin's life was normal. Then his father was charged with the abuse and murder of four young boys, and normal became a nightmare. The only things that keep him sane are his little sis, his best friend/dream girl Summer, and the alcohol he stashes in his room. But after Jed wakes up from a total blackout to discover a local kid has gone missing—a kid he was last seen talking to—he's forced to face his greatest fear: that he could somehow be responsible.

ALL THE BROKEN PIECES

by Cindi Madsen

Liv comes out of a coma with no memory of her past and two distinct, warring voices inside her head. As she stumbles through her junior year, the voices get louder, but when Liv starts hanging around with Spencer, life feels complete for the first time in, well, as long as she can remember. Liv knows the details of the car accident that put her in the coma, but the deeper she and Spencer dig, the less things make sense. Can Liv rebuild the pieces of her broken past, when it means questioning not just who she is, but what she is?

WHERE YOU'LL FIND ME

by Erin Fletcher

When Hanley Helton discovers a boy living in her garage, she knows she should kick him out. But Nate is too charming to be dangerous. He just needs a place to get away, which Hanley understands. Her own escape methods—vodka, black hair dye, and pretending the past didn't happen—are more traditional, but who is she to judge?
Soon, Hanley's trading her late-night escapades for all-night conversations and stolen kisses. But when Nate's recognized as the missing teen from the news, Hanley isn't sure which is worse: that she's harboring a fugitive, or that she's in love with one.

CINDERELLA'S DRESS

by Shonna Slayton

Kate simply wants to create window displays at the department store where she's working, trying to help out with the war effort. But when long-lost relatives from Poland arrive with a steamer trunk they claim holds *the* Cinderella's dress, life gets complicated. Now, with a father missing in action, her new sweetheart shipped off to boot camp, and her great aunt losing her wits, Kate has to unravel the mystery before it's too late. After all, the descendants of the wicked stepsisters will stop at nothing to get what they think they deserve.

FLAWED

by Kate Avelynn

Sarah O'Brien is only alive because of the pact she and her brother made twelve years ago—James will protect her from their violent father if she promises never to leave him. Until, with a tiny kiss and a broken mind, he asks for more than she can give. Sam Donavon has been James's best friend— and the boy Sarah's had a crush on—for as long as she can remember. But as their forbidden relationship deepens, Sarah realizes her brother is far more unstable than she thought, and he's not about to let her forget about her half of the pact.

WILL THE REAL ABI SAUNDERS PLEASE STAND UP?

by Sara Hantz

When kickboxing champion Abi Saunders lands a job as a stunt double for hot teen starlet Tilly Watson, she's a little freaked out. But once the wig and makeup are on, Abi feels like a different person. When Tilly's gorgeous boyfriend, Jon, mistakes Abi for the real star, Abi's completely smitten. In fact, she's so in love with her new life, it isn't long before she doesn't have time for her old one. But when the cameras are turned off, will she discover running with the Hollywood A-list isn't quite the glamorous existence she thought it was?

THE WINTER PEOPLE

by Rebekah L. Purdy

Salome Montgomery is a key player in a world she's tried for years to avoid. At the center of it is the strange and beautiful Nevin. Cursed with dark secrets and knowledge of the creatures in the woods, his interactions with Salome take her life in a new direction. A direction where she'll have to decide between her longtime crush Colton, who could cure her fear of winter. Or Nevin who, along with an appointed bodyguard, Gareth, protects her from the darkness that swirls in the snowy backdrop. An evil that, given the chance, will kill her.

THE SOCIAL MEDIA EXPERIMENT

by Cole Gibsen

Seventeen-year-old Reagan Fray is popular, Ivy League bound, and her parents are rich enough to buy her whatever she wants. But behind the scenes, Reagan is struggling to hold the fraying threads of her life together. When she's suddenly ostracized from her friends and on the receiving end of the bullying she used to dish out, Reagan fights to reclaim her social status by teaming up with outcast Nolan Letner. But the closer Reagan gets to Nolan, the more she realizes all of her actions have consequences, and her future might be the biggest casualty of all.

LOVE AND OTHER UNKNOWN VARIABLES

by Shannon Alexander

Charlie Hanson has a clear vision of his future. A senior at Brighton School of Mathematics and Science, he knows he'll graduate, go to MIT, and inevitably discover the solutions to the universe's greatest unanswerable problems. He's that smart. But Charlie's future blurs the moment he meets Charlotte. She's an enigma—and she needs his help. But by the time Charlie learns Charlotte is ill, Charlotte's gravitational pull on him is too great to overcome.

WHATEVER LIFE THROWS AT YOU

by Julie Cross

Annie's convinced she knows rookie pitching phenom Jason Brody's type: arrogant, self-involved, bossy. But when opening day arrives and both Brody and her father's jobs are in jeopardy, she and Brody call a truce that grows into friendship—and beyond. Falling for a rising star who's quickly reaching a level that involves rabid female fans is not what Annie would call smart, except suddenly she's getting hints that maybe this crush isn't one-sided after all. Could someone like Brody actually fall for a girl like her?